WES     Westall, Robert.
        Antique dust

$17.95

WES     Westall, Robert.
        Antique dust

JUN  5                    2003

$17.95 22            7      466

| DATE | BORROWER'S NAME | |
|------|-----------------|---|
|  |  |  |
|  |  |  |

© THE BAKER & TAYLOR CO.

# Antique Dust

## Ghost Stories

*by* ROBERT WESTALL

VIKING

VIKING

Published by the Penguin Group
27 Wrights Lane, London w8 5τz, England
Viking Penguin Inc., 40 West 23rd Street, New York, New York 10010, USA
Penguin Books Australia Ltd, Ringwood, Victoria. Australia
Penguin Books Canada Ltd, 2801 John Street, Markham, Ontario, Canada l3r 1b4
Penguin Books (NZ) Ltd, 182–190 Wairau Road, Auckland 10, New Zealand

Penguin Books Ltd, Registered Offices: Harmondsworth, Middlesex, England

First published 1989
10 9 8 7 6 5 4 3 2 1

Filmset in Monophoto Baskerville
Printed in Great Britain by Richard Clay Ltd, Bungay, Suffolk

A CIP catalogue record for this book is available from the British Library
Library of Congress Catalog Card Number: 88–51906

ISBN 0-670-81201-3

To M. R. James,
most economical of writers,
who could coax horror
out of a ragged blanket

# Contents

# The Devil
# and Clocky Watson

*I* DOUBT YOU'LL remember Clocky Watson. Little, with a ginger moustache. Used to hang around the antique-sales after the War. I doubt I'd remember him myself, though many a bad turn we did each other. Except for the way he died. And the story he told me before he died.

I remember the first sale he came to, at Chelford village hall. Those were the days! Rows of varnished, bulbous-legged tables and over-stuffed sofas with bidders perched on every arm, eating sandwiches cut by the village wives, massive in navy floral prints. Auctioneers had time to be witty in those days. I remember young Taberner: 'Nice pair of marble lions. Stick them on your gatepost to sneer at passing strangers! Who'll start me at two pounds?'

Thin as a rail he was, then. Who'd have thought he'd die of a heart attack at eighteen stone?

Anyway, there was Clocky, in his green pork-pie hat and demob suit, already wearing thin. I noticed him because of the way he looked at things. Pure avarice! By the time he'd picked something up and turned it over and over in his little pale hands with the ginger hairs on the back, you'd have thought it was his already. Mind you, he wasn't such a fool as to let you know what he was bidding for; he handled everything.

But mostly he handled clocks, Viennese wall-clocks. A glut on the market in those days, with their big glass cases and eagles on top, and brass pendulums swinging. Every old lady who died seemed to have at least three. They hung in rows, on the darkest wall of any saleroom. Three quid, they'd fetch, if all the decorative knobs were intact, and they were working. If some knobs were missing, the price was halved; and if they wouldn't tick when you

opened the case and swung the pendulum, they weren't worth five
bob. It can cost the earth to get a dead clock repaired, and your
profit's gone.

So there were we dealers, going along the row, twiddling and
opening and swinging the pendulums, one after another.

I'd never known a worse lot. Couldn't get a tick out of them,
and every second knob missing. I didn't bother to bid. Neither did
anybody else, except Clocky. He got twelve in succession, at five
bob each. By the end, people were starting to laugh. But Clocky
just dipped his head, with that sly little grin of his.

I was behind him in the queue to pay the auctioneer's clerk. He
interested me, because he didn't *look* like an idiot. I can tell you,
he was hard-up. He started paying in dirty pound notes, but had
to finish with pennies.

But he had fivepence left, enough for a sandwich. I hadn't seen
him eat anything all day.

I was next in line; had my cheque ready. So I caught up with
him in the kitchen, where the village women were clearing up.
Two and a half Spam sandwiches left, and two rounds of cheese.

'Sixpence the lot,' said the woman. 'I don't want to take them
home; me husband's sick of them.'

Clocky was never one to miss a bargain; but it nearly finished
him. He started to turn out all his pockets for the last penny, and
pulled out a dirty handkerchief by mistake. With it came a shower
of varnished wooden knobs. From Viennese clocks . . .

I made him turn all his pockets out; I was twice his size, and not to
be trifled with. In his inside pockets there were three gilded eagles.
I dragged him back to the clocks themselves, and felt inside the
works, and each had a little bit of paper stuffed between the cogs,
to stop it working.

Oh, he'd been busy, had Clocky; little fingers busy in the dark.
Thirty quid's worth of clocks reduced to rubbish. I dragged him
along to the auctioneer. But Clocky said he'd taken the knobs and
eagles off *after* he'd bought the clocks, to keep them safe from
thieves. And of course he knew nothing about the bits of paper.
And young Taberner was too busy counting the cheques for the
big stuff, like Sheraton tables. And everyone else was too busy

carrying stuff out to their vans. Even the village copper wasn't interested; too busy waving a bundle of brass stair-rods he'd got for two bob.

Clocky turned to me, very pale and eyes blazing. He was eating his sandwiches like a ravening wolf, now he was off the hook.

'I'll remember you. Nearly did for me at my first sale. By my last, I'll have eaten *you*.' As I said, I was a big feller then, but I shivered. He was like a starving dog you try to take a bone off. Clocky was hungry; for a lot more than sandwiches.

As I drove out, I passed him wheeling his clocks home in an old pram, like a tramp.

He took up with Joe Gorman after that. Joe and his shop were famous throughout Cheshire. He'd been a big dealer in his day; and a crafty sod. But he was eighty-three by then, and he'd given up. He had a lot of good stuff left; but buried in the middle of great heaps of rubbish, piled up to the low ceilings. Nobody knew what he had, and he wouldn't let anybody sort it. You'd see the gilt leg of a Louis XIV chair, glinting out through a huddle of old black bicycles. I used to drop in to see Joe regularly; let him go on about the way he put things over people fifty years ago, and keep on giving that gilt leg a friendly tug while he wasn't looking. It took me three months to work that chair out to the surface; then I pretended to notice it for the first time, gave a heave and out it came.

'Not bad, Joe. How much?'

'You clumsy bugger, you've broken t'back of it.'

I looked; the broken ends were filthy; they'd been broken years before.

I showed him before he got his lawyer on to me. He cackled with glee; he'd known it was broken all the time.

'Eeh, a reet battle you had getting that out, lad. *I* been watchin' yer . . .'

'How much?'

'Not for sale. Purrit back.'

It was no good arguing; that only made him more stubborn. It nearly broke my heart. I wanted that chair, for my own place.

And in another three months it wouldn't be worth having. Rain dripping down from the sagging, black-cobwebbed ceiling was lifting the gilding off the back.

'Well, be seeing you, Joe.'

'Wait,' he said, lifting a hand knobbled with arthritis. 'Ye've been good company. Ye can have it for a quid.' I paid him. He folded the note small and tucked it into a pocket of his greasy waistcoat.

'I'll not be seeing you around then? Now you've got your chair?'

I looked at him; old cloth cap; the Sheraton armchair he always sat in, making the striped brocade blacker and blacker with the years. The tabby cat on his knee, moth-eaten and purring; its brown congealed saucer of milk, that never seemed to be changed, under the chair. The glass oil-lamp without a shade, that was his only source of light because he said *he* wasn't keeping the electric board in his old age. I thought what it must be like to be old, when once you'd been young and quick and as sharp as a needle . . .

Us dealers had a bet on about Joe. Whether he or his shop would collapse first; or whether they'd go together. The damp thatch sagged; the whole house leaned with salt-subsidence, only held up by the massive central chimney. Nobody had dared go upstairs for years. People reckoned one day there'd be a rumble; then there'd be only a pile of smashed furniture, worm-eaten beams and damp thatch. And when they dug down, Joe and his cat would still be sitting there, stone dead.

'I'll come again, Joe. That table-leg looks interesting.'

He cackled. 'That's a beaut, boy. Chippendale. Got it at the Franley Hall sale, after old Franley shot hisself in 1926.'

He was joking. Or was he?

I never did find out, because Clocky Watson discovered him. Any time you went there, you'd find Clocky already sitting, listening to the old man telling of his ancient triumphs. After a bit, Clocky would bring one of his wretched clocks down to clean, while Joe talked. Pretty soon, Joe let him clear a bit of space by the window, for a workshop; Joe would sit and brew tea, and tell

Clocky he was restoring the clock all wrong. Clocky had an old blue van by that time. He was making a living running van-loads of restored clocks down to tourist towns like Stratford and Cambridge, where the first American tourists were arriving to be fleeced. He ran a stall in Cambridge market from the back of his van, which had 'Clocky Watson' painted on the side, and very bad paintings of Louis XV clocks which he'd never seen outside the Lady Lever Art Gallery. I heard he drove the Cambridge dealers wild; which made him a bit of a folk-hero locally, as we couldn't stand the southern dealers with their big Mercedes and camel-hair coats and wads of notes.

A bit of folk-hero, that is, till the night Joe's shop collapsed. People heard the rumble and came running. All that was left was the central chimney sticking out, and a pile of smashed timber, already alight because Joe always left his paraffin-lamp burning all night, to discourage burglars.

The fire-brigade could do nothing with it, damp though it must have been. By the morning, all that was left was ashes.

Halfway through the blaze, somebody said, 'Joe's not still in there, is he?' And we had an awful vision, and all went belting off to Barnton, where he sometimes slept at his sister's.

He was there all right. Dead. Someone had got there before us, and told him, and he'd died of a heart attack. Somebody said afterwards how right and poetic it was, the old boy and his shop ending on the same night, after all.

I didn't think so; because I had made a few inquiries.

The woman who kept the shop opposite said she'd heard two quick sharp bangs, before the rumble that brought Joe's shop down. And Clocky Watson's van had been parked round the back all day, which the woman thought funny, as it was a Sunday and the shop was shut.

And we all knew Clocky had had a commission in the Royal Engineers, and frequently boasted in the pub of the bridges he'd blown up in Burma . . .

Clocky and the blue van disappeared for a week. Then he turned up with a van-load of Welsh dressers, spindle-backed rockers and Wedgwood, that he boasted he'd tricked Welsh farmers out of for a song. That van-load was the basis of his real prosperity, and he never looked back.

I didn't doubt it about the Welsh farmers; there were rich pickings in Wales in those days.

But what had the blue van carried *away* from the shop, on the day before the fire? Nobody would ever know for sure. But I guessed the Chippendale table from Franley Hall, at least.

Trouble is, if you make inquiries about somebody, people tell them they're being inquired after. Clocky caught me in the back-yard of the pub one night.

'After me again, Ashden?' He was very cool, lighting up one of those little cigars he began smoking about that time.

'You *killed* old Joe, when you wrecked his shop . . . murder . . .'

'Prove it.'

I had nothing to say.

'Ashes to ashes, boyo. Dust to dust.'

The next thing he did was to buy the Allington house; a huge semi-detached villa, in the Gothic style. Alderman Allington had been the big nob in our town for sixty years, driving out in his black Rolls with the brass headlamps and chauffeur in livery. He never missed a Council meeting, right to the end. So hardly anybody grasped that his childless wife had died, his money departed, his servants gone. From the outside, it was still the grand Allington house.

He'd been dead a fortnight when they missed him; it was August and most people were away. There sat Alderman Allington, dressed for dinner, or a full meeting of the Council, with thick grey cobwebs dangling from the chandelier, and draping the knives and forks of the silver dinner-service. And all he had in front of him was bread and cheese.

Nobody rushed to buy the Allington house, with its sixty-foot ballroom. Perhaps nobody felt big enough to fill Alderman Allington's shoes. Perhaps it was the thought of him sitting there a fortnight in evening-dress, with mouldering bread and cheese in front of him. Perhaps the house was just too big for modern tastes.

None of this bothered Clocky, who got the house and the furniture for four thousand. He even got the Rolls, for there was no heir, and the lawyers were afraid of vandals. Clocky boasted he sold the Rolls within two days, for two thousand. He was the first to spot the London boom in vintage cars.

Oh, yes, Clocky Watson was riding high; but I reckoned he was riding for a fall. Even that crabbed, calloused soul could not enjoy walking that great grey house, where an old man had sat down to supper and never got up again. I said as much, in the pub. Somebody told him what I'd said. He came over to laugh in my face, and invite me across, so I could see.

It was no longer a house. A huge sign said 'CLOCKY WATSON ANTIQUES' in gilt lettering on black – like the flashier kind of funeral parlour. The old man's beautiful overgrown garden had been gouged out into a red gravel car park. The main rooms had been stripped of everything saleable, fitted with neon lighting, and filled with antiques so wonderful that I knew they must have been stolen.

But it was the rooms at the back that really broke my heart. The mahogany ballroom floor was covered with black marble clocks from one end to the other; a city of clocks, like a view over a black marble London, or a miniature cemetery of black gravestones. Not a clock ticked; they were dumb, like black cattle awaiting slaughter. Already the spiders were spinning webs between them.

'What the . . .?'

'Investment, boyo, investment. Five bob each. Nobody wants them; people are throwing them out. But in ten years' time, when there's no clocks left in the whole trade . . . forty quid, fifty? There's a thousand clocks there. You lay down your little bottles of wine, Ashden. I'll lay down clocks.'

'You're *mad*.'

'We'll see.' He showed me another room; every wall packed with Georgian barometers, exquisite things. He saw my admiration.

'They're all off to Germany next week – three container-loads.' He flicked ash from his cigar on to the floor. 'You feel pleased to sell one, Ashden. I sell by the hundred. I told you I was going to eat you, Ashden.'

'May God forgive you,' I said. 'What happens when all the antiques are gone?'

'You'll go bankrupt. I'll find something else to sell. Rosebud chamber-pots . . . Victorian postcards. I'm buying them up cheap already. Keep anything for twenty years, you'll make a fortune.'

I really hated him then. The wicked was flourishing as the green bay tree. I actively sought to do him harm. It was surprising how easily I got the chance. As they say, the Devil finds work for idle hands.

I'd taken my wife shopping in Muncaster on New Year's Eve, as a conciliatory gesture. I'd been neglecting her recently, building up my business. So I let her spend the whole day in Plensbury's. I admired the dresses she tried on, and the curtain-lengths she held up. We bought piffling household things like tap-washers and carpet-shampoo we'd needed for months. It was hot, stuffy and boring, and as we left the store I felt like giving myself a treat.

There was an antiques supermarket in a basement behind Plensbury's. It was run by a sharp young Jew who was cashing in on the rich married women who were starting to want to play at antique-dealing. My wife, glutted and laden, followed me for once without complaint.

I was disappointed; the place had gone downhill. In the old days, a bargain had always been possible because the young wives hadn't known the value of half they were selling. But now there were outbreaks of the trendy and unsaleable. Old Victorian harmoniums, dug out of the Muncaster slum-clearance areas. Victorian bloomers, sold by students in jeans wearing too much make-up. Even some modern brass guns and carthorses, the dry-rot in the body of the dying antique-trade. I was round the whole place in five minutes, despair in my heart. I had a word with Monty, the grizzled, crop-haired veteran who managed the place.

'Bad, Mr Ashden? It's downright murder. Boss has gone to pieces – lost all his business sense. These young married women – in the old days when their money ran out, and they couldn't pay the rent, he'd take their stuff in payment and throw them out. That's business. Now . . . he's letting them pay their rent in bed. Up to his neck in three divorce cases, and one of them's pregnant. That's all he thinks about, these days.'

I took a heavy-hearted look round; it's always depressing when a good source dries up. It was then I saw it; high up on an Edwardian tallboy, big as a mahogany cliff. A black clock, massive. What we call in the trade a bracket-clock, though you'd put it on your mantelpiece. Shaking with excitement, I grabbed a kitchen chair and climbed up to examine it.

It was made of ebony, or some other dark, close-grained wood I didn't know. Inlaid with ormolu. Gold feet, exquisitely chiselled. A gold mask above the dial, and five gold balls on top. It was ticking softly and evenly; no wear on the works. I turned it gently so as not to damage the pendulum. The back of the movement was engraved; an eighteenth-century fusee; the maker was John Pike of London. Pike had been clockmaker to the Prince of Wales.

Trembling, I reached for the price-ticket. If it was under a thousand pounds, I had a bargain worth taking straight to Sotheby's.

The price-ticket read £25--, and my heart sank. The owner knew its value. Though what it was doing among all this tat . . .

'Nice, innit?' Monty, coming up behind me, made me jump.

'No chance of discount for trade, I suppose?' I said bitterly.

'No discount,' said Monty, enjoying some kind of private joke at my expense. 'Twenty-five, the boss said, and no discount.'

'Twenty-five hundred, of course?'

'No, squire. Twenty-five quid; twenty-five greenbacks.'

'Is this some kind of joke?' I turned back to the clock. Cheap plastic repros were coming on to the market then, from Italy. But surely I knew real wood, a real Georgian fusee?

'It's genuine. A genuine John Pike. Boss had it to Muncaster museum – we've got a certificate.'

I scrambled down and wrote a very wild cheque.

'Geoff,' came a low voice from the shadows behind us. My wife's voice. 'Geoff, what are you buying?'

'A genuine Pike – got it for twenty-five.'

'Then you can just get your money back. I'm not having that thing in the house.'

'What . . .?

'Can't you see what it is? Are you *blind*?' She dropped her parcels and scrambled up on the chair. I couldn't help noticing her legs; which was odd. My wife has very pretty legs, but I'd lived with them for eight years. But now, as her black skirt rode up with the effort of scrambling, I noticed the plump smoothness of calf, the dimple behind the knee. I was seized with a fantasy of dumping the clock in the car, and driving home like a maniac and making love to my wife with the black clock ticking in the corner of our bedroom . . .

But nothing could have been further from her mind. She turned to me with a pale and outraged face.

'Can't you *see* the feet?' I looked closely, and was surprised. Instead of the usual lion's foot, they were gilded cloven hoofs. Her hand moved upwards, caught between a desire to show me and snaking revulsion. The gilded mask above the dial wasn't the usual goddess or lion's head, but a goat's head with tight-curled horns and oval eyes. On the silvered dial was engraved the number thirteen – XIII – below the usual number one. And the corner-spandrels round the dial contained . . . miniature male genitals. Well-draped with vine-fronds, but definitely gilded male genitals.

'So what?' I said. 'It just makes it more special.'

'Special?' she said. 'Special? Can't you *feel* it's evil?'

'Well, I've bought it now. Aren't you over-reacting?'

I was ashamed of her, going on like this in front of Monty. I wanted to punish her; put the clock in the corner of the bedroom and make love to her on the floor beneath, and if she didn't like the idea, so much the better.

'I'm not having it in the house,' she said. 'If you bring it in, I'm leaving you. I won't ride in the car with it, and I'll thank you to give me half an hour to pack and leave before you fetch it in.'

When she said the word 'leave', I suddenly knew she meant it.

'All right, I'll keep it down the garden shed!'

'No.'

'All right, I'll drive it straight to London.'

'You'll find me gone when you get back.'

I glanced at Monty, hating this scene in public. But he didn't seem surprised. Just . . . interested.

'Look,' I shouted, 'I'm not throwing up the chance of making two thousand quid. What do you know about antiques?'

'I know about *that* one.'

I looked helplessly at Monty.

'You can't have your money back,' he said. 'The sale's made.'

'Did the others want their money back?' asked my wife.

Monty shrugged.

'How *many* others wanted their money back?' asked my wife, sensing victory.

Monty shrugged again. 'In the end, they just leave it on our doorstep, when we're shut. It's a wonder it hasn't been stolen. But the dogs won't even pee on it.'

'Dogs have sense. Well, Monty, we won't even bother to take it down. You can keep your twenty-five pounds and welcome to it.' She pulled on her gloves, as if that made it final.

'I wish to hell somebody would take it,' said Monty. 'We've had no bloody luck at all since it came.'

It was then the idea came into my mind. 'Can you do a delivery?'

Monty nodded.

I gave him Clocky Watson's address. 'Put "Happy New Year" on the wrapping,' I said.

He got it, of course. I heard him boasting in the pub; though he didn't know who'd sent it. Clocky didn't make any secret of his triumphs, however dark he kept his fiddles. Then I heard he was drinking hard; that he'd sit in a corner, pale and sweating, knocking back the whiskies one after another and talking non-stop, until people just went away.

I clashed with him at several auctions, and beat him hollow. He couldn't seem to concentrate. Then he developed a nervous trick of nodding to himself . . . fatal at auctions. There was a lot of junk knocked down to him he'd never intended to bid for, let alone buy. And it cost him. Because when people saw him bidding for junk, they bid against him, thinking he'd noticed something valuable they'd missed. Then they began to force up the bidding against him for a cruel laugh, once they saw he no longer knew what he was doing. As I said, he was never popular after Joe Gorman's death.

Then he just vanished. When he hadn't shown up for three months at any auction, I began to get nosy; I went round to the old Allington house.

It looked a bit empty, a bit thin on items, like an antique-business does when it's starting to fail. The grand black-and-gold nameboard was starting to flake with the sun, the weeds were sprouting all over the car park. It was a total stranger who came out to serve me. I toyed with this and that, bought up a job-lot of 1930s novelty brass ashtrays – cats' faces, crescent moons and the like – and then said casually, 'Mr Watson around?'

'He's . . . in . . . London at the moment, sir.' The man looked decidedly worried. 'I'm running the shop for him.'

I couldn't leave it alone. 'Used to know Clocky well . . . my name's Ashden . . . got a shop in town.'

'Yes . . . I've heard him speak of you.'

'Has he still got that black clock with the cloven hooves?'

'As far as I know . . . he didn't leave it behind here, sir.'

I went round to the Allington house about once a month after that. Not so much hunting for the odd bargain as for news of Clocky. The place got slowly tattier and emptier, but it didn't close. I got to know the manager well – a Yorkshireman called Tom Ponsonby. I got a few cheap items, but never a sniff about Clocky.

Until one sultry dark day at the end of August. I was going over a mahogany chest, looking for woodworm; the wormholes were very difficult to see, in the dark wood, with no lights on.

'My, my,' said a voice. 'It's Geoff Ashden. I hear you've been round quite a bit, Geoff, asking after my health.'

He was only a shadow; a little shadow against a distant window. I couldn't see his face in the shadow, but I knew it was Clocky from the way he picked up a vase from a table and began to turn it over and over in his little pale hands, like he was going to devour it. 'I hear you've been asking about a clock as well, Geoff?'

I was silent; my mouth was dry. He was *different*, in a way a man should not be different. I had an odd fear he might be a ghost.

'Well, don't you want to know what happened to me, Geoff? After I got your little clock? Isn't that what you've been coming back for, all these months?'

He laughed; not a pleasant sound. And this is what he told me.

———

Well, Geoff, it was late when I found it on the doorstep; dark already, because the traffic out of Muncaster had been heavy. I nearly fell over it. I carried it in, and read 'Happy New Year' scrawled on the packing-box. I thought one of my old mates had left it there because it was nicked and too hot to handle.

I set it up in the little ground-floor room at the far end of the corridor. Got it going all right. Then I just sat looking at it, and drinking whisky to celebrate, till nearly midnight. Then I went to bed. My mind was full of how much I might get for it – I know one or two big collectors in the States who'd ask no questions.

I was wakened about two by the sound of water dripping. I banged on the light bloody quick, I can tell you. You know what a frost we had, last New Year's Eve, and I've got some bloody great old slate water-tanks in the roof, and the water-pipes are all lead and crumbling to crap. You know what water does to antiques, and I had a load of walnut veneer in at the time.

Anyway, I looked at the carpet, and it was bone dry. No drips coming from the ceiling, no bulge in the plaster. But the sound of dripping now seemed to come from another room. I grabbed my dressing-gown and ran from room to room, switching on lights and looking to my best stuff first.

Not a trace of damp anywhere. But there might be a leak in the roofspace, and a soggy ceiling just waiting to collapse. I searched the whole house . . . nothing.

Except that sound of dripping water; the 'plink' that water makes falling into a puddle. Then I thought it might be outside.

But when I went out with a torch, everything was frozen solid, crunching underfoot, and quite silent, the way frosty nights sometimes are. So I went back to bed and switched off the light and listened to the 'plink' of water.

Ever tried to get to sleep when a tap's dripping in the room? You lie awake, waiting for the next drip. And they never come regular, like the tick of a clock. Well, this was much worse than a dripping tap. There were, it seemed to me lying listening in the dark, at least eight different drips, all dripping at different speeds, one right beside me in the room. I kept trying to place them. And the longer I lay, the keener my ears seemed to get. I couldn't just hear drips, but *echoes* of drips, unmuffled by carpets and curtains. Wherever the drips were coming from, they weren't coming from my carpeted showrooms downstairs, or the bedrooms either side of me, stuffed with junk I'd picked up for a song and meant to do up some day.

In the end, I put the light on again and fetched a whisky. I keep some in the bedroom, for the very occasional girl who agrees to share my bed for the night. I was drinking it when the solution hit me. The frost outside must be causing condensation *inside* my ancient cavity-walling. Quite harmless to the furniture. I rolled over and slept immediately.

It never occurred to me that the echoes suggested a far bigger space than a four-inch wall-cavity.

When I woke up again, my first thought was how big the room sounded. Huge, high-domed, and somehow made of *stone*. The drips and echoes rang through it, like flights of frantic birds, backwards and forwards. A cold draught of air touched the cheek I lifted from the pillow, bringing a smell of ... damp ... underground.

Where the hell was I?

But with the stupidness of sleep, I still reached for my bedside lamp; found it in its usual place. It clicked on, and there was the whisky bottle leering at me, an empty glass and ashtray full of dog-ends. And my shirt and socks in a heap on the bedside chair, though my trousers had fallen on the floor as usual, weighed down by my pocketful of loose change.

But it didn't banish what I began to think of as the *cavern*. My eyes told me I was in my bedroom; my ears, nose and skin told me I was underground. I felt split in half; like when you wear stereo headphones, and hear the guitarist thumping away over your head, and the invisible singer's footsteps pacing the floor in front of you, and a huge audience stirring that couldn't possibly be contained in the room you're sitting in.

I normally enjoy that sensation; I didn't enjoy this. But there must be some rational explanation. The draught must have come from my bedroom door that was slightly open into the darkness of the hall. I closed it in a rush, and leapt back to the safety of bed. The musty smell? My shoes lay tumbled by the bed. I got one up and sniffed the filthy muddy sole. It smelled damp and dark and ancient. A dealer spends a lot of time in old, cold houses and damp cellars.

I poured another drink and looked at my watch. Just on three. I lay back and waited for my old friends the clocks to start chiming in the showrooms downstairs.

First came the long-case I'd inherited from old Allington. That nobody would buy, because it carried a brass plate, recording its presentation to him by the employees of Barlborough Council on the occasion of his eightieth birthday. It had been in the room where he died, and they don't like dead men's shoes in Barlborough, do they? Fools. Don't they know all antiques are dead men's shoes? Bedroom mirrors that have reflected centuries of dead men's lovemaking? If you don't like the dead, buy Danish teak . . .

Then the old white alabaster clock in the front showroom chimed in hysterically. Yes, the one from Joe Gorman's shop; green with verdigris when I rescued it from the flames . . . yes, you were right about that, Geoff. And I thought, old Joe's welcome to haunt me if he likes. Just as long as he doesn't get in the way of trade. But then a haunted antique-shop would be quite an attraction; draw the crowds. Perhaps that's why old Joe has stayed away. Out of spite. It'd be like him, that.

One by one, all my old friends joined in; and it was friendly in the night, like watchmen calling that all's well. But all dim and muffled, by the thick walls, and dusty carpets.

Aha, there's a stranger, I thought. That'll be the new one. Nice chime. But so loud. Filling the house. Must have left the door of that room open. So incredibly loud ... and the only one that *echoed*. The rest had been muffled. It was almost as if ... If there *was* a dripping cavern, that clock was in it.

Subconsciously, I'd been counting the chimes. Any buyer of a new clock does. Ratchets can wear, and the clock starts chiming and never stops. That's a pretty expensive thing to cure in an old clock, unless you cut out the chiming mechanism altogether, and that halves your profit.

It struck ten, eleven, twelve, thirteen. Damn, that'd mean taking it for repair to old Ratcliffe. And Ratcliffe knew how to charge. That'd certainly spoil my profit.

But it didn't strike again. Maybe I'd miscounted.

Then I shot upright. There were voices in the corridor, footsteps. Coming towards my door. Vigorous steps, cheerful voices, men out on the spree. It was hard to tell what they were saying because of the echo effect. But something like 'Drink up, Higginson ...' and something that sounded like 'Fay suh ki voodra, Francis, fay suh ki voodra. Eh, Wilkes?' Rich men's voices, assured, like the local Tories celebrating on election night.

Who the hell had got into my house? I leapt out of bed, shaking with rage at their cocksureness. Got my old pistol out from under my pillow; the one I borrowed from the Royal Engineers when I got demobbed. Pushed open the door.

Not a sign of anybody. I ran through the house. Everything was exactly as I'd left it; front door was bolted, all three security chains in place. No window unlocked or broken ...

As I listened, a group of people passed on the main road beyond my car park.

I laughed; it was New Year's morning. There'd be drunks parading till the small hours. And my car park was a good place for them to come and pee. It's masked by trees from the main road. Sound carries very clear on a frosty night; something to do with temperature inversion.

I might have known. The footsteps I'd heard had been crunching on broken stone. There's broken stone in my car park, but none in my house.

I went back to bed and slept the sleep of the just; or the drunk.

The following morning, I went over that clock pretty closely. I wanted to get a description typed up, for America. The more I looked at the clock, the better bargain I knew I'd got. All the ormolu was hand-cut, not mass-produced. A one-off job for a very rich guy. A well-off kink with a very nasty mind. Not just the cloven hooves and goat's head. But the egg-and-dart moulding wasn't really egg-and-dart, but alternate male and female genitals. And the handle at the back was in the shape of a woman's breast. I began to see sexual symbols everywhere. Disturbing. I began to think I'd been without female company too long . . . but I kept on with my note-taking.

Lastly, I had a grope around inside the ebony case. Sometimes people leave spare clock-keys in there – even spare pendulums. Hair-clips, any old thing that in the past has helped the clock to work. I once saw a Tompion kept going by a Morris Cowley split-pin.

But in this case all I found was a piece of folded paper. I thought from its shape it had been used to wedge something – the handle on the rear-door was a bit loose and the door tended to swing open. The paper was brown with age, but the middle was less brown as I unfolded it.

It was a disappointment; just a series of numbers:

4/1/44
205
339
67
404
Ps 83

And it was signed, in a large spindly hand:

P. S. Melmerby – Dean

But it was old – I judged Victorian. Very copperplate, like old clerk's ledgers. Anything old will be valuable one day. So I didn't throw it away; I put it in an old tankard on the fireplace.

I spun the hands right round the clock, to test the striking mechanism. Worked perfectly, one through to twelve. I tried to get it to strike thirteen but it wouldn't. I sighed with relief; no need for the expense of old Ratcliffe. But the odd thing was, when I examined the dial, the numeral one had been shortened, and the numeral thirteen had been slipped in underneath. It wasn't a later alteration, but Georgian work, elegantly done.

I posted off my offer to three gentlemen in America, and forgot all about it.

I went to bed that night hoping for a good night's sleep. If you remember, Geoff, the thaw set in on New Year's Day, and water, perfectly normal water, was dripping from every gutter. And I hoped the jokers who'd been peeing in my car park would be in bed too, sleeping off their hangovers.

But again I wakened, and all the echoes and drips were back. And I realized I was waiting for that damned clock to chime thirteen . . . bloody ridiculous, considering my watch said twenty past two. I had just told myself not to be a stupid bugger when it started chiming.

Thirteen.

Oh, what the hell, I thought. I'll see Ratcliffe. And rolled over . . .

Then, through the cavern of drips and echoes, I thought I heard the sound of voices again. Female voices this time, indecipherable through their whispering and giggling. Soft feet – somehow I knew they were bare; and thick cloth swishing and rustling. A seductive sound that drew me, made me get up. I like women; especially women tip-toeing about in the middle of the night on bare feet, giggling.

But by the time I'd got up there was nothing to be seen or heard.

A dream; a nice dream; pity it ended so soon. Ah, you'd better get a permanent woman, Watson, I thought. You can afford one now. Before you turn into one of those dirty old men that hang around nude statues in auction-rooms they haven't got the money to bid for.

I got back into bed and tossed and turned.

Then that damned clock started chiming again; and it went on and on and on. And there's nothing worse than a clock chiming on and on in an empty house. It was like a church bell, chiming, summoning . . . summoning to what?

I was frightened by then; not inclined to go padding along all those empty corridors in bare feet. I buried my head under the bedclothes. It would soon run itself down and shut up.

It took me a while to realize it wasn't just the clock that was chiming. My bedside phone was ringing as well.

I embraced that phone in my loneliness like a long-lost friend. But it wasn't a long-lost friend. It was my next-door neighbour, from the other half of the haunted mansion, beyond the party-wall. Bloody man had never bothered to speak to me since the day I'd moved in; cuts me dead when we're getting our cars out in the mornings.

'That you, Watson?' he says. 'That your bloody clock that won't stop chiming? What've you got there – Big Ben? You've got me awake, my wife awake, and the kids are screaming. For Christ's sake, can't you *hear* it, man? Are you *dead* or something? Stop it, or I'll ring the police and report you as a public nuisance.' Then before I could say a word, he hung up. But I knew he'd be behind his little party-wall, listening, with the phone in his hand, ready to ring the police. And I can't afford to have the police nosing round, the business I run.

I dragged on my dressing-gown, and swigged a mouthful of whisky straight from the bottle. I even took my pistol with me. And that bell went on tolling me . . . to what? I kept on praying it would stop before I reached that half-open door, and had to feel round for the light-switch in the dark.

It didn't stop. I had to reach round. I had to walk in and see its broad green pudding of a dial grinning at me. And the cloven hoofs . . .

Then it stopped chiming. Just like a bossy human being that summons you to the front of the shop to make a complaint, then tells you to get lost and walks out.

I'd stop its rotten little games. I turned it round and took the pendulum out. But then it began to tick away like a mad thing, as any good clock deprived of its pendulum will. It was doing an hour every five minutes. In four more minutes it would be chiming again.

I laid it on its back. It kept on going. I laid it on its dial; on its side. It kept on stopping and starting again. I nearly threw it out of the window; but I'm a dealer with a profit to make. I looked round for something to wedge in the works. And thought of the bit of browning paper I'd found that morning. As I wedged it home, I had a strange feeling that that was exactly what the Victorian gent had done, to stop it too.

'Perhaps now I'll get some peace!' I said to myself.

I couldn't have been more wrong.

I got back into bed with the light on, and hunched over another whisky. It took a long time for my panting to die away; but finally the drink took hold, and I began to relax.

It was then I felt the bed move behind me. Just a little tremor in the mattress, as if someone lying beside me had moved an arm or leg. I don't go home every night to an expensive wife like you, Ashden; but I've had enough women to know when there's someone in bed with me.

Then I thought, oh, *rubbish*! It's my own leg giving one of those twitches that I've had ever since I fought the Japs in the War, in the Arakan Box. I often twitch, on the verge of sleep; especially if I've had a hard day.

But I waited, with the last of my whisky held to my lips. Waiting for it not to happen again.

It happened again, stronger; it felt like somebody turning over on their side. My back, you understand, was turned towards the rest of the bed. I was facing the bedside light. I desperately wanted to turn round and look, to see what it was. And I equally desperately didn't. So I stayed frozen. Till the bed moved a third time. Whatever it was was moving nearer. It's a big, big bed.

My body leapt of its own accord. My feet caught in the bed-clothes, and I sprawled full-length on the bedside rug. My whisky-glass flew from my hand, rolled across the floorboards, and finished up with a hollow rap in the corner. In a second, I was in the corner with it, crouching, the stupid revolver pointing in my trembling hand. I knew it would be quite useless, against whatever was in my bed; but it gave me the courage to stand up and look.

The bedclothes were tossed back on my side of the bed; but the other side, where the movement had been, was as flat as a board. Furthermore, right in the middle of the flatness was a big fat copy of Miller's *Guide to Antiques* that I'd been consulting before I went to sleep. It's a big bed, as I said. Too big for an ordinary house. That's why I got it cheap.

I walked back to the bed. Pulled back the bedclothes . . .

Nothing. Then I remade the bed, absolutely flat. Poked every inch of the flatness with my gun-barrel, wondering about rats. Nothing. Then a little cold draught from under the bed caught at my ankle. I think I screamed, and leapt away. Then I crept back on my knees, and lifted the counterpane with the gun-barrel.

Nothing; except the floral chamber-pot I keep under there as a joke.

Eventually, when I had stood and shivered long enough, I called myself a stupid bastard, and got back into bed and put the light off. There I lay, waiting and shivering.

There was another wriggle in the mattress; and another. But by that time I'd conned myself into a mood of scientific curiosity. I reached for where the wriggle had come from, and grabbed a handful of it.

Now if it had been the kind of thing you read about in horror-stories, like cold bone, or rotting rags, or slimy filthy flesh, I'd have been out of bed and down those stairs and in the hands of our local constabulary before you could say knife. Still in my pyjamas . . .

But it wasn't anything like that. It was warm, plump, female flesh, breathing gently. And it lay absolutely still, as a young rabbit will 'freeze' if you catch it out in the open, when it's too late to run away. I felt up it, I felt down it. I found a smooth hip, a plump thigh, then a generous breast. Then long silky hair, a face with smooth cheeks and a turned-up little nose. I remember the eyelashes batted against my fingers like a captured butterfly. But otherwise the creature didn't stir. And oozing up out of the bed-clothes as my arm stirred them came a smell that wasn't me; the warm smell of girl. A bit thick and animal, but not unwashed. Better than some of the living ladies I've had in that bed, with their stale reek of gin and cheap perfume.

Only this one smelt a little bit afraid. I got to know the smell of other people's fear in the Arakan Box.

A small hand reached out and clasped mine; slightly sweaty but warm and firm. The other hand began to fumble with the top button of my pyjamas.

I nearly let it happen. Lonely men aren't choosy, Geoff. But then you wouldn't know that; you've probably never been lonely in your life. The body was pressing close to mine, now. Then I thought of the flat bed, with the copy of Miller's *Guide* lying on top . . . Only suckers take the goods and ask the price afterwards, and Clocky Watson's not a sucker. I detached the yearning hands gently, and got out of bed yet again, and put the light on.

The bed was absolutely flat and the copy of Miller hadn't moved. I'm proud to say I got dressed properly, though pulling my shirt over my head was a panicky moment. And all the time the bed stayed absolutely flat.

When I had my raincoat on, I suddenly felt ridiculous. I'd had a bad dream . . . no, a very pleasant dream. I was a fool. It was cold and wet outside, even if the thaw had set in. I was bone-weary. The bed looked more inviting than ever, and it was *my* bed. I walked across in a no-nonsense mood, and thrust my arm in.

Immediately, under the flatness, two warm hands clutched my arm gently, beseechingly. I tried to pull my arm out, but those hands were pretty strong. I had to put in my second hand to release the first. We struggled, silently, and somehow, under the bedclothes, my struggling arms made the shape where a woman might have lain.

Then suddenly I was free and running down the stairs, leaving on every light in the house.

I walked till morning.

The first thing I did, after I'd had an Irish coffee with plenty of whisky in it, was to box up that clock. I took it to a friend of mine I call Floradora. Her real name is Mrs Eunice Pearce, but she has the faded good-looks of an old music-hall star. She's been a fine woman in her day, and although her blonde hair is now out of a bottle, she can get a chest-of-drawers into the back of a shooting-brake as well as anybody in the trade.

'Keep this in the back of your shop a couple of days, Flora?'

'Hot, is it? Fell off the back of a lorry?' She lit up a cigarette and coughed appreciatively.

'Somebody gave it me for a present.'

'I'll believe that when I see it. Well, mark it "Property of Clocky Watson – to be called for" and I'll find a place for it. I don't even want to know what it is. Then I can't be done. I'm a bit old for scrubbing floors in an open prison . . .' She thrust the clock into a dark hole, and piled some Edwardian corsets on top.

I went home and had a good sleep; disturbed at teatime by two Dutch dealers hammering on my door wanting a gross of pewter candlesticks at three pounds apiece. Then I went back to bed and slept the night away too. But by the following morning, I was feeling bored. That was the trouble with that clock; I got bored without it. And though I might fret on about its immense value, and the fact that Flora is both nosy and was a bit light-fingered in her younger days, and her shop's about as burglar-proof as a 1930s piggy-bank, and she carried no insurance, the truth was I was wanting to examine again the thing that had been in my bed. I had a sick desire to muck about. I drove round to her shop.

'It's not here,' she said. 'You can't leave a thing like that *here*. You must be out of your mind – it's worth thousands.'

'Where is it? I thought you didn't even want to know what was in it?'

'I had to have a peep – I had to know what you were letting me in for. Might've been a bomb. I've got it at home. And I've got it going for you. What d'you think of that? Some fool had stuck paper in it.'

'Chiming?'

'Chiming beautiful. The budgie loves it.'

'How . . . did you sleep last night?'

'Like a top. Why – thinking of coming to join me? I don't snore, you know!'

Well, I knew one thing, now. That clock had no interest in well-preserved middle-aged ladies.

'I'll take it now,' I said.

'But I've just opened me shop. I'll miss trade . . . there's always a German looks in on Tuesday mornings, and I've got a couple of whatnots for him. Besides, it's a responsibility, looking after a valuable clock like that.'

I knew what she was after. I reached for my wallet and took out a fiver. 'Storage expenses.'

She took it. '*And* I got it going for you . . .'

We took my car.

The clock sat huge in the corner of her small sitting-room, surrounded by Staffordshire figurines and lace antimacassars. It looked trapped, like a caged tiger at a children's tea-party.

'Here,' said Flora, 'he was a randy old sod that made it, wasn't he? All those boobs and pricks . . . funny the things these vicars get up to.'

'Vicars?'

She handed me the folded bit of brown paper that I'd used to stop the works.

'What's this, then?'

'Haven't you never been to church in your life, then, Clocky? That's a list of hymns and psalms for a church service, that is. See – Ps 83 – that's the psalm.'

'Which church?'

'How the hell would I know? I'm not the Archbishop of Canterbury – I just look like him. Must've been a few years ago though, mustn't it?'

I stuffed the paper in my top pocket and forgot it.

Later that day I got the clock set up and going, in exactly the same place, then went to bed early, trembling with excitement. It was the stupidest thing I've ever done in my life; but I suppose getting rid of it so easily to Floradora had given me a false sense of security. What I'd failed to notice was how quickly I'd grabbed it back off her again. That's always the same when you start an addiction, whether it's drink or drugs. You always think you can kick the habit any time.

I lay reading Miller's *Guide*. The massed photographs of clocks, chairs, figurines, swam before my face pointlessly. I wasn't really reading at all; I was waiting. But the clock struck ten, without anything happening but the rumble of a passing train. And at eleven, there was only a distant dog barking.

I suppose I must've dozed off; those sleepless nights had taken more out of me than I'd thought. Because I never heard the clock chime midnight at all.

But in my sleep I became aware of someone getting into bed with me. Only she did it in such a matter-of-fact way that I didn't really waken up. I'd had a skinful of whisky again, to calm my nerves. And I always drink whisky when I have a woman up to my bedroom, and I suppose I thought it was one of those.

'Maggie,' I murmured drowsily, groping for the warmth. When she spends the night, Maggie's always tripping out to the loo.

But it wasn't Maggie; Maggie's a real big armful, and her skin's slightly rough. This skin was too smooth and young.

'Clare?' I asked, querulously, thinking I'd dropped a clanger, calling Clare 'Maggie'.

The body shook, as if giggling. So I knew it wasn't Clare. For Clare, bed is always very serious, earth-shattering. Besides, she's thin, and her shoulder-blades stick out. This person snuggling under my armpit was just right . . . smooth, well padded. Fuddled with drink, I couldn't think who it was at all. Oh, well, said my whisky-sodden brain, what the hell? Whoever it was certainly knew how to make love . . .

And then the clock began to strike. It more than struck. The sound marched up and down the corridors of my house like great boots, getting nearer and nearer. No mortal clock could strike so loud. It was a noise that would shatter windows. I tried to struggle upright, full of rage that anything should so disturb my house. But sleep and whisky held me down; and the warm twining form that burrowed deeper into the angle of my shoulder and neck, almost totally enfolding me.

Then the sound of real boots in the hall, crunching on loose broken stone. Doors were being thrown open, banging against *my* plastered walls with a force that made me break out in a cold sweat. Again I tried to struggle upright, reach the pistol under my pillow. But my companion weighed me down.

Shouts; great jagged angry shouts, so full of rage I couldn't understand what they were saying. And a terror filled me, far greater than my own fuddled outrage. It oozed from the shape wrapped round me, that was now shaking from head to foot, and exuding a cold sweat that made it feel like a corpse.

There was banging and shouting right next door now. The terror coming from the thing wrapped round me filled my whole body, so that I went down into the black pit with it . . .

Then came a new noise, drilling through the rest like a workman with a road-drill; off, on, off, on. A cool, hard, sane modern noise that drilled deeper and deeper into my mind, forcing me to open my clenched-shut eyes.

My own bedroom ceiling, with its familiar pattern of cracks, looking deeper in the glow of the bedside light. My closed bedroom door, with my dressing-gown hanging from it. Whisky bottle, full ashtray . . .

And the bedside telephone ringing.

It was Floradora. I managed to gasp out 'Hello'.

'You OK?' she said in her old nicotine croak. 'You sound funny.'

'I was asleep.'

'Bet you weren't having a very nice dream.'

'Had some whisky.'

'You'll ruin your bloody liver.'

'Man's got to have some consolation.'

'You'd do better coming over here.' It was good to hear her voice, normal as catching a bus or buying a packet of cigarettes. 'Hey – I forgot to tell you. There was something engraved on the back of your clock movement.'

'You ring me up in the middle of the night to tell me *that*?'

'S'only half past eleven. Some people don't get to sleep as easy as you. Now when my old man was alive. . .'

'What was engraved on the clock?'

'Fay suh ki voudra.'

'You what?'

'It's spelt . . . you gotta pencil handy? . . . F-A-Y C-E Q-U-I V-O-U-D-R-A. It's French . . . but not spelt quite right . . . not unless my girlish schooldays have let me down.' She gave a sexy giggle; I reckon she'd been at the whisky as well.

'How girlish were your schooldays? No – don't tell me.'

'All right, Simon Pure. Sounds like a family motto though, doesn't it? Of the guy who had the clock made?'

'Something like that.' Now I felt sane again, I wanted to get off the phone and see what had been happening in my house. Though I could've done with her there, to hold my hand.

'See you,' she said abruptly, and hung up. She's like that; very brazen up to a point, then she gets hurt and goes like a streak of lightning. I'll never understand women.

I went through what was by now a weary routine. Put on my dressing-gown, tie the cord with trembling hands. Search the bed, under the bed, find nothing. But as I searched my long, empty, undamaged corridors, full of closed doors and ticking clocks, I seemed to hear echoes, of footsteps and whispers and giggles. Fading, fading.

I made up my mind; I would not give that clock house-room a moment longer. I packed it again in its wooden box, stuffing crumpled newspapers all round it. Then I carried it out to the garage and locked it in my car, then locked the garage and went back and sat in my bedroom wicker chair.

I dozed a bit, towards dawn.

Next morning, I drove into Muncaster. I knew I had to get rid of the clock. But I was Clocky Watson, and I was determined to make a profit on it. I went round every dealer I knew. And I swear they'd all heard of that clock. They'd be all interest as I walked in with the box, because although I've got a bad name, they know I get some good stuff. But the moment I took off the wrappings . . . Not only did they not want to know, but they took a grim enjoyment in my frustration. By the end, I knew they were phoning ahead of me. I didn't even bother to start taking off the wrappings. I kept a civil tongue in my head, till the last shop, because I knew my raging would only have added to their pleasure. In the last shop, which belongs to an old Jew I know, I really blew my top.

'But Marcus, it's bloody *Georgian*!'

'Is Georgian,' he agreed with a shrug.

'Look at the craftsmanship!'

'Superb craftsmanship,' he agreed.

'Worth thousands!'

'Worth what you can get for it . . .' He smiled tinily. 'I am sorry for you. But I am also glad you bought it from my nephew. Perhaps now Moshe will get his business back in order. Perhaps now he will save his marriage. He was stubborn, like you. He insisted on making a profit . . . nobody profits from the Dean's clock. Leave it up some nice quiet little back alley – it will come to no harm. Only, please, do not try to sell it back to Moshe for a pound. Three years he has suffered, and if it got hold of him again . . .' He drew the edge of his hand across his throat.

'What did you call it?'

'The Dean's clock. In Muncaster, in the trade, it has always been known as the Dean's clock.'

'Which Dean?'

'A Dean who has been gone for many years. I first heard of the Dean's clock as a young boy. Which Dean?' He shrugged. 'Colleges have Deans, cathedrals have Deans. The telephone directory has two whole pages of men called Dean . . . Leave it up some back alley, Clocky. When no one is looking. As far from here as possible – I have to live with my neighbours . . . I don't want them hammering on my door.'

'Be damned to you,' I shouted. 'I *will* make a profit!' I shouted because tears of frustration were growing in my eyes.

'*Shalom*,' he said, softly, as I staggered out with the clock, kicking his door open in front of me.

After that, I drove aimlessly, trying to think of some other place to take it. But the evening rush-hour had started, driving me round in frantic, hooting, exhausted circles. It was getting dusk, a pale-green dusk, with clouds of windblown starlings hovering over the black spires and chimneys of Muncaster. And the cars and the scurrying people seemed to be fading, growing distant with the day, leaving me alone with the night, and the clock sitting in the middle of the back seat behind me.

I kept on coming back to the traffic-lights by the cathedral. That's a trick of the one-way system. If you're lost in Muncaster, or drifting, you always come back to the traffic-lights by the cathedral. Each time I came round, the cathedral windows were lit up, golden, inviting. There was one empty place in the car park outside; a place to stop and rest my brake-foot. I pulled in, stopped the engine.

And behind me (it might only have been the jar as I jammed the brakes on) the clock boomed once, a jangling, angry, discordant boom. I thought . . . full of imprisoned anger.

I was out of that car like a shot; didn't even bother to lock it. I ran for the big, lit, open door of the cathedral.

A handful of people streamed down the steps past me; women with umbrellas and solitary well-dressed old men. Beyond, the organ was playing a voluntary. I had come in at the end of a service. I stood there, as the last worshippers slipped past me. It seemed to my desperate mind that they too knew about the clock, and were leaving because I'd come. I'd often felt lonely in my life; but never as lonely as then.

The organ music was soaring, soothing. For a second, I closed my eyes, and let myself get lost in it. But I knew it was already ending, like a dying wave that would recede and leave me stranded. Alone.

The music stopped; the organist closed his keyboard and put his light out with a click of a switch that echoed up and down that nave like a full-stop. I watched him too walk away, with a rolled newspaper and a bagful of groceries with a celery-head sticking out of the top. He looked at his watch as he passed. Lucky man, he was going somewhere.

I just stood, waiting for someone to come and throw me out. Then I saw the man who was going to do it. He came down the centre aisle, a tall thin negro in a long black cassock. But he wasn't a forbidding figure. He walked, smiling and staring about him with pride, like a child left in charge of a sweet-shop. He had the most marvellous teeth I ever saw in a man.

'Hello,' he said with a beaming grin, taking my hand between both of his. 'Welcome to our great cathedral.' I suppose it was a very Christian thing to do, but I wondered how many staid Englishmen it had frightened away. 'Can I help you in any way?' His eyes were brown, a bit moist with emotion, but very kind. It was like having a warm bath. 'I am Father Eagle St John Smith. My father named me after the eagle of St John, in the Gospels. But just call me Eagle.'

I was speechless. I'd never seen anyone less like an eagle in my life; a dove would have looked more ferocious. I warmed to him. I wanted to say something, but didn't know what to say. So I finally said, 'You're new here?' That from me, who'd never been to church in my life. But he *seemed* new; he had a glossiness that doesn't last long in Muncaster.

'Yes, I am new. I was ordained in our great cathedral at Barbados six months ago today, and now I am assistant priest in this great cathedral. I am going to write a book about it. There is *so* much to write; I learn some new things every day. Let me show you round some of these marvellous things.'

I let him lead me round; not really listening, just saying 'Yes' and 'How curious' and 'I see', stupidly. At last he ran down to a stop. Concern crossed his face. 'But I've done all the talking. I think you wanted to ask me something.' And he really wanted to know. Suddenly, his face was serious.

I couldn't start telling him all about my life; he was too happy. But I didn't want to disappoint him; he so much wanted to help. Then I saw, on one of the pillars, a hymn-board with numerals. Just like the piece of paper in my top pocket. So I got it out.

'I'm an antique-dealer. I found this in a clock I bought. I've been wondering what it is? It's pretty old.'

He took it, then produced a pair of gold-rimmed spectacles from a hidden pocket. Suddenly, he was all scholar.

'Oh yes. An order of service, written out for the organist. I write them out every day myself. But this is old, as you say. And written by a Dean – look – 'P. S. Melmerby – Dean'. Why, it is from this very cathedral. Mr Melmerby was Dean from 1817 till 1864. He is featuring largely in the book I am writing! How exciting!'

A sudden hope squeezed my heart. A way out; with profit.

'The clock I found it in – it's called the Dean's clock. Must have come from this cathedral. Would you like to see it? I've got it in the car.'

Again, that smile of pure delight. I felt – I swear – a pang of conscience. He was so *happy*.

'I would certainly love to see your clock. What an exciting place this cathedral is to work in. Someone shows me a new thing every day! Where is your car, Mr . . .'

'Watson. Clocky Watson. They call me that because I sell clocks for a living.'

'Let us go and see your clock then. It must be a fascinating job, selling clocks. I expect you find you always have plenty of *time*.' He laughed uproariously at his own feeble joke and, putting his arm around me, led me from the cathedral.

We opened the two rear doors of my car, one from each side. It was full night, now. And although I switched the courtesy-light on, it was very dim inside. I don't think I'd have dared to strip off the wrappings if he hadn't been there. The clock glimmered, black and gold, the Devil's colours, in the semi-darkness. As I pulled off the last wrapping, I joggled it and again it chimed, faintly, janglingly, angrily.

'That's one magnificent clock. And I think I've seen it before. In one of the old photographs in the Deanery. To think of it coming home like this! Let me just lock up the cathedral, then come to the Deanery and see the photograph.' He clasped me and hugged me in a transport of excitement.

I drove round to the Deanery; a tall, classical terrace-house behind the cathedral. There was an entrance portico with blackened stone Doric columns, six ill-washed milk-bottles, and a notice pinned to the door saying: 'Dean at Diocesan Board of Social Responsibility – back at seven'.

'Would you mind?' said Eagle. 'Can we give the Dean a pleasant surprise? On the photograph we have, your clock is standing on the mantelpiece in this very hall. Can we return it there, for half an hour, in all its glory?'

I got the clock from the car gladly, if shakily. His idea went along beautifully with what I had in mind.

'That looks just magnificent,' said Eagle, standing back with his hands on his hips and head on one side. 'Just like the old photograph. Even the chairs are still here. Most of those old Deans were bachelors, and when they died they just left their furniture behind. You'll like this place, Mr Watson. I'll bet we've got more old things than your shop!'

'I'd like you to have this clock,' I said softly, hardly daring to breathe. 'It seems right it should come home. Of course, I couldn't just *give* it to you – I've got a living to make. But I got it cheap, and I could pass the benefit on to you. I could let you have it for fifty quid.'

His face was a study. 'That's generous. Such a beautiful old clock. But there are so many good causes to give to.' He looked doubtful. 'But maybe the Lord will provide.' The brilliant grin came back on his face. 'The Lord will provide for all our rightful needs, Mr Watson. And maybe the Dean's got something in a fund . . . I'll go and get that old photograph.' He streaked upstairs and was back in a second, on his long jubilant legs. And there was the clock in an old sepia photograph, rather blurred and out of focus, but as much its diabolical self as ever. Leaning on the same mantelpiece, head on hand and looking like a repressed Victorian volcano, was the Very Reverend P. S. Melmerby, with that slightly manic look that so many Victorian portraits have: Wagner looking like a madman . . . Gladstone looking damned . . . Freud looking like a demented Jehovah. They say it's only caused by having to stand perfectly still for twenty minutes while the photograph's taken, but I've always had my doubts. We were still looking at the photo and giggling when the front door opened again, and a squat figure stepped in and wiped his feet very firmly on the doormat.

Most of Eagle's exuberance dropped away. He said, 'Good

evening, Mike,' in a subdued tone. Then his high spirits broke through again.

'Don't you notice something different, Mike? About the hall?'

The Very Reverend Michael Wilbraham, Dean of Muncaster, took off his threadbare naval duffel-coat, hung it on the back of an Adam chair, and wound his long maroon scarf on top. He gave a sense of weary and disabled power. The lines on his balding face said he'd seen too much, thought too much, been disappointed too often. I just knew that I'd never sell him anything.

'What's that thing doing here?' he asked in an awful voice.

The smile faded from Eagle's face; he looked like a hurt child. 'It used to belong here, Mike. It's in this old photo.' He held out the photograph hopefully. Wilbraham dismissed it with a curt wave of the hand. 'I suppose that thing had to turn up again sometime. I just hoped we'd seen the last of it – in my time, at least.'

'What you mean, Mike?' Eagle's voice was querulous.

'Have you really *looked* at it, Eagle?' Wilbraham's voice was savage with disgust. 'Have you seen the decoration on it?' His pale, plump fingers flicked the cloven hoofs and the goat's head; the obscene frieze of genitals.

'Mr Watson was going to let us have it cheap. For the church.'

Wilbraham looked at me as he'd looked at the clock. 'I'm sure he was. You will oblige me, Mr Watson, by taking this clock away from the Deanery as soon as possible, and yourself with it.'

Full of sinking dread, I stepped up and took hold of the clock. It seemed impossibly heavy as I tried to lift it.

Next thing I knew, I was lying in the fireplace among the fire-irons, and Eagle was splashing water on my face so liberally I thought I was drowning.

'He's a sick man, Mike! We gotta help him!'

'Sorry about this,' I said weakly, trying to get up. 'I was in too much of a hurry to have any breakfast, and I forgot to have lunch.' But the world kept going dark, and I *couldn't* get up. I just lay there, listening to the battle going on above my head.

'Where in God's name do you find these people, Eagle? Do you have to bring them here?'

'Yes, I do.' Eagle was suddenly defiant. 'Like you said, in God's name. I'm not turning away people in need. What's the point in having a church if you do that? How can this poor fellow drive, in this condition?'

'All right – one night. He can stay here tonight. See to him yourself. And see he's gone by the morning.'

Gently, tenderly, Eagle helped me up the worn-carpeted stairs. I sat in an armchair while he made up a huge feather-bed, whistling to himself now he'd found some good to do. He even helped me off with my shoes and trousers. I was afraid he mightn't even leave me my shirt.

'Now you lie there peaceful, while I get us something to eat.'

I lay staring at the high, bare room; there was a dark patch of wallpaper over my head where a picture had recently hung.

When Eagle, still whistling, brought up the laden tray of supper, there was a small picture lying between two plates of steaming bacon and beans. He hung it back in its place above my head.

It was the photograph of the Very Reverend P. S. Melmerby . . .

She was there again; the warm little body snuggling in under my armpit. For some reason I was quite unable to move, except my head. I looked upwards; the Reverend P. S. Melmerby glowered down. He looked even madder upside-down.

But what light was I seeing him by?

I glanced across at the black marble wash-stand.

There was a lighted candle, in an old brass candlestick.

And by its light, the Reverend P. S. Melmerby knelt in prayer; bearded as an Assyrian, in a voluminous white nightshirt.

He took not the slightest notice of me; gabbled into his hands, like a man in the last stages of desperation. He sweated great drops of sweat, wept, implored his God, tore at his long, greasy, slightly curling locks and beat his great beefy hands, still clenched together, against the cruel edge of the black marble wash-stand. Then he was off his knees and pacing. Then down to prayer again, without hope.

I seemed to watch him for ever. Terrified though I was, I felt sorry for him. He became if anything increasingly desperate. He looked at a watch that hung from the pocket of his dark day-clothes, draped hugely over a chair. He looked often across to the bed; but whatever he saw, he didn't see me.

Then, down in the hall, the Dean's clock began to chime. Together the kneeling figure and I counted the strokes; he with tiny nods of his great greasy head.

Eleven, twelve, thirteen . . .

Then, with a huge sigh drawn from the bottom of his lungs, the Reverend P. S. Melmerby arose and walked across to his bed; starting to lift his nightshirt and disclosing great tree-trunk knotted legs, he climbed on to the bed.

The whirling whiteness of his nightshirt covered my face, and I passed out.

'How are we this morning?' asked Eagle, splitting his white grin over a fine-smelling tray of bacon and eggs. And yet . . . that grin did not have its usual brilliance. There was something a little forced, a little guilty about it. Like he was covering something up. 'How did you sleep?'

'I had nightmares.'

He wiped the side of his face ruefully; his grin was now smaller but a lot more real. 'It was quite a night for dreaming, wasn't it?'

'You too?'

'I haven't dreamed dreams like that since I got ordained. I was back in Barbados being a bad, *bad* boy. I lived a bad life, Mr Watson, before I became an altar-boy at the cathedral and gave my life to God. After last night's dreaming, I'm wondering if the Lord hasn't said to me, "Eagle, take your rotten old life back – I don't want it no more."' He rubbed his gleaming blue-black hair and whistled. 'What were your dreams, Mr Watson? Or shouldn't I ask?'

'Clergymen. Clergymen getting into bed in long white night-shirts.'

'You've been looking at our friend up there too much.' He glanced at the photograph.

'Oh, it wasn't just him. There were several more. A little guy with a bald head and long white hair. He had rather a sweet smile; a simple soul. But there was one real nasty piece of work, with cropped ginger hair under a wig. He put it on a wig-stand by the bed.'

Eagle leapt to his feet, the glint of scholarship again in his eye. 'Hang on, hang on. That's just incredible.' He swirled out of the door, and swirled back equally abruptly.

'Were they any of these?' He had an armful of small framed pictures which he dealt out all over the bedcover, like a pack of cards.

Some were faded photographs, some faded pencil-drawings. I scanned them, and picked out two, like I was going through mug-shots of criminals at the police station.

'The Very Reverend George Tait, 1871–1901. He was a real sweety . . . did great things for the poor children, but he never married and had children himself.' His face lit up; then darkened as I handed him the second picture. 'He looks *mean*. The Very Reverend Gregorious Halloran, 1785–1802. Started off as a curate at West Wycombe. Not a man of God. Lots of funny stories – found dead in his chair, one New Year's Eve. They said he died of a stroke, but I have my doubts. Paah!' He threw down the picture, as if it had suddenly turned slimy. 'Well, isn't that strange? You picking them out like that. I wonder if I should mention it in my book?'

'Better not.' I shook my head at him. 'I doubt the Dean would like it. You've annoyed him enough about that clock.'

'Been looking at that clock. It's real evil. Feels *bad*. Bad as fetishes I've seen on Haiti. I tried to pick Mike's brains about it over breakfast, but he isn't saying anything, except get rid of that clock quick. I'm sorry. Eat up your breakfast.'

He came to the car with me, swinging the car door to and fro, thoughtfully. 'If there's anything else I can do.'

'Eagle, you've done plenty. You've been great.'

'I hate to leave you like this.' He glowered blackly at the clock. 'Tell you what – here's my phone number. Any time you need me . . .'

'Thanks, Eagle.' I put his beautifully engraved clergyman's

calling-card in my top pocket – along with the folded hymn list. And drove away.

I got back to the shop, and a rush of business. Letters, slips of paper pushed under the door, asking me to phone people. Dealers rang up, demanding, it seemed, just the very things I had to sell. And not only offering to meet my price, but offering more than I would've asked. It was suddenly a seller's market. They stripped my shop bare; I was down to those silent ranks of black marble, and I even had tempting offers for those.

I didn't have time to do anything about the Dean's clock, which was sitting in my car. Several times I thought of having it in, to try and get rid of it quick on this seller's market. But I swear there was never *time*.

So when I closed up it was already dark, and I was feeling very much the Big Wheel of the antiques world. If things went on this way, I'd soon be very rich indeed.

I locked up and poured myself the first drink of the evening, too tired to cook myself anything to eat. And again, I thought of the Dean's clock. It was too vulnerable, sitting out there in the car by the front door. Anyone could nick it; kids might steal the car for a joy-ride. I'd better get the clock in to safety.

And then I shuddered, and thought, *no way*. Let it sit out there all night. If it's stolen, I can make a good profit on the insurance . . . several thousand quid. Plenty of people could vouch it had been Georgian. And it couldn't do me any harm, outside the house. I'd proved that.

I walked to the Alvanley Arms for a meal, and a few drinks to celebrate. As I said, I *walked* to the Alvanley Arms, even though it was a mile away, and it was pouring with rain. I could no more have driven the car with that clock on the back seat than fly.

Coming home again, I tiptoed past that darkened car like there was a person inside. That should have warned me it was later than I thought.

In the world that clock came from, it's always later than you think.

I wakened to the sound of dripping water; echoing in stony places underground.

Oh, God, I thought, not again. Please not again. It's not fair. The clock's in the car outside. It's not in the house.

The echoing and dripping did not listen to my arguments. I tried to reach over and put my bedside light on, but I couldn't move. All the fight was drained out of me, and not just with lack of sleep and too much drink and food. I went without sleep and food for days in Burma . . .

I could only wait.

Female giggles, the swishing of robes against soft skin.

Then shouting; arrogant male shouting.

Then the bed moved; and the warm and trembling thing snuggled in, sending its terror into me. And all I could do was lie there.

Then, I must have opened my eyes. A white cowled figure, nothing but cloth, stood astride me. With a slow gesture, he lifted up his robe and displayed . . .

With all my strength I kicked out.

It didn't scream; it gurgled. It gargled and gasped for breath and fell off the bed with a thud and lay gurgling and gargling and gasping in the corner. I knew it was dying; I've heard men die; but it took a very long time. It kept on trying to crawl towards the door.

Then my phone was ringing, hauling me out of the horror like a flung rope. I grabbed for it in the dark.

'Mr Watson?'

'Who's that?'

'Eagle. You O K? You sound rough.'

'I'm O K.'

'You sure? I'd come out to you, if I could. But I can't drive – I've got no licence.'

'What's worrying you, Eagle?' I looked at my watch; it was well gone midnight.

'I've been doing some research since you left. On that clock. In our old records. I found an inventory of Gregorious Halloran's worldly goods, made for the Church Commissioners in 1802 after he was found dead. The clock was his. He must have brought it to the house – the other Deans just inherited it. You know, the nasty guy with the cropped red hair – he must have brought it from West Wycombe.'

'What's so bloody marvellous about West Wycombe?'

'Don't you know? The Hellfire Club? Sir Francis Dashwood? Cabinet ministers they were, and so corrupt they make Aleister Crowley look like a Girl Guide. I think Dashwood had your clock made for the Hellfire Caves, where it all went on.'

'Caves . . . wet, dripping caves?'

'How'd you know? You been there?'

'I can hear the water dripping; the house is full of it.'

'Jes-as. I'm getting my clothes on. I'm coming to you, if I have to *walk*.'

'But Eagle, it's twenty-four miles!'

'I'm on my way!'

'No – wait!'

'Yeah?'

'Just wait there, while I put the light on and check.'

'Check what?'

'That there's nothing . . . here.'

'What'll you do if there is?'

'Scream blue murder.'

We managed some sort of laugh, between us. I switched on the light. Where I had heard a man crawl and die, there was just a rather nice Edwardian towel-rail, and a stretch of grubby wall-to-wall carpet.

'OK, Eagle. I'm OK.'

'I'm starting now. Wish me luck.'

It came out of the blue. I was still sitting up in bed, with the light on, and the dead phone still in my hand. I was staring at my legs under the bedclothes and thinking, rather stupidly, 'How could I have kicked that . . . thing, when my legs were in bed all the time?' Then I looked up, and they were in the room. Five of them, and they brought the darkness with them. One still wore a robe, with the hood thrown back, revealing a muscular neck. The others were naked and powerful and hairy. The heaviest-built one was going bald.

'Here she is,' said one, looking at me.

'She's done for Ormandby,' said another. He had a snub nose, a round brow below his cropped hair, and womanish curling lips. I never saw any living creature I liked less.

'Steady, Frank,' said a third. 'She may have a family.'

'She has no family. Charlotte says she's an orphan, and the girls will be paid to keep their mouths well shut. No whore kills a Franciscan and gets away with it.'

And all the time the invisible female thing clung to me in terror; blended into me, closer than my own body.

'*Finish* her,' said the one called Frank. He was sweating all over; his mouth hung open, displaying gold in his lower teeth.

And then they went to work on me. I'm not fooling you, Ashden, when I say that I went through what no living man has ever suffered, and I hope few women. I did not think it was possible to suffer so much, and continue to feel. And at last I felt death tear my body and mind apart, and it was a blessed darkness and silence. And I was *changed* and will never be the same man again.

But, at the end of it all, there I was, sitting up in my own bed, with the dead telephone still in my hand. I remember feeling myself all over, moving my arms and legs one by one, wriggling my soul round inside my skull and amazed I still existed, physically untouched.

And the dripping was gone, and the echoes were gone, and somehow all my fear was gone. The worst had happened, and I was still here. So gone was my fear that I put out the light, and lay back. Totally shattered; but relaxed. And immediately, that female thing was lying against me; relaxed, trusting, asleep. It murmured, just as any sleeping woman will murmur.

'What is your name?' I asked. I'd read that somewhere, once. That you must always ask a strange spirit its name. Like Christ asked the Devil in the Bible, and its name was Legion.

The voice, when it came . . . it was like only one thing I'd ever known. The time I bought up the old church-clock at Addeston. It hadn't gone for donkeys' years – but when we started to take it apart, in the darkness of the tower, putting oil on the screws to loosen them, it chimed for the last time. A great creaking, a thin ghostly screeching, whirring, and then, faintly, the clock spoke.

'My . . . name . . . is Susannah . . . sir. I . . . am . . . a . . . good
. . . girl. I . . . did . . . not . . . mean . . . to go . . . to Mistress
Charlotte's house . . . but she . . . offered a bed . . . and I had no
money . . . sir. She . . . said . . . it would be nothing . . . to affright
a young maid . . . sir . . . just a few . . . gentlemen . . . and singing
. . . and dancing . . . and lots to eat . . . and rowing on the river in
boats, sir . . . I didn't mean . . . the . . . gentleman no harm . . . sir
. . . I was afrit o' what . . . he was agoing to do . . . to me. I didn't
intend no harm . . . when I kicked him . . . there . . . sir.'

'And so they killed you?' I said, in a creaky whisper to match
her own.

'Aye . . . sir . . . as the clock was chiming, sir . . . and I was afrit
to go to . . . my Saviour, sir . . . because . . . I'd killed a man . . .
and I was afraid of hell, sir . . . so I went an' hid in the clock . . .
sir . . . I remember thinking . . . it was like a little house . . . where
time itself lived. And I've lived there . . . ever since . . . sir.'

'And are the ones in this house . . . the other girls . . . the men
who killed you?'

'No . . . sir . . they be . . . just my memories . . . sir . . . what I
can't help thinking of . . . sir. There's only me . . . sir. Will you . . .
protect me, sir? I will . . . be good to you . . .'

'Like you were *good* . . . to all the old priests who came after?'

'Aye, sir. I was very . . . good and faithful, sir . . . to most of
them . . . 'cept that Halloran, sir . . . he were a devil, and the
Devil took him . . . They were not displeased with I . . . most of
them . . .'

'Didn't they ever tell you you could be forgiven . . . that you
could go on . . . to heaven, without fear?'

'No . . . sir . . . they never told me that . . . not in all the years
. . . Could I, sir?'

'I'm sure you could.'

'They told I . . . I must stay in their beds, sir . . . or I'd go to
hell, sir. If it be all right . . . could I stay with you, sir . . . an' go
on to heaven when you go, sir? Then it won't . . . be lonely, sir.'
She snuggled in tight; she was very warm and loving.

'You feel so real . . . how do you do that?'

'I touch . . . your mind . . . sir. Nobody else could feel or hear me, sir, if they was here. Only you, sir. If you like . . . I can touch your eyes . . . so you can see me too, sir.'

'As you were before they killed you . . . or after?' I repressed a shudder.

'Oh, before, sir . . . for you . . . they did tell me I was pretty . . . back home. I only showed myself . . . as I was after I was killed . . . to Halloran, sir. 'Cos of what he did to me . . . '

We spent a happy night, Ashden . . . the happiest in my life, till Eagle came hammering on my door at six in the morning. I'm sorry about Eagle, but I could never have made him understand. We had harsh words, and parted bad friends.

Well, what do you say about the little present you gave me now, Ashden? You've made me happy, and you've made me prosper, so I owe you something. That's why I've told the manager to give you a good discount on anything in the shop.

———

'You're *insane*,' I shouted at him. But when I looked up, he was no longer in the room. And, not having heard him go, I began to wonder again if he'd been a ghost. But being a realistic man, I went to have a talk to Ponsonby, the manager.

'I've just been talking to Mr Watson, Ponsonby.'

'He's gone, sir.'

'So he was *here*?'

'He never stays long, sir. This shop is just a backwater to him, now . . . more for buying stuff and storing it than selling. He's mainly busy with his other shops.'

'Other shops . . .' My voice acquired an incredulous squeak. 'What other shops?'

'London . . . Brighton . . . Stratford. Paris is next, they say. He's a big man in the trade now, sir.'

'And he told you to give me a good discount?'

'Yes. Very warmly he thinks of you, Mr Ashden. Says you made his fortune.'

I stormed out, and didn't go back. But I did a fair bit of detective work. There *were* Watson Antiques branches in London, Brighton, Stratford and Paris. And later in New York and in the

South of France. Clocky indeed had the luck of the Devil. And I even paid a call on the Hellfire Caves in West Wycombe. They exist; they're a spooky tourist attraction now; not to my taste – a bit garish, with their shop-window dummies dressed up in monks' habits, and their canned spooky music conveyed over a loud-speaker system. And there was indeed a Francis Dashwood, and a Higginson, though I could find no trace of a Franciscan called Ormandby . . .

But the oddest thing of all is that the caves, being carved from chalk, are pretty dry, without the sound of dripping water any-where.

So I shrugged, and forgot the whole business. Until the day Clocky died.

He died in his Rolls-Royce, on a road called the Grande Corniche; on the Riviera, where he had a villa. The Corniche had some pretty steep hairpin bends, and on one of them, at the age of sixty-six, Clocky met his death in the form of a large tourist-coach.

His death wouldn't have caused much fuss, even though he was by that time a multi-millionaire, except for what the coach-driver said at the inquest.

He said that Clocky was on the wrong side of the road, wasn't looking where he was going, because he was laughing and fooling around with a young girl in the front seat of the Rolls. The young girl was plump and pretty, with rosy cheeks and long fair hair, and she had her arms round Clocky. And they were still laughing when the Rolls went off the road, and fell a thousand feet down the cliff. The driver was deeply shocked, kept on saying, 'That young girl, and that old man.'

When they got to the crashed Rolls, Clocky was dead, still with, they said, a smile on his face. And the doors of the car had not jolted open – they were still locked shut. In fact, they were jammed, and had to be prised open. And of the young girl who had been laughing, there was no sign. Neither in the car, nor on the hillside, nor for many miles around.

# The Doll

*I*T STARTED with the bloody-mindedness of Henry Prendergast, auctioneer and valuer (established 1852). Working in our market town, Henry's burning and only interest is in auctioning farms and livestock. But sometimes, when somebody's inconveniently died, he has to sell off the contents of the house as well. Which brings him perilously near the realm of antiques. And in Henry's estimation, antiques are of interest only to poofters.

So he doesn't so much sell furniture as insult it. A chair is simply a chair to Henry, whether it's a Chippendale or 1940s Utility. Cups are cups, whether Spode or chipped mugs. He's fond of creating large cardboard boxes, of mixed contents: anyone start me at a pound? I've had a profound respect for Henry's boxes ever since I found, under the red plastic orange squeezers and aluminium hardboiled-egg slicers, a hand-blown ruby-glass jug I sold for twenty-five pounds.

He does house contents first, so he can settle to the real business of the day; and does it at such breakneck speed that he frequently knocks down stuff to people at the front while there are still some London guys waving frantic catalogues at the back. He likes faces he knows and names he remembers, like mine; I am the poofter he sells mixed boxes to. Like the box with 'Old Clocks' scrawled on it; in the depths of which, under a long-dead Sectric wall-clock and a two-bell alarm rusted solid, I found the blackened works of a Tompion.

But on this occasion, the box was marked 'Dolls'. Now I've always hated dolls, and Henry knows it. But since two of the 'dolls' were classical Parian-ware statues of fair size, and still with all their fingers in spite of the cavalier way Henry had treated them, I bid up and got the box for fifteen. The Parians I went and sold immediately for seventy; I had a buyer before I bought them. But that left me with the rest of the lot, a doll I immediately christened Rosebud. I threw Rosebud on to the back seat of the Merc. By chance, she fell sitting upright; her china eyelids rolled up, exposing china-blue eyes, and she sat watching me drive all the way home. In spite of the quick profit on the Parians, I loathed her. Nearly three feet high, plump and smug. Neither a baby nor a little girl nor a grown woman, but uneasily a bit of each. If you undressed her, God knew what twee prudery you'd find; but I had no desire to, though her sumptuous brocade and lace petticoats had plenty of inviting buttons and poppers. As I watched her in my driving-mirror, I felt more like taking a hammer to her smug china face. But you don't make your way as a dealer by smashing things . . . dolls, even nineteenth-century dolls, were not antiques in my opinion, but I reckoned some indulgent and pressurized parent would fork up a couple of quid. So when I got home, I threw her on to a Regency sofa I hoped would fetch five hundred.

The next day, who should roll into the shop but Martin Tyzack. He looks like Billy Bunter, height six feet four, with a fringe of red beard, a darned green zipped cardigan and a green combat jacket they probably issued to elephants in the Burma campaign. A fat slob, you might think, and you'd be dead wrong. That paunch is solid muscle; I've seen him walk out of a sale with a mahogany *chaise-longue* under each arm. And slob he is not, either. He says his ancestors were Dutch pirates, and I'm inclined to believe him. He just fills your shop, in body and spirit, poking into everything like he owns the place, and his insistence that the world is as he says it is is so strong that he rolls over you like a tidal wave. The first time I met him I was green, and he nearly talked me into selling a bureau for half what it was worth. Only the telephone ringing saved me, gave me time to throw off his spell, and I sent him packing. We haven't got on well since.

Anyway, he came in like his usual horde of locusts, pawing this and that, poking at a Viennese regulator hanging on the wall that he reckoned was ticking off-beat, and threatening to knock it off altogether with his sausage-like fingers.

The only thing he didn't look at was the Regency sofa.

'That sofa's five hundred to you,' I said, 'and no discount for trade . . .'

He uttered his usual hurt yelp, and walked across to it. 'You must be joking!' He poked the delicate, fraying original upholstery.

'Five, and not a penny less,' I said, 'and if you burst that upholstery I'll sue you.'

He picked up Rosebud instead. 'And this?'

'Two,' I said, meaning two pounds. Now if you name a price too high for Tyzack, he yelps. And if you name one that's lower than he was going to offer, he gloats unbearably. But when you catch him on the *very* fringe of what he's really willing to pay, he writhes silently; a sight that gladdens my soul.

'Come on, have a heart,' he moaned.

'Two.' What a fuss to make about a doll!

'I'll take it,' he said, fetching out his greasy cheque-book. And wrote me out a cheque.

For two hundred pounds. Then he told me the doll was a thirty-six-inch Jumeau, and he had every hope, at the next London doll fair, of getting five hundred for it.

And so I came painfully to realize that dolls were big money. That night I put a permanent advertisement in the local paper for china-headed dolls. I was venturing into a field where I knew nothing; and loved even less. That was the first time I ever did something purely for money. In view of what happened, I suppose you can say it served me right.

It was always a game that left me feeling dirty. So often the dolls had belonged to somebody who'd died; so often they were being sold by old people, who didn't produce the doll till they'd finished telling their long, sad tale; or worse still, sat clutching it, so that I couldn't see it clearly. Sometimes the owner had just died, sometimes many years before . . . those tales were even longer and sadder. And often, when the whole story was told, with me sweating to be off to an auction, the doll turned out to be broken, or merely wax-headed, or in some cases, plastic. And yet not to make an offer seemed like insulting the dead . . . twice I had to stop myself buying total rubbish for far more than it was worth. I'd decided to cancel the advert, when the telephone call came through.

It was late. I was just about to turn in. But the voice was youngish, female, intelligent, cultured.

'Yes, a lot of dolls . . . oh, there must be four dozen. I used to collect them, you see. There's an Armand Marseille with the original wig . . . and a closed-mouth Kestner . . .'

'Where do you live, Mrs . . .'

'Westover. I'm a widow. We're the manor house at Westover. My husband's family have lived here for donkeys.'

It sounded a happy hunting-ground. I reached for my dealers' guide. 'I could call about eleven, tomorrow morning.'

'I'd rather you came tonight.' Her voice positively crackled down the wire, sharp with anxiety. The kind of sharpness I tend to associate with stolen goods. But the manor house at Westover? Hardly a likely receptacle for hot stuff. I looked at my watch.

'It's nearly eleven, Mrs Westover. It must be thirty miles.'

'It's a good road, empty at this time of night. I don't mind waiting up. I'm a late bird.' Then, almost coyly, though the sharpness hadn't gone from her voice, 'I might sell you my big Steiner.'

I looked at my Miller's *Guide*; a Steiner had just gone at Sotheby's for eight hundred.

'What kind of prices are you asking?'

'Oh, I'll look after you, young man. I'm tired of them . . . sick to death of them.'

I sighed. I'd had a long day at the sales, and my back was killing me. 'All right, I'll come; if you're sure *you* don't mind.'

'Just be *quick*.' She regained control of herself, poured back the honey into her voice with a conscious effort. 'Turn right by the parish church.'

I couldn't have missed it. A big house, standing well back in its own heavily-treed grounds. Every light was on, from top to bottom. There was a car parked outside, with the driver's door open and the right winker still winking. It had a disastrous look about it. But the grounds were a picture of disciplined calm, in the light thrown from the windows. Neatly clipped topiary, velvety lawns below classical urns.

She answered my ring so quickly that she might have been hiding behind the door. She had a half-full glass in her hand, and a strong smell of whisky on her breath. I began devoutly wishing I hadn't come. She said in a whisper, 'Come into the sitting-room. Would you like a drink? I'm just having a nightcap.' From the way she lurched against the sideboard, making the bottles rattle, she'd had a lot more than a nightcap. But she didn't look a drunk. Neat tweed suit, pearls, highly polished court shoes, and her hair hadn't been done this side of Muncaster. She gave me a drink, sat on the sofa facing me, clutching her own drink in both hands as if she was afraid she might drop it. Then she seemed to fall into a daze. Of course, my dealer's eyes were discreetly everywhere.

And I didn't much like what I saw. The hearthrug was Persian, I'd swear; but marred with two-inch burn-holes, as if coals had leapt out of the fire. There were five oval-framed paintings on the wall, portraits, possibly eighteenth-century. Or rather, there were four paintings and the oval fade-mark left by the fifth, which was tucked away behind the sofa, with its glass broken.

The silence drew out, unbearably.

'The dolls,' I said gently.

She came to, with a start. She must have been about forty; a real classy looker, except that something, maybe the drink, had pulled her face apart, feature by feature, and she hadn't been able to quite pull the pieces together again.

'My husband always hated the dolls . . . but of course you want to see them. They're upstairs. On the bed.'

Alarm bells began to ring in my head. When an attractive widow of forty, having got herself half drunk to ease her tension, invites you up to her bedroom at nearly midnight . . .

'I find it hard to judge dolls by artificial light,' I mumbled. 'Their colouring . . .'

I think she really saw me, then, for the first time; realized that I was a human being, with feelings of my own, with whom some relationship was essential. She smiled, looked a little embarrassed at my embarrassment, then shook her head. 'Not tonight, Josephine,' she said, ruefully. And, in that second, I really could have fancied her; she had been some looker. Then the odd fixed look came back on her face. 'Come and see the dolls – they're really there. This is a business arrangement, pure and simple.'

But still she spoke in a whisper, as if there were someone else in the house she didn't want to hear us.

So we went up the old, well-polished oak stairs. There was a magnificent grandfather-clock on the landing, brass-faced, worth a real packet. Except it had stopped, and the glass was gone, and the hands were twisted together, and the inlaid case was split at the corners, as if it had just fallen over in a very expensive accident.

'What a shame!' I burst out.

'Yes, isn't it?' she said.

'You're covered by insurance, of course.'

'Oh, yes, my husband saw to the insurance,' she said; and shuddered.

We went down a corridor, which didn't contain much but a long dark old table. On which stood a row of Parian-ware statues of a size that took my breath away, except that every one had been broken. The snapped-off arms and heads lay neatly beside each. I screwed up my eyes. I felt I was walking into a nightmare; when I opened my eyes again, the nightmare was still there.

She stopped outside the door. 'They're in here,' she said, in a lower whisper than ever. As she opened the door, I braced myself, expecting anything.

Except what I saw.

A four-poster bed, with old grey antique hangings. And on the bed, a mass of china-headed dolls. And each one had been systematically pulled to pieces. Their pink fat-bellied bodies lay naked and bulging, above a mass of disembodied arms and legs. Their heads peered at me from one heap, like the skulls in a charnel-house. All pink and smug, neither baby, child nor grown woman, but a little of each. And they lay on a mass of jumbled silk and brocade, lace and velvet, that must once have been their clothes.

'They've been naughty,' said the woman. 'Terribly, terribly naughty. So they had to be punished.'

It's one thing being alone with a sex-hungry woman. In my trade, along with plumbers and TV repair men, I see quite a bit of that. But even desperate sex has rules; you can withdraw from the game. In madness, there are no rules; or you might say the mad make up their rules as they go along, and they never bear any resemblance to *your* rules. I began to back warily towards the door.

But some of the mad use two sets of rules; some are very good at playing sane. She spotted what she'd done, quick as a cat, and changed the rules again, without visible effort.

'Sorry!' Her smile was very charming, very appealing. 'I've had a bit too much to drink. Now . . .' She began holding up dolls' heads briskly. 'This is my Steiner . . . big, isn't she? And this is a Bébé Bru No. 7 – I paid three hundred and fifty pounds for her . . . and here's a Schoenau and Hoffmeister.'

She achieved her purpose; the dolls had been worth a king's ransom. I began to look at them more closely, comforting myself that everybody has their funny little ways. She assembled a big Jumeau, swiftly and expertly, from the massacre on the bed. 'See, it's all here . . . nothing damaged . . . they just need sorting and reassembling. They're all complete and unbroken; you have my word on it.'

Oddly enough, I believed her. Mad she might be, but she was no swindler. Now she was running swiftly on, every inch the brisk businesswoman. 'I've put out an old trunk of my husband's here. They'll all go in there, easily. We can pack them in their clothes, so nothing will get broken.' The old trunk was very battered, plastered with labels from the Riviera, Florida, Singapore; an antique in itself. I wondered why her husband had been such a widely travelled man. Which had come first, her madness, or his travel?

But even in that strange house, at that unearthly hour, I remained a dealer. 'How much are you asking?' It was a good question to ask; from the world of daylight and sanity.

Her hand flew to the pearls at her throat. She hadn't even worked out a price; she was having trouble thinking of one now. And that, in my dealer's world, was unheard of. The first thing sellers ever think of is the price. From the moment they think of selling to the moment you pop the question. It may be a totally unrealistic price; they've probably revised it up and down for days. But boy, they *think* about it.

She swallowed and said, 'Would five hundred be too much? You could get that back on the Jumeau, once you got her back together. Then the rest is pure profit.'

I picked up various heads and looked at them, playing for time. I knew enough about the dolls by then to know it was all marvellous stuff . . . but the whole thing felt wrong. I may be hard, but I hadn't descended to cheating madwomen. Besides, she might change her mind. I might have her hammering on my door in the morning, wanting everything back. Probably with the alleged dead husband.

'All right,' she said 'Two fifty. I'm *sick* of them.' On the word 'sick', uttered with terrible violence, the madness surfaced again momentarily. I suddenly wondered whether the dolls were really her husband's . . . and the husband away; perhaps with a new mistress. That would be enough to make her break up the dolls, then try to sell them. We get a lot of people trying to sell us other people's things cheap, for spite. I was in two minds, between fear and desire, and it made me cruel.

'Are these your husband's? Are you selling them to spite him?'

I shouldn't have said it. The dam burst. 'My husband is dead,' she said, with a chalk-white stretched face. 'Do you want to see his death certificate? Do you want to see his grave?' Then she dropped her whisky-glass on the floor, and put her head in her hands, sitting on the doll-littered bed. The whisky spilled across the carpet; other drops spattered down beside it, tears falling through the cracks in her hands.

'I'm sorry,' I said, wanting to put an arm round her shoulders and not able to dare. So instead I added, 'I'll give you two fifty.'

In a second her head was up, and she was smiling radiantly through her tears in a childlike, affectionate way that was truly horrifying. I'd have paid a thousand quid to get out of that house then, let alone two fifty. But my troubles seemed to be over. She got up and began packing the dolls in the trunk, interleaving the delicate limbs between the layers of velvet and brocade with a deftness I couldn't have equalled. Instead I sat on the bed, with that craven gratitude you feel when the mad leave you alone; and wrote my cheque with fingers that trembled so much that I wondered whether the bank manager would recognize my signature.

Then I just sat and watched her finish, full of that limp relaxed warmth that creeps over you after stress; I hadn't felt that way since the bombing runs we made in 1940, when people fell fatally asleep on the way home.

In the end, there was just one doll left lying on the bed; a very odd doll indeed. For one thing, it was the only one that hadn't been pulled to pieces. It was quite whole and undamaged. For another, it seemed to represent some kind of negro child. It had a moulded china head, like all the rest, but covered closely with warm brown velvet, the kind you sometimes find on old armchairs. Its hair, long and frizzy, looked like real human hair, nearly the same colour as the velvet, but a tinge redder. The eyes were nearly closed, under puffy velvet lids, but you could see the slitted glint of eyes. And lower down, inside the slitted mouth, the glint of little browned ivory teeth. The body seemed clumsily made and looked like a well-stuffed velvet bolster; the arms and legs were chains of little brown bolsters, like a string of sausages.

I knew instantly that this was one I didn't want. But she looked up at me, impatiently, and said, 'Bring that last one over and pop it in. Then we're finished, and you can get to bed. The trunk won't take much carrying downstairs – it's an awkward size, but it's not heavy.'

'I don't want that one,' I said. 'I think I'll leave that with you.'

Her face, which had become reassuringly sensible, began to fall apart again. I remembered the storm I'd just suffered; I remembered, cruelly, the phrase about humouring lunatics. I could always throw the brown thing in the bin when I got home. Or maybe sell it to Tyzack . . . I picked it up, walked over and threw it into the trunk on top of the rest. She clicked the clasps of the trunk shut with three resounding snaps and said briskly, 'Let's go. I'll write you your receipt downstairs. I'll go first.'

We got the trunk into the back of the Merc. She seemed to relax all of a sudden, and offered me another whisky while she wrote the receipt in businesslike fashion. Then stretched out her legs, without much regard for her skirt. She had good legs, neat plump knees. And she didn't look insane any more, just terribly, terribly tired. Irrationally, I felt a twinge of desire. Perhaps she spotted it. It didn't displease her. But she only stretched, yawned, and said, 'I think I shall sleep tonight. Can you let yourself out?'

I drove home slowly and carefully; but it was late, and I met nothing but signposts.

I had another whisky and went to bed, but I was a long time in sleeping. My head was still in a whirl; I didn't know what to make of any of it. I dozed once or twice, and dreamt I was still in that house, by that bed, sorting dolls' arms and legs endlessly. The last time, I jolted awake; something was different, something was not quite as it should be, in my bedroom. For a long time I lay, mind half awake, body nearly asleep, sluggish, unmoving, wondering what it could be. Then I realized it was the bright light coming round the edges of the curtains. Dawn? I looked at my watch. Five a.m. No way. Besides, the light was too artificial, a piercing grey-blue. That got me out of bed, and to the window.

Outside, nothing stirred. My Merc was still parked on the gravel, facing the house.

With its headlights on. I cursed myself for a drunken sot. The battery must be nearly flat. I *never* left my headlights on . . . I pulled on a dressing-gown and stumbled downstairs. When I got the front door unbolted and unbarred, I found it was raining lightly. The cold wet gravel stuck up into my bare feet as I limped towards the car. What a cock-up! None of the doors locked, ignition key still in. I must have been more drunk, or upset, than I thought. And with dolls worth ten thousand quid in the back, waiting for the first light-fingered johnny. I glanced nervously at the trunk of dolls. In the glow from the courtesy-light, I could've sworn the trunk lid was open. Oh, God, thieves. And I wasn't at all certain the insurance covered stuff left in the car overnight. I hobbled round to the tailgate. That wasn't locked either. And it had sprung slightly open.

But the charnel-house of dolls was still inside; their glass eyes stared up at me, in mute, plump appeal. The woman hadn't fastened the trunk properly . . . she'd been drunk as well. Or else it was an old trunk, and the catches had sprung under the pressure of the bulk inside. Anyway, relieved, I re-fastened the trunk. Then locked the tailgate. As I did so, my bare foot came in contact with something furry, flabby, soft and wet. Looking down, I saw it was the brown velvet doll. Must have fallen out of the sprung trunk and then out of the car when I opened the tailgate. I considered unlocking the tailgate again, but I was too tired. I picked up the wet body, and as I was passing through the shop I threw it on to the sofa where Rosebud had once lain. I remember my hand didn't like it; it felt . . . *unpleasant*. But what else could you expect of wet velvet?

I walked upstairs congratulating myself on a lucky escape.

Strangely enough, I wakened in a good mood, though pretty late. But that didn't matter; it was Sunday, blessed Sunday. I listened to the bells of the parish church, ringing for eleven o'clock matins. I never go to church, but I like the bells and the idea of other people going to church, while I slump around in my dressing-gown.

After a good breakfast, I dressed in my oldest sweater and jeans, dragged the trunk into my living-room, and began to try to sort out the dolls.

It was hopeless. I managed to get together the bits of the big Jumeau, because she'd packed those close to one another. But otherwise, all I could manage was to sort out bodies, arms, heads and legs separately in descending order of size, pairing off the arms and legs where I could. By lunch, after a lot of sweat, I had four neat rows of arms, legs, heads and bodies stretching right across my lounge carpet, where they certainly couldn't remain for ever. The clothes were just a heap of pointless jumble.

Exasperated, I rang Tony Blackbarrow, who earns an idle penny lounging about Christie's at Chester most of the week.

'Tony . . . cheers . . . do Christie's have such a thing as a dolls expert?'

'We have someone who knows a bit about dolls,' he said primly, leaving me suitably crushed. Dolls weren't antiques, weren't worth an expert. But there was money in them, so somebody would know *something* about them . . . typical Christie's.

'Actually,' he added, 'you may be in luck. We had a rave-up in the Chester saleroom yesterday – some of the London top brass up before the sale Tuesday week. Most of them are still scattered round the Cheshire countryside enjoying your local *dolce vita*. Point-to-point at Tarporley, matins at St Matthew's, Wilmslow.' He yawned. He was only out here in the sticks with us because he'd said something rude to a boss-man in London. To Christie's lot, Cheshire is Siberia. 'Leave it with me,' he said. 'I'll ring you back.'

He didn't, actually. Instead, it was a very brisk young female voice. 'I hear you have a doll problem?'

I explained. 'Sorry to bother you – a bit of a drag on Sunday.'

'Not so bad as an outing to Hilbre Island to watch the damned seagulls, with my cousin's four sticky toddlers. Where do you live?'

Which was how I came across the first great love of my life, Ursula Spilberg. She was on the doorstep within half an hour. Tall, and about twenty-seven, but with a figure like a teenager. Black polo-neck sweater, black skirt, black nylons, black flat-heeled shoes – her only concession to her height. Black hair worn long and dead straight; said she always washed it herself, and it was true. Not a trace of make-up, and an olive skin clear as a pearl. An imperious but delicate nose, and eyes . . . brown, but otherwise, words fail me . . .

'Where are the dolls?' she said. And brushed past me and went to find them herself.

I showed her into the lounge, and watched her reaction.

Stillness. That's always the way with the real experts. Lesser men like Tyzack will poke, pry, turn things upside-down, wave their arms, go on at great length to impress. But when an expert's with an object, *you* don't really exist. They're like a worshipper with a god. At last she said, 'Are all the clothes complete?'

'I was assured they were.' That's something else; her kind of expert makes you careful what you say, like having dinner in a Cambridge college.

'A great collection, once. You may have twenty thousand pounds here; if we can get it together.'

And again, she lost all interest in me, kneeling on the floor, moving about on her knees along the pale pink, shining rows of limbs, her hands busy sorting, mostly as quick as a typist's, but sometimes pausing so long, considering, that I thought she'd gone to sleep. At last she got up and stretched, long slim olive hands pressed in to the small of her narrow black back. Now, the room was scattered with individual dolls, still in pieces, but complete. I moved myself from where I'd been sitting in a chair, and found I could hardly stand for stiffness and tension. I looked at my watch and discovered, amazed, that nearly two hours had passed.

'All complete except one,' she said. 'This Jumeau is beyond saving.' It was only a small one, thank God. But rather frightening. The top of the skull was caved in like a breakfast egg, but still attached to half the body. The other half of the body was still attached to a leg and a broken stump. The rest was missing.

'Vandalism,' she said. 'Someone has torn it apart. Why should anyone do that?'

'A child?'

'That is not the work of a child.'

For some reason, I shivered; perhaps I'd just got cold, sitting so still. 'Would you like some coffee?'

She relaxed, stretching her arms above her head with the carefree grace of a handsome boy. 'A lot of coffee – not Nescafé, I hope. And scissors and glue and elastic – you have elastic? – dressmaker's elastic? – yards and yards. It isn't perfect, but it will do. We have a long day ahead of us, Geoff.'

'I can get you elastic – but – we'd better come to some financial arrangement . . .' I felt things were getting out of hand – she looked a pretty expensive lady.

She looked at me, one eyebrow cocked. '*Dealer!*' she said.

'I've got overheads,' I said. 'You look a pretty massive overhead.'

She looked down at her own slimness. 'Massive?'

'Sorry. I mean . . .' I hated talking money with her, and she knew it.

'Look, Geoff, you will let Christie's sell these for you? Very well, then, Christie's will get their usual commission off you, and then they can pay me for working on Sunday. Go and get coffee and elastic and leave me in peace.'

'What about a bite to eat?'

'When I have finished – not while I'm working.' And she began to sort out the dolls' clothes.

I went down and knocked up Mrs Turton, who runs the village general store, and bought a lot of ground coffee and all types of elastic, which caused her to give me a very funny look. On the way home, I kept an eye open for Mirabelle. Mirabelle is my cat, or rather the cat that drifted in and took me over. Large, fat, tabby, middle-aged and utterly determined, she just wore me down with persistent sitting on my doorstep. When I discovered she didn't claw the antiques, or disgrace the fitted carpets, I let her stay. I suppose that sometime in her life she must have been neutered; she was certainly a female, and hadn't yet produced kittens.

I was a bit worried about her; I'd never known her miss a meal, but she'd missed one that morning. And cars come very fast through our village.

Anyway, there was no sign of her.

I worried about Mirabelle all day, off and on; there wasn't much else to do, except brew endless pots of black coffee and wash up, and watch. Ursula had an insatiable appetite for work, and no time for clumsy apprentices. Occasionally I was summoned to hand her a tool out of reach, or put my finger on a knot while she tied it. She'd indicate what she wanted with a nod and a mumble, because she had some tool or material held in her mouth most of the time. Half-cups of cold coffee proliferated along the lines of dolls, but when she happened across one, in the course of her travels, she drank it, hot or cold, regardless. I tried her with chocolate biscuits which she left half eaten inside their red and blue wrappers; I tried her with ham sandwiches, which she left to curl up and go brown.

So mostly I sat, feeling cold. I wanted to light the log fire, but the way was barred with recumbent, shiny pink bodies, and when I tried to cross them, I was instantly, malely and clumsily, in the way of important work.

I kept my ear cocked for the return of Mirabelle, feeling oddly disorientated, a stranger in my own lounge. Once or twice I thought I heard her upstairs, the soft tread and leap of velvet paws on carpets and furniture. But when I went to look, there was no sign. The door to the shop was open, and I looked in there; but she wasn't there, either. As time went by, and I fell into a cold daze, I thought I heard her upstairs more and more often. Except it seemed to my drifting mind that there was only half a cat upstairs, or a cat that ran on two legs, like Puss-in-Boots. But every time I went upstairs, looked, called, no Mirabelle.

Finally, I heard not just the velvet footsteps, but a gentle, sharp tapping, slowly diminishing. I knew what *that* was, all right. She'd done that before; rubbed in passing against a big Greek vase I keep at the top of the stairs, and set it rocking. I rushed out to greet her, with the kind of chiding a lonely man gives his cat.

Nothing. Except the pad of paws retreating along the upstairs corridor to the back of the house. At least I had her cornered now; no way she could nip out through the cap-flap in the back door.

'Mirabelle, you naughty girl. Where've you been? You've missed your breakfast.' If I had any worry in my mind, it was that Ursula might think me mad, talking to a cat.

At the top of the stairs, I stopped, listened.

'*Mirabelle?*'

A soft thump from the smaller spare bedroom.

'All right, all right, I'll come and fetch you, if that's what you want.'

The room was empty; I looked in every place a large, fat cat might get herself. Nothing.

Then I looked out of the closed lattice window. And there was Mirabelle sitting on the roof of my garage opposite, as large as life, washing her tail in the last rays of the sunset. I called to her, and she looked at me, inscrutably. I could tell she wasn't purring.

At the same moment, something soft-footed slipped out of the bedroom door behind me . . .

I rushed in pursuit, but the hallway was full of shadows, and my eyes were full of sunset, and I couldn't see much. I nearly fell downstairs in my pursuit of the strange cat. I knew it hadn't left the house; I'd have heard the bang of the cat-flap.

But the strange cat was nowhere downstairs, either. I thought for a moment I'd caught it in the shop; there was a dark bump on the top of the Regency sofa against the outside light, that hadn't been there before. But when I reached out in the gloom it didn't move. It was only the head of the brown velvet doll . . .

'Such a fuss about a cat,' observed Ursula from the floor. 'Like an old maid. You ought to get married, Geoff; give yourself people to worry about.'

'You offering?' I snapped. I was a bit put out about the strange cat; my sense of humour had suffered.

'Me? You couldn't afford *me*. You have me for a day and you're worrying about becoming bankrupt! Anyway . . . look!'

She indicated the floor with a sweep of her arm. Not only were all the dolls whole again, but one was actually dressed in black bombazine, with lace at the throat, and a little black straw hat pinned to her golden curls. 'Most of the clothes carry the maker's mark, thank God. The end is in sight.'

'Well done. Come and eat. Can I do you a mushroom omelette?'

'I could eat a horse.'

I cooked; Mirabelle glowered at me through the kitchen window from the garage roof, making no attempt to come down; Ursula prattled about how brilliant she'd been at sorting various dolls – a Heubach Koppelsdorf, an S F B J with hand-painted eyes – mainly in technical terms that were Greek to me. She was sitting at the kitchen table, still working at dressing another doll. 'Hey, that smells good. But listen, is that your prodigal Mirabelle returning? She must be wearing clogs.'

Well, it certainly wasn't Mirabelle, who was still glowering down outside. But there was a tapping of something hard on wood, coming from the lounge. I thought of every possible house-noise I could remember, and it was none of them. It was like some heavy-footed, uneven clock ticking . . . or something walking on two legs.

I ran to the half-open door to the lounge. Behind me, the kitchen lights were on; but the lounge was in shadow, now the sun had set. I have a low line of oak cupboards along one wall, on which I keep the antiques I want to live with before I sell them. Along that ledge a little figure in black was walking, with her back to me, and a black straw hat still perched on her golden tresses. The movements were jerky, not like real life, the arm movements small . . . but without doubt, in a mechanical way, the doll was walking. As I watched, she reached the end of the cupboards and stopped.

And then slowly and awkwardly she turned to face me. Even in the gloom I could see the fat china cheeks, the over-large blue glass eyes, the rosebud simper.

Then she began to walk back towards me.

'Oh, very well done,' I said to Ursula. I blamed her, you see, because she'd drawn my attention to it. 'Automated dolls – radio-controlled, is she? With a mini-chip?'

'What are you going on about?' I heard Ursula say. Then I heard her get up, and felt her standing behind me. And heard her sharp indrawn breath as she saw the doll. For the first time I felt a little nervous.

'Come off it – have mercy on an old man's nerves!'

'It has nothing to do with me!' she said sharply. 'It is just an ordinary Jumeau.'

'That just happens to walk, the moment you finish her. You'll have to do better than that.'

The doll turned a little sideways, so that her tiny china tottering steps took her behind a large hand-blown glass jug. She seemed to be pressing herself against it, like an automatic toy when it runs up against a wall. And then the jug began to rock, and then it began to slide towards the edge of the cupboards.

And we both stood and watched, pressing closer together, Ursula saying over and over, 'It has nothing to do with me.'

And then the glass jug tipped; and fell with a terrifying crash and scatter of fragments.

The doll turned and looked at me; then made off down the cupboards to the next object.

And I remembered Mrs Westover saying, 'They've been terribly, terribly naughty. So they've had to be punished . . .'

The next object, an art nouveau bronze figure, began to totter. As I reached it, it fell on my foot. Without doubt my foot saved it from damage, but it certainly damaged my foot. I saw red and grabbed at the doll, which was heading for the next object. The doll leapt from the cupboards, and scuttled across the floor with a dry rattling like a crab, and with surprising speed. I could not catch it. I chased it round and round; a tall standard-lamp that I valued crashed over. Round and round the room, ridiculously, we went. The doll had the trick of moving as you reached down for it, rather like a cat that doesn't want to be picked up.

In the end, I cornered it. It fluttered within my hands with dry, cold life . . . obscene. I held it hard by one leg, and raised it to smash it against the cupboards. Then I felt a hand on my wrist. A warm human hand, very determined.

'How much was that jug it broke?' asked Ursula, fiercely.

'Twelve quid,' I said, amazed at the question.

'And you would break a five-hundred-pound doll for a twelve-pound glass jug? You won't get rich that way, Geoff.'

That stopped me; that and the fact that the doll now lay quite motionless in my hands, smiling up at me.

'You hold it, then,' I said.

'I will.' She tucked it very firmly under her arm. 'We need a good cup of coffee.'

I sipped my coffee while Ursula held the doll upside-down and inspected it, inside its froth of petticoats.

'Perfectly ordinary legs,' she announced. 'Held together with my elastic.'

'But it *walked*.'

'There is another explanation,' she said. She held the doll upright and made it walk on the table top, in a hideous facsimile of its former behaviour. 'I can make it walk. So could something else. I think this poor expensive doll is quite innocent.'

'What do you mean?'

'I think you have a mischievous poltergeist.'

'But poltergeists throw things.'

'They don't, actually. The best authorities, like Wilson, say that they *convey* things through the air at great speed.'

'What's the difference?'

'A poltergeist can seem to throw a stone at you, but when it hits, it seldom hurts. And poltergeists can make a thrown object turn at right angles, like a flying saucer.'

'You mean, when I grabbed it, I was struggling with a poltergeist?'

'When it was wriggling in your hands, did it feel as if it was moving itself, as if it had a life of its own?'

'No,' I said, after thought.

'Well then,' she said, 'it is best if we get this little one to a place of safety, from great brutish brainless men.'

'But what about all the others?'

As if on cue, there came a tapping from next door. As of tiny china feet . . .

We went back in, slowly. Before we did, I switched on the light, for it was now quite dark.

And as the light went on, we saw them. Doll after naked doll, rising upright, faces smiling primly, rounded pink bellies glistening around navels, little pink limbs tapping out a stately dance in rhythm together, like an obscene chorus-line. There was a crash as some other precious object fell to the floor. I went berserk, remembering all the broken things in Mrs Westover's house.

'Damn that woman! She's wished these things on to me. She knew – she knew. I hope she'll roast in hell for this!'

As I said it, every doll collapsed gently back to the floor and all was still.

In the stillness, I heard the cat-flap in the kitchen behind us bang once. The way it does when a cat leaves the house, which is quite different from the noise a cat makes coming in. I could have sworn I had a sense of something leaving . . . then shook my head angrily to clear it of such rubbish. I went across and picked up my other broken treasure – thankful it was only a ruby wine-glass, part of a set of six.

'Was that your cat going out?' asked Ursula, shakily. But it hadn't been, because Mirabelle had just walked in. She walked from doll to doll, casually sniffing them, then indignantly demanded her supper. There was a fresh layer of drizzle on her coat, and her fur was cold from the outdoors. I knew she had not been inside the house before.

'Why the hell should she choose to come in now? She wouldn't before. She fought me!'

'I think she came in,' said Ursula, with a careful attempt at scholarly detachment, 'because something rather unpleasant just left.' But her voice broke before she finished, and she shuddered violently.

It's a funny feeling when something like that happens to you. I righted the standard-lamp (no damage, except the shade a little dented) and picked up the broken glass, glad the damage was less than twenty pounds – and the insurance would cover that, if I made up the right story. The real old ordinary world came flooding powerfully back (along with a smell of burning – Ursula ran into the kitchen and managed to save some of the omelette).

Or, rather, the old ordinary world came flooding back along the surface of my mind. But beneath, the darker part of my mind stayed occupied by something darker still.

'What *was* it?'

Ursula nodded at Mirabelle, hungrily finishing off last night's dried-out Whiskas. 'Whatever it was, it's gone. Or the cat wouldn't have come home.'

'What if . . . it . . . comes back?'

Again, Ursula nodded at Mirabelle. 'I think we shall know –
that one will tell us.'

'She'd better stay indoors, then.' I brought Mirabelle and a recharged saucer into the lounge, and closed the door. Mirabelle,
miffed at being mucked about, gave me one contemptuous look,
then went back to her meal.

'Why did it go so suddenly?' I asked. 'Was it something we did?
Something I said?'

'Well, you were getting pretty ferocious.'

I thought of all the damaged objects at Westover Manor. 'I
don't think it's impressed by human rage, somehow. What can we
*do?*'

Ursula got up briskly. 'I know what I'm going to do.' She
rolled up the sleeves of her black jumper. 'Get those dolls finished,
and in a place of safety. Have you got a big cabin-trunk?'

I showed her the trunk they'd come in. 'The locks are a bit
dicey – they sprang open on the way over here.'

'Did they?' She fiddled with them. 'They seem all right to me.
Still, have you got a couple of spare padlocks? Leather straps? We
could fasten them up, double sure.'

'They might . . . burst out.'

She looked at me, narrowly. 'When you grabbed that . . . doll
that was . . . walking . . . how strong did it feel?'

I thought; and the gooseflesh ran up my arms from where my
hands had gripped it. Then down my back, like someone walking
over my grave. But I had to admit: 'Not very strong. About as
strong as a mechanical toy. Not as strong as me.'

'Not as strong as straps and locks, then. And if we pack them
tightly in with newspaper, they won't hurt themselves. I'll dress
them; you pack them. You might as well do something to earn
your living.'

'What about that omelette?'

'You eat it – I'm busy.'

And so we worked, while Mirabelle slept, paws fatly beneath
her, just batting her ears occasionally at any unusual rustle we
made. I'd managed to get a roaring fire going by then, and of
course she slept in front of it. As midnight went through till one,

then two a.m., it grew perilously cold. And still we dressed the dolls, and packed them tight in the trunk in rows like sardines. The job seemed endless, but it kept us from thinking, and I for one didn't feel at all like sleeping.

By six, we were finished. The last doll went in. A last layer of tightly crimped newspaper, and then the lid went down. It was a bit like closing a coffin – the same feeling of relief. Locks clicked, padlocks turned, straps were tightened. We ate corned-beef sandwiches, cut thick with tiredness.

Ursula went to the window, hesitated very slightly, then pulled back the curtains with a decisive ruthlessness, as if she might confront something outside. But there was only my garden, in a dim pink light.

'Dawn,' she said. I realized that birds had been chirping outside for some time. And there was the accelerating sigh of the electric milk-cart, and the solid clink of bottles. Suddenly, I felt safe.

Ursula yawned and stretched, with that boyish lack of self-regard. 'God, I could sleep for a week. So much for a weekend's rest. Have you a rug?'

I brought her one, and she flopped on to my studio-couch, pulled the rug up to her chin, placed both narrow, elegant hands smoothly under her head and fell asleep as softly as a child.

I wasn't so inclined to sleep. Certainly I had no intention of going upstairs to bed on my own. I made up the fire and settled in the big wing-chair, not hoping to get in a wink. But Ursula slept on, and Mirabelle slept on, and the noises of the day began outside – cows in the lane, driven by old Harry Acton who was burping and belching and coughing off the results of another good night at the pub. I just closed my eyes for a moment. I felt my hand and bare arm (my sleeves were still rolled up) droop over the arm of the chair, like it always does. I heard Mirabelle stir and get up; then I must have dozed again. Gradually, I became aware of a small, soft creature brushing against my bare arm. A hot tongue licked my skin. I stirred, half awake, moved my arm irritably.

'Oh, lay off, Mirabelle!' She seemed to stop; I slept again. Then there was a little hot rough tongue rasping at my arm again, making the skin slowly sore.

'Lay *off*, Mirabelle!'

Then I slept once more, my arm drooped again, and there was a little flash of pain, as if she'd playfully nipped me with her teeth, the way cats do. But before I could move, it was suddenly all right. It didn't hurt any more. A kind of warm pleasurable numbness ran up my arm.

And then the dreams started, crazy dreams. A courtroom; rows of people dressed in black, with big white collars; a man pointing at me, accusingly. I started, and wriggled out of that dream. But the next one was worse: a scaffold, in a dreary, empty wasteland with nobody about, but with a hanged body swinging and turning in the wind. There were black birds perched on its shoulders, and when the wind turned it to face me, the eyes had been pecked out. But it had a skirt and long fair hair: it was a woman.

I struggled, trying to waken, to shake off the warm weight that dragged down on my arm. But I could not waken, and the last dream was the worst: Mrs Westover, in her nightdress with lace at the throat, screaming, choking. In smoke and flame . . .

Then someone was shaking me. I opened my bleary eyes, and there was Ursula, huge-eyed, shouting, 'Wake up, Geoff. For God's sake, wake up.'

I leapt up, half stupefied, half panicky, feeling sick. 'Sorry, I was having a nightmare.'

'Some nightmare. What have you done to your wrist?'

I looked down. The inside of my wrist was bleeding, from where the little blue veins are. Blood dripped down my fingers and on to the carpet.

Ursula knotted the clean white handkerchief round my wrist and said, 'I'll put it in a sling. You must keep it still, or it'll start bleeding again. What happened?'

'It sounds silly,' I said shakily, 'but I think Mirabelle bit me, while I was asleep. Except I couldn't wake up and stop her. She's never done that before.'

'And exactly where is Mirabelle now?'

The door into the hall was ajar; we'd left it closed. 'Funny – I didn't know she could open doors. I know some cats can.'

Ursula went and looked out of the kitchen window. 'She's back on the garage roof, glowering at the house. Same as she was yesterday . . . I think . . . that thing's back. I think we've got company again, Geoff.'

'Don't be stupid. Go and get her in.'

I watched from the window. Mirabelle came off the garage roof willingly enough, into Ursula's arms; she's a bit of a slob for a cuddle. But the moment Ursula moved towards the house, Mirabelle began to struggle like a mad thing. In the end, in spite of Ursula's efforts, she broke away, and leapt back on to the garage roof. Ursula came back, her face bleeding from a scratch. 'We've got company all right.'

'Perhaps she just feels guilty about biting me.'

'I don't think that was Mirabelle,' said Ursula, slowly.

'What d'you mean, not Mirabelle?'

'The wound was the wrong shape. It was more as if something had *sucked* you. I've seen Asian doctors using leeches, out in the Far East. It's like the wound leeches make.'

'Oh, come on. A leech crawling in here . . . Mirabelle would've killed it.'

'I think Mirabelle saw whatever it was, and ran away to the garage. It's back right enough, Geoff.'

'Oh, God, I feel sick.' I sat down suddenly, my injured wrist throbbing like mad. Then I jumped up again, in a fury. I picked up a poker. 'Let's find it, and kill it.'

We looked everywhere; searched the house from top to bottom, with every window and door locked, and the cat-flap blocked by the cabin-trunk. Every dark space we searched, every cupboard, drawer. Nothing.

Except, as we came back into the kitchen, a rustling . . . as of paper. It nearly drove us mad, till Ursula traced it. Then I wished she hadn't. It was the cabin-trunk. Small pervasive rustlings, as if, in their beds of newspaper, the dolls were trying to turn.

I snatched at the straps wildly; I'd beat the things to a *pulp*!

'No, Geoff. We know it's not the dolls – the straps are still fastened. They're harmless now. No, Geoff. Something left the house last night, and now it's come back and it's trying to move the dolls . . . What was your dream?'

I told her. We gazed at each other too long, too solemnly.

'Mrs Westover . . .'

'D'you think I'd better ring her?'

'It would certainly ease my mind,' said Ursula, bluntly.

But when I rang, a strange voice answered; a man's voice, slightly coarse and slow, but full of authority. It had to be a policeman's voice. It asked my name and address.

'It's strange you should ring, sir. I was just going to ring you.'

'Me? How did you know about me?'

'We found your name on a cheque in her handbag in the hall, sir. We got your address through your bank manager. From the date on your cheque, you may have been the last person to see her alive.'

'She's *dead*? She was quite well when I left her. She hasn't been . . . *murdered*?'

'No, no, sir. Nothing like that. Her bedroom door was still locked when the brigade broke it down. And the window wouldn't open wider than to let a cat through. You don't know if she had a cat, sir? A stray she'd just picked up? She didn't keep any animals that the charlady knows of.'

'I saw no cat.'

'No, sir. Well, I just thought . . . She had a paraffin-lamp alight in her bedroom apparently. She was frightened of the electricity going off all of a sudden in the middle of the night, the char said. It got knocked over, and the place went up like a torch, with her inside. Half the upstairs is gutted. I thought perhaps a cat had got in and knocked the paraffin-lamp over while she was asleep. But maybe she knocked it over herself, poor soul. She's been drinking pretty heavily, the last year. Were you a friend of hers, sir?'

'Well,' I kept my voice straight with a terrible effort, 'not a friend. I only met her two nights ago. I bought some dolls off her. I'm a dealer.'

'Oh, yes, the dolls, sir. She was very keen on dolls, Mrs Westover. Gave talks to the Women's Institutes about their history, and that. Will it be all right if I call on you later this morning, Mr

Ashden? As I said, I think you may have been the last person to see her alive.'

'Yes,' I said weakly, and put the phone down.

'What's up, Geoff?' said Ursula.

'She was killed by a fire in her bedroom. Just after I'd wished she'd roast in hell. I didn't *mean* it . . . What happened?'

'I think you'd better sit down and listen, Geoff. You may say I'm quite mad, but what I think is that something heard you make that wish . . . and went and carried it out. Those dolls here stopped moving the moment you made that wish.'

'Oh, that's crazy.'

'There's a way you can test it.' She nodded at the cabin-trunk, which was still gently rustling. 'Wish those damned dolls to stop moving.'

'I wish to hell those dolls would stop moving,' I shouted to all the empty rooms in my silent house.

The rustling stopped.

We sat around the kitchen table, just drinking coffee and waiting; kidding ourselves that we were waiting for the police. We couldn't seem to find anything to say, except I kept bursting out that I hadn't *meant* Mrs Westover any real harm, and Ursula kept assuring me she knew that. Once she said, 'I won't leave you alone in this house till . . . it's all over, Geoff.'

'Thanks,' I said, and meant it. As if finally to reassure me, she rang up Christie's and cancelled her appointments for the next two days, merely saying calmly that she was on to something 'interesting'.

When she came back to the table, I said to her, 'You know more about this than you're letting on.'

She raised one eyebrow. 'Perhaps. You can't be around dolls long without coming across some funny things. They're images of people, you see.'

'So are toy soldiers . . . so are bronze statues.'

'Toy soldiers are too little . . . and European statues are empty, somehow. People don't have feelings about them. They're just *art*.'

'What about crucifixes?'

'Crucifixes know their Master. So do most Buddhist statues. I wouldn't be without my Buddhas – they're better company than a cat. But Hindu stuff can be nasty. And there are the little Eastern cults. I've seen one or two things out of Mesopotamia I wouldn't give house-room to, at any price. Be careful of anything with wings and little moveable arms.'

'But dolls . . .' Even in a near panic, I was scornful.

'The French for doll is *poupée*. Did you ever hear of something called a poppet?'

'Some might say you're rather a poppet yourself.' Feeble, but the best I could do in the circumstances.

She smiled wanly. 'How the meanings of words do change. In Salem, Massachusetts, in the 1690s, you could be hanged as a witch for having poppets. Little figures made of cloth or wax, in the image of some neighbour you didn't like . . . stick a pin in them, the neighbour got sick. Melt them, the neighbour died. That's what the witchcraft tribunals reckoned, anyway – and hanged people on the strength of it.'

'Oh, come on, this is the twentieth century.'

'What difference does that make? I am sick and tired of people telling me it's the twentieth century, as if that ever solved anything. Aleister Crowley happened in the twentieth century; Adolf Hitler happened in the twentieth century.' Such a look came over her face that I was glad to answer a knock on the door.

The police. Uniformed constable, carrying his notebook; plain-clothes sergeant, CID.

I introduced Ursula; they were duly appreciative. Then the damned woman excused herself, saying she'd do some shopping while I was busy. At least she was keeping her word, and not leaving me in the house alone. The police gave me a searching look, but it was envious rather than censorious . . . then got abruptly down to business.

'You seem upset, sir. Nervous. Has something been upsetting you?' Why do books always make the police out to be fools?

'Well . . . I am upset about Mrs Westover, naturally.'

They did not look convinced.

'And, as a matter of fact, I've been awake most of the night.'

It was all too obvious what they were thinking, with those little smiles. I had a reputation as a sober citizen to keep up.

'We've been up repairing those dolls I bought off Mrs Westover. They're going to London for sale. They're pretty valuable.'

'Yes, we knew that, sir. She had them insured for ten thousand pounds. She sold you the lot, did she, sir? We couldn't find any round the house.'

'Yes.'

'For only two hundred and fifty pounds. That's what the cheque said. We thought it was a bit odd, that.'

'She'd . . . damaged them . . . pulled them to pieces. That's why we were up all night, repairing them.'

'*All* night, sir?'

'Till six this morning.'

'And the lady will vouch for that?' They notably relaxed, and I felt wrongfully acquitted of the crime of murder; but absurdly, almost tearfully glad, just the same.

'Mind if we see the dolls, sir?' I took them into the kitchen and showed them; almost hoping that the dolls would rise up and dance. Not just for the looks on their faces; not for the thought of what they would write in their notebooks; but because Ursula and I wouldn't be alone any more.

But the dolls lay quite still, in their beds of newspaper.

We returned, for some reason, to the shop, where I'd first let them in. The sergeant, whose name was Weatherill, sat down heavily on the Regency sofa. Then he noticed the brown velvet doll, sitting next to him. He picked it up.

'Nasty-looking sod, that one. Not going to London with the rest?'

'We forgot about it. It was the only one that wasn't broken, and I just tossed it down here.'

'That was the last one she bought. I remember her showing it to me – the night her husband died. She'd left it lying on the stairs and we reckoned he'd tripped over it when he came downstairs in the middle of the night, looking for burglars.'

'Burglars?'

'That was the sad thing about it. They thought they heard burglars moving about downstairs, and he went down to look, tripped over the doll and broke his neck. But when we looked there was no sign of burglars, every window and door tight shut and nothing missing – a tragedy that. A well-liked couple, they were. She went to pieces after he died – took to the drink. Never looked like getting over it. I don't know how often she had us out to the house in the middle of the night, that last year. She'd ring us up, quite frantic, but every time we got there, there was nothing. It got embarrassing . . . sad, really. Ah well, give my regards to the lady when she gets back.'

Again, the little knowing grins. I watched them get into their Panda. The sergeant made some kind of remark about what a smashing doll Mr Ashden had acquired, and the constable said 'Lucky for some', I think – I have a certain gift for lip-reading. Then they drove away.

Leaving me alone . . .

But before I had time to do more than go and slam the lid on the dolls and fasten the straps, there was a reassuring tooting of a car horn outside the shop. Ursula was back.

She came in triumphantly, bearing a large faded book that she said she'd conned out of the public library on a temporary ticket, using my name. She laid it on the kitchen table, put on reading spectacles that made her look a lot more scholarly without diminishing her attractiveness, and opened it at a certain page.

'Listen, Geoff. And don't interrupt till I've finished.' She pushed the spectacles further up her proud nose. 'Have you heard of someone called Matthew Hopkins?'

'The Witch-finder General? The one who burnt a lot of harmless old women during the Civil War?'

'I think,' she said, 'that *most* of them were harmless. But Hopkins was certainly nobody's fool – he knew a lot about witchcraft. And when he was trying a witch, he always attacked on two grounds, the first of which was that witches kept familiar spirits – cats and frogs and such, that went out to do their evil work for them. Carry out their wishes . . .'

'But . . .'

'Shhh. Listen to this. "Evidence against Goody Mercer, by Thomas Applewick, farmer. Item. That early one morning, about four o'clock, he did pass Goody Mercer's door. It being a moonlit night, he did perceive the door to be open. He did look into the house, and presently came four things in the shape of black rabbits, leaping and skipping about him. Having a good stick in his hand, he struck at them, thinking to kill them, but could not.

'"But at last he caught one, by the body of it, and did beat its head against the ground, intending to beat the brains of it. But when he could not, he took the body in one hand and the head in the other, and endeavoured to pull off its head. But the head stretched and slipped through his hands like a lock of wool.

'"Yet he would not give up his intended purpose, but knowing a pool to be nearby, he went to drown it. But as he went he fell down and could not go, except crawling on his hands and knees, till he came to the water. When, holding the thing fast in his hand, he did plunge his hand down into the water, up to his elbow. After a good space, he conceived it was drowned and let go. Upon which it sprang from the pool high into the air, and so vanished away."'

'Oh, go on. Black rabbits! What's that got to do with it?'

'I think you've somehow got hold of a familiar spirit, Geoff. That carried out your wish against Mrs Westover. I think it made the dolls dance, to get your attention, then . . .'

'Oh, *rubbish!*'

'Rubbish? Listen to this, then. Hopkins's own speech for the prosecution. "The land is full of witches; they abound in all places. I have hanged many of them. Few of them would confess. But they do have on their bodies divers strange marks at which – for some have confessed – their familiar devils have sucked their blood."

'This thing, Geoff, having worked your will on Mrs Westover, came back and . . .'

I glanced at the white bandage on my wrist. Beneath, the wound was still throbbing.

And, diabolically, it all came together. I remembered the odd little velvety footsteps upstairs, that I'd spent half of yesterday looking for. The thing that sounded like half a cat – the thing that ran on two legs – while Mirabelle crouched terrified on the garage roof. I remembered wishing Mrs Westover harm, and the dolls stopping dancing, then the cat-flap banging, as something that was not Mirabelle slipped out. Then Mirabelle daring to come back into the house, ravenous with hunger. Then Mirabelle fleeing again, and the little velvety thing sucking at my wrist. And the dreams of what must have been a witchcraft trial, and the witch's body hanging, and Mrs Westover burning . . .

A doll? It had come with the dolls . . . but the dolls were all locked up.

Except the brown velvet doll, lying on the sofa in the shop. The doll that had tripped up the late Mr Westover and broken his neck, having lured him with soft noises downstairs . . .

'It's in the next room – in the shop,' I said. I don't know how I kept my voice as steady as I did.

'Yes,' said Ursula, with a matching, vulnerable steadiness.

It lay there, quite still. It was, as Sergeant Weatherill had said, a nasty-looking sod.

'The doll itself,' said Ursula, clinging to her scholarship like a drowning man clutching at straws, 'is certainly nineteenth-century. The china head bought, the rest made by somebody.'

'But that dream was seventeenth-century.'

'It's not the doll itself – it's what's inside it. What the doll was made to hold. And the hair.'

The frizzy red hair, that went so ill with the faded brown velvet, was certainly human.

I picked up an antique pistol from a shelf; like poor old Farmer Applewick must have brandished his stick at the black rabbits.

'I'm going to finish it,' I said. 'The Aga's on – I'll smash it and burn it.'

'No,' said Ursula, urgently. 'No. It's on your side at present. It thinks it's your servant – and while it thinks that, you're safe. If it turns against you . . . It's probably indestructible anyway. Oh, you could probably burn the velvet, even the hair . . . but . . . who knows how old it is? Maybe thousands of years. They had familiar devils in Mesopotamia three thousand years before Christ. Don't *touch* it, Geoff.'

But she said it too late. I did not go to it, but it stirred, got up on its tiny bolster legs and feet, and began to walk towards me. Its tiny teeth glinted in its near-closed mouth; its tiny near-closed eyes were fixed on my bandaged wrist.

I stayed transfixed, till it touched my hand. Then I went berserk; if I paid with my life, it would not have any more of my blood willingly. If it killed my body, I would keep my soul.

I hit it several times with the pistol; then the barrel of the pistol broke off from the butt, leaving me with a handful of useless broken wood. It tried to run behind the sofa. I grabbed at it; felt, inside the velvet, bone . . . and sinew . . . a terrifying life, quite unlike the automaton movement of the other dolls. It wriggled like a rat . . . and bit me like a rat. I felt a sharp pain in my hand, and the blood flowing down my fingers again.

Then as if satisfied with the taste of my blood, as if it had shown me who was master, it climbed back on to the sofa and was still.

But it had broken my nerve; I stood there whimpering like a child.

And then the bell on the shop-door rang.

It was Tyzack, mountainous in his green jacket.

'You hurt yourself?' he asked, with more curiosity than sympathy. 'You want to get that seen to – it looks deep.' He proferred a handkerchief, much dirtier than Ursula's. 'And broken a good fake pistol too – you *have* been in the wars!'

Somehow his heartlessness steadied me more than the deepest sympathy would have done. I wrapped his filthy hanky round to stop my hand bleeding on the wall-to-wall carpet, and said nastily, 'What can I do for you, squire?'

'Harry Prendergast said you'd acquired a lot of dolls from a woman who's just died over Westover way. He's been chatting to the police about who's going to auction her stuff. You know how keen he is on house-clearances . . . when there's real money in it.' He leered at Ursula lecherously.

'Those dolls,' said Ursula stiffly, 'are now the responsibility of Christie's.'

'And I suppose you're going to be the best doll in the auction,' said Tyzack. 'I wouldn't mind bidding for you.' He looked round in his usual predatory way, and picked up the brown velvet doll.

'This one going to Christie's as well?'

'No,' said Ursula. 'That doll is for sale. Isn't it, Geoff?'

'Not good enough for Christie's. But good enough for old Tyzack,' said Tyzack, to no one in particular. 'How much?'

'Fifty,' I said weakly. If I asked too little, he'd smell a rat.

'Twenty,' he said insultingly.

'Thirty.'

'Done!' He stuffed the brown velvet doll into the capacious sagging pocket of his combat-jacket, and began peeling fivers off a greasy wad. 'Tara then. Seeya. Don't do anything I wouldn't do!' He looked from me to Ursula, and lumbered out to his Volvo estate.

'You're free, Geoff,' said Ursula. 'He took it voluntarily; you gave it voluntarily. Like with you and Mrs Westover. It's passed on – you're shot of it.'

'What about old Tyzack?'

'It's his worry now. I should think he can look after himself.'

Tyzack drove away, waving triumphantly.

'Will you marry me?' I asked her. It just popped out.

She frowned, half smiled. 'Come on – you're just overwrought. You couldn't afford me, little dealer – I'm the enormous overhead. But I'll make you some fresh coffee. Then I must be on my way.'

I still see her for lunch, when I go up to town.

I expect you're worrying about Tyzack?

You really needn't have bothered. After a decent interval, I rang him up.

'It's gone, old lad,' he said. 'Got a hundred for it. How's that for a quick profit? You're too soft, Ashden.'

'But it was . . .'

'I knew what it was. D'you think I'm a fool?'

'So who did you sell it to?'

'A witch, old mate. She's had me looking out for something like that for years.'

'Which witch? Where?'

'Don't you worry your head. She lives up Huddersfield way – old girlfriend of mine, when I was in the army. It's in good hands, Ashden. Don't worry, you've seen the last of it.'

And I suppose he was right. That was ten years ago, and I haven't touched a doll since.

# The Last Day of
# Miss Dorinda Molyneaux

*L*IFE'S IRONICAL; but sometimes nice-ironical. Take the time
I was struggling with all my might and main to overtake Clocky
Watson in the antique trade. As you know, I failed. What I never
noticed, in the middle of my exertions, was that I was becoming a
very solid, prosperous citizen in the eyes of my fellow-citizens.

Not, that is, until people began having a quiet word with me,
putting in a quiet word for me, ringing me up and conducting
rambling, ambiguous, awkward conversations that always ended
up with me being invited to join something.

The Freemasons I refused; if I have one belief, it's that I must
make my own way by my own bloody efforts, and my sense of
humour would never let me appear in a funny little apron. The
invitation to be a magistrate I put off for years; in my game the
line between crook and Honest John is drawn in some very funny
places (as it is in most games, if the truth be known) and I would
not play the hypocrite. But I joined Rotary without a qualm,
though I never did much apart from eat, drink and gossip. My
starring moment always came in their annual sale of second-hand
goods in aid of the hospital radio. I think at first they hoped I'd
find a long-lost Rembrandt. But in the end they put me in charge
of the old lawn-mowers, in the rain outside. (It always seemed to
be raining.) And if I got the odd sideboard as a bargain, or a set of
good Victorian chairs, I always paid more than the price they'd
put on them, in their ignorance. Of course, *they* reckoned they
were making my fortune . . .

But the invitation I liked best was to be a school manager at
Barton Road Primary. I was still unmarried at thirty-four – though
not from lack of wining and dining young women – and having

despaired of ever having children, the chance to acquire three hundred at one blow was too great a temptation.

The third meeting I attended was to appoint a new teacher. I found it amusingly boring at first. My fellow-managers were not a brilliant lot, being mainly the weaker hangers-on of the local political parties. Each seemed to have a set question which he asked every candidate in turn, with an air of profound wisdom. We interviewed three worthy female mice, in tweed skirts and jumpers, and the only difference I could make between them was that one was rather tall, one rather fat, and one amazingly minute.

The fourth candidate was Miss Dorinda Molyneaux. That caused a stir, I can tell you. The Molyneaux were a county family, living five miles away at Barlborough Hall. There were five daughters, born one a year over twenty years before, while their mother was getting breeding over with so that she could return with undivided interest to riding horses, all duty done. The girls had a name for being spirited. One had run off to South Africa with a Count Clichy, who had once tried to run our local country club. Another went far left, emigrated to America and got involved in the Berkeley campus troubles. I looked forward with interest to what eccentricity the eldest, Miss Dorinda (or rather, to be correct, Miss Molyneaux), should display.

Miss Molyneaux's eccentricity was doing good; to the children of the underprivileged workers. For I must explain that although Barlborough is a pretty half-timbered little town, it has its black spots, and most of them are centred round Barton Road.

She came in, closed the door behind her decisively, and shook hands firmly with our madam chairman, without giving her the option to shake hands or not. She then shook hands with the rest of us, with that raised eyebrow of privilege that requires introductions. She followed up the introductions with questions as to our occupations and well-being, and her general thoughts on life. She was definitely interviewing us. In all it must have taken up nearly a quarter of an hour. And we had allowed twenty minutes for each candidate.

Then she sat down, crossed her legs, and gave us, with a smile, her undivided attention.

The first thing I noticed was how remarkably fine those legs were . . . Miss Molyneaux was a very fine young woman indeed. Long, glossy hair below her shoulders, expensively cut to look casual. The pearls would be real, and old. A tan not acquired in English weather. A big girl, though not fat, and eyes as bold a blue as those of the first Baron Molyneaux who had crossed with the Conqueror and stolen his bit of England.

They asked her their usual questions. Did she believe in corporal punishment? She put her head on one side, crinkling up her face in schoolgirl thought.

'I'm not *against* it. Not *really* against it. But I believe in training by kindness. I had a horse once . . .' She kindly explained her theory of animal welfare to Councillor Byerscough, who was not half as senile as he looked, and a near Communist to boot . . . I sat back, waiting for her to lose one vote after another. Pity; she was by far the brightest person we'd seen that afternoon.

But it wasn't as simple as that. I wasn't allowing for the weight of prejudice. There were four left-wingers who wouldn't have voted for her if she'd talked like Ernest Bevin and sung like Caruso. There was the Headmistress, who sat with a look of spreading outrage on her face. But there were also five Tories, shopkeepers mainly, though they called themselves Independents, who were not only almost touching their forelocks to Miss Molyneaux but asking to be remembered kindly to her father. And both sides would have voted to spite the other, if the candidate had been the Queen herself.

And then there was me. I'd sat quiet, as Miss Molyneaux had swept out with a final gracious smile round the table, and hostilities had commenced. I'd sat quiet as old battles were re-fought, and old wounds, like the Dinner Ladies' Christmas Present, re-opened. And in the end, deadlocked, they turned to me.

Which class, I asked gravely, might she be destined for?

'Upper year, bottom stream,' said the Headmistress, her eyes going remote and frosty, sensing a traitor in her camp. 'Our worst problem – they need an experienced teacher who will keep them in hand – not someone fresh from training college, like . . .' She stopped herself just in time. 'I can't upset the whole school system in mid year by moving my staff about.'

Why did I vote for Dorinda Molyneaux? To begin with, I fancied her. Then, I had slightly cruel curiosity about what she and 4C would do to each other. But above all, I thought Barton Road needed a good shake-up. I longed to set a cat among the mice . . .

So she got the job, and thanked us graciously. And I earned the Headmistress's undying hatred.

School managers do not have a lot of say in the daily running of the school; but Dorinda's arrival was so spectacular that stories kept reaching me, third-hand.

The class horror (there's one in every class) moved in on her quickly. By the end of the second morning, during an altercation concerning a broken ruler, he called her a silly tart . . . Now Dorinda might be opposed to corporal punishment, but the Molyneaux did not get where they are today by not knowing how to cope with English peasants. And the vigour with which 'Molly' Molyneaux could hurl a lacrosse ball still lived as a legend in the halls of Roedean.

The class horror, Henry Winterbottom by name, was back-handed across the ear so hard he teetered on his toes five yards before he hit the painting-cupboard, which was rather insecurely fixed to the wall. Then he fell down, and the cupboard fell on top of him. The noise was heard as far off as the caretaker's house.

The Head rushed in and extricated Henry from the wreckage. Miss Molyneaux's teaching career looked doomed to early death. But blows were the coin of affection in the Winterbottom family, the only coin in an emotionally bankrupt household. And besides, the disaster had been so widespread as to bring renown on Henry's head also. Both he and Miss Molyneaux would linger in legend . . . So he uttered the gallant words, 'I just opened the cupboard door and it fell on me, Miss.'

The Head, sensing she was being robbed of her great opportunity, swivelled her eyes around the class, looking for a dissenting verdict. But the class was too firmly under Henry's thumb; and

Miss Molyneaux's violence was much too treasured a possession.
Not a lip moved. But Henry Winterbottom became from that day
on as faithful to Miss Molyneaux as any of her many family dogs.

And that was the way it went. Miss Molyneaux was used to
being firm with dogs and horses, and 4C became her foxhounds.

From 4C's point of view, she was the greatest of treasures, a
genuine eccentric. Where the earnest little mice would have
nagged 4C about bad handwriting, or not handing in their home-
work in time (death to any child's soul) Miss Molyneaux gave
detailed instructions on how to groom a horse, generously brandish-
ing a curry-comb in huge strokes that carved an invisible horse
out of the air.

Then there were those thrilling moments of silence, after Henry
asked such questions as: 'Have you ever drunk champagne, miss?'
Which were rewarded not only with the news that Bollinger '48
was the best champagne to buy, but that Miss Molyneaux had
actually consumed a whole jeroboam with a feller in a punt on the
river at Cambridge, at the incredibly aristocratic hour of four in
the morning.

The Head tried a few sneaky tricks. Classes had to be marched
in crocodile to the playing-field a mile away for games. It was said
that many such journeys had turned the Deputy-Headmaster's
hair grey.

But Miss Molyneaux had a good eye and a vigorous disposition.
She not only took over the girls' hockey team, but joined in the
boys' soccer in her flaring-blue tracksuit, laying out the school
captain with a magnificent foul.

Soon, the whole school was eating out of her hand, and to 4C
she was a goddess. Several parents complained about requests for
ponies at Christmas . . .

It was at about this time that I came back upon the scene. She
nailed me at the Autumn Fayre, held in aid of a school minibus.

'Their minds need broadening,' she said. 'No good teaching
history without *showing* them. I hear you know about old things.'
So I turned up one afternoon with the least breakable items from
my shop. And, as we've learnt to say now, she counted them all
out and she counted them all back, heavily thumb-printed. And

Henry Winterbottom got the silver salt-cellar back out of Jack Hargreaves's trouser-pocket before I'd even missed it. Henry gave Jack a well-aimed kidney-punch by way of retribution, saying, 'You can't nick off him – he's miss's *feller*, ain't he?'

Miss, who also overheard this infant dialogue, had the grace to blush, and I suddenly felt I had a chance. 'We ought to take them round a stately home,' I said, ever the good citizen.

'How nice,' she said, with the kind of smile you give the Spanish chargé d'affaires.

'But we'd better spy out the land first,' I added. 'So you can make up a project. Do you know Tattersham Hall?'

'No, I don't know Tattersham,' she said, suddenly sharp. 'Who lives there now?' I felt I was moving into a different league.

'A lot of butterflies.'

'Oh, that silkworm lot,' she said ungraciously. 'They bought out Bertie Tattersham after he'd got the DTs, silly old sod.'

The Headmistress passed, giving a look that would cheerfully have crucified us both.

'You free Saturday afternoon?' said Dorinda. She was never one to wait to be asked.

I drove up to Barlborough Hall prompt on two. Dorinda was in the formal garden with two rather disreputable Pekinese called Marco and Polo; she was either teaching them to pull up weeds, or instructing the flowers how to grow. Something was certainly getting it in the neck.

Marco peed on my best cavalry-twill slacks, by way of greeting.

'Not used to animals, then?' asked Dorinda brutally. 'It's a sign of affection – he's marking you out as his property.' Obviously, Polo felt hurt about Marco's pre-emptive strike on my garments; he walked up casually and buried his teeth in the tatty fur round Marco's neck. Together they rolled into some rather depressed laurels, making a sound like feeding-time at the zoo.

'They're *great* friends,' said Dorinda.

She looked at my Chrysler station-wagon, parked on the rather thin and rutted gravel. 'Is it foreign?'

'It's illegitimate,' I said gravely. 'Its mother was a Rolls, but they left her out one night and she was raped by a rather common single-decker bus.'

'I suppose it will get us there?'

'And your best Sheraton commode, six Chippendale dining-chairs and all your family portraits.'

'Oh, yes, you're a dealer, aren't you?'

Not a propitious start, and the trip got steadily worse. We walked into the entrance-hall at Tattersham, which is lined with dead and glorious foreign butterflies in celluloid boxes, which some people will pay up to four hundred pounds for.

'Yu-uk!' said Dorinda; a noise of disgust so explosive it would have made Earl Harold flee the field at Hastings. It turned every head in the room.

'I thought your lot liked dead animals?' I said.

'Only ones we've shot ourselves. Anyway, when . . . if I ever invite you for tea, you won't find a single dead animal at Barlborough. We are not a "lot" – we're individual people, and I've never met the Duke of Edinburgh, either.'

I had hoped it might be romantic in what the Tattersham people call the Jungle: the old palm-house, still full of palms and little tinkling power-driven waterfalls, but now alive with huge tropical butterflies that will actually settle on your hand.

'Bloody hot in here. Worse'n a Turkish bath,' said Dorinda. A blue swallowtail from Malaya settled on her shoulder. 'Tatty-looking thing,' she observed. 'Falling to pieces. Should be put out of its misery.'

Then she dragged me from room to room, questioning everyone she could lay her hands on about the processes of silk-farming. I left her side for a moment. It was a mistake. I heard her hoot, 'You mean they have to *kill* the poor things, to get the silk? Kill them by boiling them alive? Monstrous. Should be abolished. I'd rather wear nylon knickers, now I know.'

I got her away from the blushing curator with, as the RAF used to say, maximum boost.

'Not bringing the kids here,' she announced, as we tumbled down the front steps. 'Nothing but a bloody abattoir. What's that?' She stopped abruptly, so that I banged into her, which was not unpleasant.

'That's Tattersham church.'

'But it's three miles from the village.'

'But very close to the Hall. The gentry could walk there without even getting wet. The villagers could walk it in an hour – nothing to peasants.'

The blue frost of her eyes travelled slowly up and down my face.

'I wasn't aware there was a Peasants' Union, Mr Ashden,' she said at last, 'and I wasn't aware you'd appointed yourself shop-steward. I suppose your father was a docker or something, and you're not going to allow me to forget it. I suppose you left school at twelve, and worked polishing the gentry's boots for two shillings a week, and a half-day off every fortnight.'

'My father,' I said, 'is a bank manager in Cottesden, and I took a second in History at Durham.'

'More the Petty-Bourgeois Union, then?'

'Do you want to see the church?'

It might have been the sudden frost in the May of our relationship, but I shuddered as we approached that church. It wasn't the sort of church I like. It might have been medieval once, but it had been badly got at during the Gothic Revival. The worst thing they'd done was to re-case the outside in some pale, marble-like stone, as smooth and nasty as a marshmallow. The years are not kind to that sort of stone; green algae had gathered in every crevice and ledge, and dribbled its pale-green-ness down the walls. It looked like a hollowed-out tombstone, with windows.

The door was open. In fact, from the rusted lock and the porch-ful of dead leaves, I guessed nobody ever bothered to close it; the nearest village was three miles away, and there was no fear of vandals. All the notices flapping on the notice-board were yellow and held on with drawing-pins that had deteriorated into blobs of rust. The vicar, the Reverend Ernest Lacey, lived five miles away, at Tettesden: if it was still the same vicar.

We pushed on, through the inner door. Inside, purple and blue windows, in the black darkness. We stood for a moment, unable to see even our feet.

Then the family tombs began to loom towards us out of the darkness. They reared up to left and right, the whole length of the wall, a flowering of white marble pillars and marble faces lying on gilt cushions, trophy of shield and sword and trumpet, and pot-bellied exulting cherub with dust piled in his navel. They crowded inwards across the black-and-white tiled floor, like a crowd at a road accident, bare white marble arms outflung pleadingly in frozen futile gestures; white marble eyes seeing nothing, but seeming to know a great deal. Between them, the space for the living, a few short box-pews, seemed to cower and shrink. Even if that church was packed, the dead would surely outnumber the living.

> IN THE FAMILY VAULT UNDER THE ALTAR
> ARE DEPOSITED THE REMAINS OF
> JOHN ANSTEY ESQUIRE
> SECOND SON OF THE LATE CHRISTOPHER
> ANSTEY ESQUIRE
> AND ONE OF HIS MAJESTY'S COMMISSIONERS
> FOR
> AUDITING PUBLIC ACCOUNTS
> WHO DEPARTED THIS LIFE THE 25TH NOVEMBER
> 1810

So many wanting to be remembered, and so few coming to remember them. It struck me that the ignored dead might get angry, like tigers in a zoo that have been left hungry for too long.

'Oh, that's *beautiful*,' breathed Dorinda. She was staring at a grille that bordered the altar; a thing that the blue window behind reduced to a skeleton, but which on closer inspection still disclosed a lick of gilt. I went up and fingered it. Very fine wrought-iron work, of curiously individual design. It closed off a pointed arch, and seemed to my bemused gaze to be almost woven out of odd-shaped distorted crosses, overlapping, and weaving through each other.

'It is by Tijou?' whispered Dorinda, awed for once.

'Too late for Tijou – Tijou's your 1680s – St Paul's. This is more your 1760s. Still, a good piece of blacksmithing.'

'Peasant! But the children could make rubbings of the patterns on it – they could copy out the words on the tombs, and draw the cherubs. And Henry would love to draw all those spears and shields.'

'And there's a couple of monumental brasses, I'll bet.' I pulled back a faded red carpet, unpleasantly damp to my fingers, to reveal a six-foot knight and his lady, engraved flat in brass, inlaid in the black-and-white marble of the floor.

'Oh, this would make a *lovely* project – we could have an exhibition in the school hall. But how can we get them here?'

She turned to me, flushed with enthusiasm, mouth open. I wanted to kiss her, but settled for saying, 'Well, the school's getting the minibus soon. Can you drive it?'

'Of course.'

'And if I bring my illegitimate Rolls, I can park twelve into that.'

'Will it be safe?'

'Never lost a grandfather-clock yet, and they're worth money.'

'Oh, let's *do* it, Geoff!'

One part of me was elated; she'd never called me 'Geoff' before. But the other half of me, the antique-dealer, was doubtful.

This church felt wrong. I do not say this lightly. Dealers are undertakers of a sort. When a man dies, the undertaker comes for his body, and quite often the dealer comes for the rest. How often I have been left alone to break up the home a man has built up over fifty years, and sell the pieces where I can. As I break up the home, I know the man. I have known a cracked teapot yield enough evidence of adultery to satisfy ten divorce-court judges. I learn that he was mean from his boots; that trapped for ever inside the sepia photographs are seven of his children. From his diary, that he believed in God or the Devil or Carter's Little Liver Pills. I deal in dead men's clocks, pipes, swords and velvet breeches. And passing through my hands, they give off joy and loneliness, fear and optimism. I have known more evil in a set of false teeth than in any so-called haunted house in England.

And this church felt wrong . . . I tried to temporise. 'It's . . not a good example of the style. I have a friend, a vicar, with the most beautiful church. He's studied it for years. He'll explain everything to the kids . . . it's got bells they can ring . . .'

She set her chin stubbornly. 'No. *I* found this. If you won't help me, I'll come on my own. Hire a coach . . .'

I disliked the idea of her and the kids being here alone even more. So against my better judgement, I said 'O K.'

Then she said, suddenly more sensitive than I'd known her, 'You don't like the place, do you, Geoff?'

'It feels wrong.'

'We're not going to *feel* it; we're going to draw it.' And the brave invulnerable smile came back, like a highwayman putting on his mask. I think, in that moment, I fell in love with her.

And knowing that, I still didn't stop the awful thing that happened.

'Cor, sir, there ain't half a niff down there,' said Henry Winterbottom, sticking his nose through the gilded grille. 'What is it, the bog?'

'Clot,' said Jack Hargreaves. 'That's the Crip. Dracula's down there.' He started chewing avidly at Henry's filthy neck, until Henry gave him a punch that sent him rattling against the ironwork.

'Yer mean . . . bodies?' Henry's eyes glowed with what might have been described as an unearthly light. 'Bodies all rotting, with their eyes falling out an' the flesh hanging off their bones, an' *skulls*.'

'Can we go down an' get one out of the coffin, sir?' asked Jack Hargreaves.

'No,' I said firmly.

'Aw, sir, *please*. We wouldn't do it no harm. We'd put it back, after.'

'It's unhygienic, shows no respect for the dead, and besides, the grille's locked,' I said.

'Oh, yeah,' said Jack Hargreaves, rather professionally. 'Reckon you could pick that lock, Winterbottom?'

'Try me.'

But I shooed them on and got them distracted in brass-rubbing a knight in armour, to the sound of tearing rubbing-paper, and cries of 'Stupid bastard' and '*You* did that.'

I prowled on; I couldn't keep still in that place. It wasn't just the cold. I thought I'd come prepared for that, with a quilted anorak and three sweaters. No, I kept having, not delusions, not even fears, but odd little anxieties . . . preoccupations. I had the conviction the walls weren't vertical . . . or was it the floor, that seemed to slope down towards the middle of the nave? Certainly the floor was hollow; no one could walk on it and listen to the echo of his footsteps without realizing that. Then . . . the windows didn't seem to be letting in as much light as they should. I kept going outside to check if the sky was getting cloudy, but it was still bright and sunny, thank God, and I went back feeling the better for it.

Then I stared at the cross in a side-chapel. It just looked like two bits of wood nailed together. I mean, it *was* just two bits of wood nailed together; but though I'm not a religious sort, I tend to see any cross as a bit more than two bits of wood nailed together.

And that smell. Or niff, as Henry would have it. It wasn't strong, but it was everywhere; you never got it out of your nostrils. The only thing I can liken it to was when I got in a new lavatory-bowl at the shop; it had to be left for the sealant to dry overnight, so the builder stuffed wet paper down the hole, but the biting black smell of the sewer filled my shop and dreams all night.

For a while, till lunch, the children made things better. There's an atomic bomb of enthusiasm in a lively class of thirty-five let loose from school for the day. I could almost feel their vitality invading every part of the dark affronted silence. But, little by little, the silence absorbed it . . . Lunchtime was still happy, with the children asking what the big house was for. But they were curiously reluctant to get back to work afterwards, and then the grumbles started.

'Miss, this Sellotape won't stick!'

'Sir, me pencil's broken again.'

Dorinda was a tower, a fury of strength, coursing round the church non-stop. I began to realize just how hard a good primary teacher can work. But the complaints began to overtake even her speed. Soon, in spite of both our efforts, only half the children were working; the rest were standing round in little dispirited groups.

Then there was a god-awful scream from the chancel: one of the younger girls screaming, on and on. Dorinda ran, I ran. The child was standing tearing at her cheeks with her fingers, eyes shut and a noise issuing from her open mouth like a demented steam-whistle.

'It's a spider, miss. Behind that man's head.' They pointed to the recumbent effigy of the tenth Lord Tattersham, who had a smirk of dying satisfaction on his face, and who appeared to have been carved from some singularly pale and nasty Cheddar cheese.

'Garn, only a spider . . .' Henry flicked with his hand behind the tenth lord's ear and the spider dropped to the floor. We all gaped; it was impressively huge. Henry raised his hobnailed boot . . .

'No,' I said. 'It's just an ordinary spider – just got rather old and big – a grandspider, maybe!'

There was a thin and nervous titter; then I picked up the spider and let it run up my anorak. 'They're very useful,' I said. 'If it wasn't for them, the flies of the world would poison us all.' I carried the spider out, saying encouragingly to him, 'Come on, Eustace.' It seemed important just then to dispel fear, discourage killing. When I got back, most of them were working, and the cheerful noise was back.

'Thanks,' said Dorinda. 'You wouldn't make a bad teacher, you know.'

'Thanks' I said. 'But I *am* a good dealer. Eustace'll fetch a pound for somebody's stuffed spider collection.' She looked as if she half believed me, then turned away laughing. That was good, too. Though I thought there was something a little shaky in her laugh.

I went to check my pile of gear by the door. Cameras, gadget-bag. But also my first-aid kit and two big lanterns. I had come pre-pared for a siege. Two large thermos-flasks of coffee; a box of

Mars bars. I hadn't the slightest idea what I was expecting, but nothing good.

A memorial on the wall caught my eye.

TO THE MEMORY OF THOMAS DORE

AN HONOURED AND PAINEFUL

SCHOOLEMASTER

LAY PREACHER AND BENEFACTOR OF THIS

PARISH.

HE PUBLICKLY REBUKED VICE AND

DISCRETELY PRACTISED VIRTUE

AND LEFT HIS INTIRE ESTATE

TO BUY TRACTS FOR THE POOR.

THIS MONUMENT WAS ERECTED BY

PUBLICK SUBSCRIPTION

AMONG HIS GRIEVING FRIENDS AND

PUPILS

MDCCCX

BLESSED ARE THEY THAT REST IN THE

LORD

There was the crash of a drawing-board, the tinkle of paper-clips and a wail of 'Oh, miss, he's tore it!'

'Thomas Dore, where art thou,' I muttered. 'We could do with some reinforcements.'

But there was no crack of thunder in response, no rending of the tomb, only echoing cries of 'Henry's took my rubber, sir.'

I did my utmost; I whizzed up and down with my flashgun and camera, taking pictures of everybody working; I gave out coffee, then followed up with a round of Mars bars. But more and more, in my rounds, I came across a scatter of work abandoned. And more and more I found children gathered miserably in the shelter of the porch, on any excuse: a stone in the shoe; the need for a loo; feeling faint, feeling sick. I ferried many across to the loos in the house. Their eyes caught the butterflies in the entrance-hall. The demands to go to the loo reached epidemic proportions as word of the butterflies got back; one would have thought cholera or dysentery was raging.

In the end, I made a bargain with them. If they'd go back and finish their work and clear up nicely, I'd fix a quick trip round the butterflies.

'That's bribery,' hissed Dorinda in the live-silkworm room.

'Do you want to put on a good exhibition or not?' I hissed back, reaching forward just in time to stop Henry stuffing three live silkworms into an empty cigarette packet (though all the display-cabinets appeared locked and sealed . . .).

I must admit I was glad to see Tattersham church fading back into the dusk in my rear-view mirror as I herded the minibus towards home like an anxious sheepdog. I was just grateful that nothing really bad had happened . . . even though the minibus ahead seemed full of the fluttering shapes of swallowtail butterflies.

They tumbled out of the transport happily enough in the school-yard. In fact, they'd sung the first two lines of old pop-songs over and over, all the way home, a sure sign of well-being.

'Where's he taking you tonight, miss?' inquired Jack Hargreaves, loudly.

'What do you mean?' bridled Dorinda.

''e's taking you to the flicks, ain't he? Your feller? I mean, 'e's not stingy . . . they've got Elvis on at the Roxy.'

'It's a cowboy film, miss – "Love me Tender".'

'Oh, it's lovely, miss – he gets killed in the end,' chorused the girls.

'It's dead wet,' chorused the boys.

'Let me run you home,' I said to her tactfully, as she was about to explode.

When I dropped her, I said, 'What about old Elvis, then?'

She invited me to a point-to-point at Meersden on Saturday; and it poured all afternoon. I can't think of a worse punishment than that.

There, the whole thing might have died. But it rained all Sunday as well, and I spent the time in my little darkroom, developing the photographs I'd taken in the church. They'd come out remarkably sharp, for flash, and I blew them up to ten-by-eight,

to console her. They'd look quite nice round the classroom walls
. . . the one thing I couldn't make out was a face that appeared in
one, peering round one of the tombs. It wasn't my face, and it
certainly wasn't Dorinda's. Far too ugly. And as it had a bald
head, it certainly wasn't one of the children's.

It was well back in the harsh shadows thrown by the flash,
watching two of the girls rubbing a brass-lettered tablet set in the
floor. The girls were very intent (or pretending to be very intent)
on what they were doing, and were obviously quite unaware of
being watched. The face didn't look like a real person, somehow;
I might have put it down as the face of an effigy from one of the
tombs, except that the eyes were dark and alive and watching. It
worried at my mind all the time I was printing and developing. I
kept on going across to the print where it was hanging up to dry,
and staring at the face; I think I was trying to reason it out of
existence, as a trick of the flash on a piece of crumbling stonework.
As a projection of my own eye and mind. But it looked . . . it
looked, let's face it, hungry and evil. I didn't like the thought that
I was making it up out of my own imagination; I've always had a
down-to-earth trouble-free imagination.

Anyway, I ran down to the school with the photographs on
the Wednesday and the kids were pleased to see me, and so was
Dorinda – and so, by a miracle, was the Headmistress. The kids
had been busy, working from what they'd done in the church,
and the lively results hung all over the walls. It appeared that
as soon as they'd got back into the classroom, they'd come back
to rumbustious life and produced the best stuff ever seen. So
good that an inspector had been summoned. I was introduced
to him: a pushy young man who went wild over my photographs
and said it was seldom that a school manager took such an interest, and who went on about having the whole exhibition laid
out in the foyer at County Hall. I wondered whether he was
just angling to get a date with Dorinda, but his enthusiasm
seemed genuine enough and had sent the Head into seventh
heaven.

I pointed out the strange watching head in the photograph.
Dorinda insisted it was a trick of the light. But Jack Hargreaves

said 'Yeah, sir, he was there. An old bloke. He didn't say nothing. Just hung around in the shadders, watching the girls, dirty old sod. I thought 'e was the caretaker.'

The Headmistress gave Dorinda a very funny look, and Dorinda went a bit pale. The Inspector changed the subject rather quickly, and went back to his praise of the drawings of cross-eyed cherubs and the very fine picture of a tomb that Henry was busy on. It had a mournful draped lady on top, in the Regency style, and the inscription:

TO THE MEMORY OF MARY CRAIG

A WOMAN OF EXEMPLARY PIETY AND

DISCRETION

WHO WAS CALLED HENCE AT THE EARLY AGE OF

29

YET HAVING IN AN EMINENT DEGREE ATTAINED

THAT

'You'll have to hurry and finish this,' said the Inspector.

'Can't sir – this is as far as we copied. We had to rush at the end.'

'Pity,' said the Inspector. 'It certainly can't be hung up in County Hall in that unfinished state.'

I saw a look pass from Henry to Jack Hargreaves; I thought it was a look of pure disgust. How wrong I was, I was only to discover later.

On Monday morning at the shop, the phone rang, sounding like trouble. It was the Head, and even over the phone I could tell she was tight-lipped and shaking with fury.

'You'd better get down here straight away, Mr Ashden. I knew this church business would lead to nothing but trouble. I feel I must call a meeting of the managers, but I think you are entitled to be consulted first.'

I covered the mile to school in record time. The Head was waiting just inside the entrance, and pounced immediately. She *was* tight-lipped and shaking. She led me to the hall where Dorinda's exhibition had been hung before going to County Hall. She gestured a quivering hand at the big central exhibit. It was Henry and Jack Hargreaves's drawing of the Regency tomb; the draped lady on top still looked like a wilting lettuce-leaf, but the inscription had been completed:

TO THE MEMORY OF MARY CRAIG

A WOMAN OF EXEMPLARY PIETY AND

DISCRETION

WHO WAS CALLED HENCE AT THE EARLY AGE OF

29

YET HAVING IN AN EMINENT DEGREE ATTAINED

THAT MATURITY

WHICH CONSISTETH NOT IN LENGTH OF DAYS

DIED MCCLXXX

Unfortunately, other words had been scrawled over this chaste message, huge words in a wild hand. Words like 'whore' and 'strumpet' and 'doxy'.

'That,' said the Head, 'is what comes of ill-advised expeditions.' She led me to her office. The Inspector was there, rather white round the gills in the face of such massive female wrath. And Dorinda, who if anything looked rather red in the face, and defiant.

'Have you faced the lads . . . with this?' I asked.

'Certainly not.'

'Can I see them?' I asked, as calmly as I could. 'I think it might stop us making fools of ourselves.'

'What *do* you mean, Mr Ashden?'

'I mean these are not words commonly found in the twentieth-century child's vocabulary.'

The Inspector nodded; he was no fool. The Head picked up that nod, and Henry was duly summoned.

'Henry,' I said. 'Suppose I was to send you out for a strumpet . . . where would you go to get one?'

Henry looked at our assembled faces warily; too old a hand not to smell trouble coming a mile off. But then a look of genuine bafflement came over his face. 'Music-shop?' he offered.

'That's a *trumpet*, Henry.'

'Cake-shop?' A flicker of a grin crossed his face.

'That's *crumpet*, Henry.'

'Dunno, sir.' His face was utterly still again.

'So, Henry, what would you call . . . a woman . . who took money for going with men?'

Henry's face froze in a look of pure horror. Never had such words been uttered in this holy of holies.

'You may answer, Henry,' said the Head, without moving her lips at all.

'A . . . tart, miss. On the game. Or a scrubber.' The whites were showing all round his eyes.

'So if you didn't know what a strumpet was, Henry, why did you write it on your picture of the tomb?'

'Cos it was on the tomb when Jack an' I got there, Saturday afternoon, sir. We didn't know whether to copy it or not, but we thought it must be official.'

I beat the Inspector to our cars by a full ten yards . . .


'Never in my forty years as a servant of God have I known such a thing,' boomed the Reverend Ernest Lacey. 'One opens one's church to schools for the benefit of the community as a whole, and *this* happens. Children today . . .'

'Can you suggest,' I said, 'how children today could possibly have reached up that high? I mean, is there a ladder available that they could have used?'

The young police-sergeant whom Lacey had brought with him nodded thoughtfully.

'There is no ladder,' said the Reverend Lacey. 'They must have brought one with them.'

'On their bicycles?'

'That's an adult's work, sir,' said the sergeant. 'You can tell by the sweep of their arm, in the lettering.' He stood up on a pew, and stretched up. 'Big fellow – almost as big as me. That's adults, Reverend.'

'Disgusting.'

'Henry,' I said. 'Was that bald man here again, when you came?'

'Yeah,' said Henry, very chastened. 'He was hanging about, peeping at us. Didn't say nothing. I thought he might stop us, but he didn't say nothing. He's only really interested in girls . . . He was a rum 'un, though.' Henry blushed delightfully, and stopped.

'Why, Henry?'

'Can I whisper, sir?' He drew close. 'Jack Hargreaves reckoned he were only wearing a shirt . . . a raggy shirt, all dirty. Reckon he was one o' *them*, sir.'

'One of what, Henry?' asked the Head in dire tones.

'An escaped lunatic, miss,' said Henry, dissimulating. 'A nutter.'

'Nutter or not,' said the sergeant, 'if it's adults, it's a crime. Now if you'll pardon me, Reverend, I'll take evidence. Then you can get the place cleaned up.' He went to the tomb and began to scrape some of the black paint of the vile lettering off with a knife, into a little envelope. I noticed the paint could not have been dry; it came off the white marble too easily. I saw the sergeant wrinkle his nose.

We left him and drove back to school, the Head emitting sighs all the way, like a dragon cooling down after breathing fire; and Dorinda making subtle little self-righteous noises that seemed to be demanding an apology from her superior.

My shop-bell rang while I was brewing coffee. It turned out to be the young uniformed sergeant from the church. I offered him a cup; he drifted round my shop looking at things.

'It's all paid for, sergeant,' I said, half sharply, half a joke.

'That's all right, sir,' he said soothingly. 'I'm into old things a bit myself. That's a nice Viennese regulator . . . the trade price is twenty pounds, I see.'

I raised my eyebrows. 'Nineteen to you, sergeant. Or is that bribing a policeman in the course of his duties?'

Surprisingly, he laughed, and got out a cheque-book. 'I'm afraid I'm not the usual sort of police-sergeant; I've got A-levels. It worries my superintendent. He doesn't think I'm quite human. First he sent me off to Bramshill College to get rid of me, and now he keeps me at headquarters for dealing with the nobs, and anything funny that crops up, like this church business.'

'There have been developments, then?'

'Oh, yes. Of a sort. We know he's got a key to the church.'

I gave a grunt of surprise.

'The vicar got a woman in to clean up, then he locked the church; thought he had the only key. A week later he went to look round, and the joker had been at it again. And three times since, in the last fortnight. I've been spending a few sleepless nights in that vestry . . . but nothing happens while I'm around. Then the first night I'm not, it happens again.'

'I don't envy you,' I said. 'It's a nasty building. I don't think I'd spend a night alone there for a superintendent's wages.'

'I wasn't alone, sir,' he said with a wry grin. 'Local bobby was with me.'

'What does he think?'

'Hasn't a clue. He's new – came last year from Stropping. I'm afraid village bobbies aren't what they were. I'd like you to come and see the place again, sir, if you will. I'd like your professional opinion.'

'It wasn't those kids, you know.'

'I know it's not kids.'

As we went, I slipped the pictures I'd taken in church into my pocket. Or rather, one of them.

I looked at the interior of the church aghast. Every tomb seemed to have been vandalized.

WILLIAM TRENTON

VICAR OF THIS PARISH FOR FORTY YEARS

AND AN INDUSTRIOUS HARBINGER OF CHURCH

MUSICK

THE SWEETNESS OF HIS HARMONIES CHARMED

THE EAR

AND THE MILDNESS OF HIS MANNERS THE

HEART

DIED MDCCCV

That one carried, scrawled in furious letters:

THEEFE. EXTORTIONER. GIVE BACK THE TITHES
YOU RUINED JACK BURTON FOR

And, on the tomb of a lady of Invincible Virtue and Great Condescension:

SHE PLAYED THE HARLOT WITH HER OWN SON

I walked from one to the other.

'Nasty,' I said. 'But not brainless. It's almost as if he knew all about them. A mad local historian?'

'It's funny you should say that. I've checked the church records. There was a farmer called John Wilberforce Burton – died in 1783. Dispossessed of his land – killed himself – not buried in sacred ground. And the lady he made that comment on, she had a son who never married. She outlived him. The comments are all *relevant*. Almost like he'd known them personally.'

'Has everyone copped it?'

'He's left the Victorian ones alone . . . and the schoolmaster, Dore.'

'Oh, the pillar of virtue, yes. Well, he would, wouldn't he?'

'Funny thing is . . .' the sergeant paused in embarrassment '. . . I had a writing expert in – a graphologist. Superintendent went mad about the expense of getting him over from Muncaster. I got all the kids in that class to scribble stuff down for me. He went over them – that's how I know it wasn't the kids – but he did say one funny thing. Apparently the writing's very old-fashioned. It seems that every century makes its own kind of mark . . .' He ground to a halt.

'You mean, like the young Georgian gents who carved their names so elegantly on the pews at Newhurst during the long sermons . . .' And I ground to a halt too. We looked at each other in the gloom of the nave, then shrugged, as men do, and changed the subject. How different Dorinda's story might have been if we hadn't.

I pulled out my photograph. The one with the bald head, watching the little girls brass-rubbing. I suppose now we'd got on to daft topics, I wasn't afraid to raise the matter.

'What do you make of that, sergeant?'

'Oh, this is the famous photograph? I'd meant to ask you about that. Only I reckoned the lads were making up a tale, to get out of trouble. Rum-looking bloke, if it *is* a bloke . . . hard to tell . . . could be a lump of marble . . . statue's hand or something . . .'

'Let's line it up from where I took it.'

We looked. There was nothing on any of the tombs where the 'head' appeared in my photograph.

'Could be anything. Maybe one of the kids left a packet of sandwiches on a ledge. It looks crumpled . . . crumpled and yet . . . bloated . . . bit like a turnip lantern. Could even be the head of another kid.'

'A *bald* kid?'

'Could be a trick of the flash, making him look bald. If he's real, I wouldn't fancy meeting him up an alley on a dark night.'

We both laughed uneasily. Then he said: 'D'you mind if I hang on to this? I'll get some copies made. Somebody in the district might recognize him. Somebody who's been to Madame Tussaud's maybe.' We laughed uneasily again.

And there we left it.

I must say the official opening of our exhibition at County Hall was quite a do. That was in the days when money was no object; the catering was elegant, and the whisky flowed like water. The exhibition looked great; they'd borrowed my negatives and blown them up to a yard square and very sharp, and the kids looked far keener and more industrious than they really had been. But their work was good, and beautifully mounted; good mounting can make a thing look worth a million dollars.

You must remember that was also in the days before kids were taken out of school a lot; I think the county was trying to encourage project work in the primaries. There were a lot of teachers there that evening, and a lot of inspectors and organizers and advisers, and a lot of councillors who'd mainly come for the whisky (which they drank at incredible speed, never batting an eyelid;

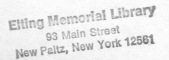

they must have had a lot of practice). Form 4C were there as well, brought by the Head from Barlborough on a coach, with four other teachers as reinforcements. The children looked incredibly clean: I didn't recognize them till they spoke.

Dorinda, I remember, came straight from home in her white Mini. She looked so happy and excited. There was such a press of people round her, complimenting her, or just touching their forelocks and asking to be remembered to her father, that I couldn't get near. But I remember to this day how happy she looked . . .

Working round the exhibits, I came face to face with my police sergeant, every inch the gent in natty thornproof; Mike Watkins as I knew him now, from his name on the cheque.

'How's your Vienna regulator doing?'

'Fine. That's about all that is.'

'Not caught your mad local historian, then?'

'Nobody recognized the photograph. Though I got some damned funny looks. You know, what strikes me is the way it all started after 4C had been to the church.'

'It wasn't them!'

'I know it wasn't. But things started happening immediately after . . . like they'd *disturbed* something. Something pretty nasty. I've got one new piece of evidence.'

All the time we'd been moving round the exhibition. Now something old and beautiful and shiny caught my dealer's eye, among all the cross-eyed cherubs and dim brass-rubbings. A padlock, thin and elegant, and polished with Brasso half out of its life.

'Hang on,' I said. We went across together. The notice under the padlock, rather wildly written, read:

A MEDIEEVIL LOCK. ON LOAN FROM
TATTERSHAM CHURCH FROM THE CRIP
(DRACULA) DONE UP BY J. HARGREAVES
AND H. WINTERBOTTOM.

The lock was not medieevil, or even medieval. It was elegantly Georgian, with an interlacing pattern of crosses: the lock from the grille of the vault under the altar.

An awful premonition gripped me.

'What's your nasty piece of evidence?' I asked. He shuffled uncomfortably.

'Well, you remember I scraped some of the black paint off that first tomb that was vandalized? I sent it to Forensic, and they couldn't make head nor tail of it, so they sent it on to the Home Office. Lucky I'd scraped off plenty.'

'Well?' I asked sharply.

'Well, old Sir Bernard Spilsbury got to the bottom of it. It wasn't paint at all – it's the decomposed remains of tissue. Animal or human, they can't really tell . . . it's so old.'

'How old?'

He gulped. 'They reckon . . . centuries old . . .'

'Oh, my God, the lock . . . the crypt. Somebody who knew the owners of the tombs personally . . . It's crazy, sergeant. If we say anything, they'll throw us in the nuthouse.'

He became very constabulary, the way even the best ones can. 'I have evidence, sir, that party or parties unknown have entered the crypt and violated the cadavers, and are using their remains to write graffiti on the tombs. All of which are crimes.'

As from another world, the voice broke in on us: from the cosy world of pretty girls handing round drinks and art-advisers plotting, and councillors knocking back whisky.

'Ladies and Gentlemen, in honour of this unique occasion, the Chairman of the County Council, Councillor Neil Fogarty, will present certificates of merit to each child who took part.'

It went quite smoothly until the name 'Hargreaves, J.' was uttered. No Hargreaves, J., came forward.

'I'm certain he was on the bus,' said the Head, tetchily.

'Perhaps he's gone to the . . .'

'Carry on,' said the Head.

They carried on, until they came to the name 'Winterbottom, H.'. He was not only missing also, but a thorough search of the cloakrooms and corridors had revealed no trace of Hargreaves, J., either.

'Where are they?' hissed Dorinda, realistically taking the form-monitor on one side and shaking the life out of her.

Eventually, there were tears. And the appalling admission that the two had slipped away from the bus, having asked to stop for the loo at Tattersham. The whole form had got off: Jack and Henry had deliberately not got back on. Others had answered their names on the roll-call. Jack and Henry had brought sandwiches and torches. They were going to lie in wait in the church for the bald-headed man who wrote the dirty words.

The next second, Dorinda was running for her car; and the sergeant and I were pounding down the corridors of County Hall behind her.

We nearly caught up with her in the car park; she drove off from under our very noses.

'We'll take my car,' I shouted. Which we did, and by putting my foot down on the by-pass, I nearly overtook her at Selmerby. But at that point she took to the little winding lanes that she'd known on horseback since a child. And on those bends, the Mini left my shooting-brake standing.

'We've lost her, sir,' said Sergeant Watkins. 'Drop me at the next phone-box and I'll summon help straight to the church.'

But I couldn't bear to stop. One thing kept ringing through my head: Henry Winterbottom saying that whatever the thing was, it didn't bother *boys*. It was the little *girls* it was interested in.

In the end, Sergeant Watkins took the law into his own hands (as he had every right to do), and jumped out as I slowed down at a crossroads. At least he had the courtesy to slam the door, so I didn't even have to stop. But the minutes ticked away; I took a wrong turning and got lost. And still the minutes ticked away.

It was half an hour before I pulled up by Tattersham church. The white Mini was parked by the porch. No light on in the church, or in the big house; but in the moonlight, the church door gaped wide. Henry's skill with a lock had worked again.

I ran through the inner door; into pitch darkness.

'Dorinda?'

There was a kind of mindless animal sob.

'Dorinda, for God's sake!' I shouted.

Then I heard a slithering noise, somewhere among the box-pews; I was just beginning to see the outline of the windows now, but nothing else.

Then Henry's voice came, quavering, 'Careful, sir. We're in the corner, here. Watch it, he's prowling round.'

'He'd better not prowl round me,' I shouted, 'or I'll break him in half.'

'Watch it, sir. He's all slippery . . . pongy . . . he sort of falls apart when you touch him.'

Oh, God, the lights. Where were the lights? I realized I'd never known.

'Where are the lights, Henry?' I was moving towards him, slowly, stealthily. Listening for the slithering that was moving between us.

Dorinda began to sob again, softly, mindlessly.

'The lights don't work, sir,' quavered Henry. 'They must have cut them off.'

My outward-groping hand came into contact with something upright, round and hard. I knew what it was; one of the churchwardens' staffs that are set upright at the end of the back pews. I got it loose, and felt for the top; a heavy brass bishop's mitre; it would make a good club. I felt a little better, and moved on. The sound of Dorinda's sobbing, the boys' heavy breathing, came nearer. So did the slithering. And I could smell him now; the smell that had always been in this church, but a thousand times stronger. The smell of death; I had smelt it, plunging into the bowels of a crashed bomber in the War.

I could smell him, I could hear him; but I hit him because I *felt* him: a sudden drop in temperature on the right-hand side of my face as he came at me – as if he drew the warmth out of the surrounding air . . .

I had never struck a blow like it before, and I hope never to strike one like it again. It would have killed a man; but I could never have brought myself to hit a living man that hard. It had all the fear in me, all the rage, all the hate. And I could tell from the feel of it that the churchwarden's staff hit him where his neck joined his shoulders. It felt like hitting a rotten marrow, with bone splintering inside. Cold drops splashed my face. But there was no shudder, no gasp of pain or groan; it was hitting a dead thing, and instinctively I gave up hope.

The next second the staff was snatched from my hands so fiercely that I lost all use of my fingers. And the second after that I was flung against the pews with such force that the seat-back, like a horizontal axe, drove all the air from my lungs, and I thought my back was broken. But I had felt the large hands that flung me; cold as ice, even through my trench-coat. I lay on the floor and listened to the slithering go past me towards the corner where Dorinda was.

I don't know how I got back to my feet, but as I did so, a sound came to me from the sane world outside: the wail of a police-car siren. The windows of the church lit up from without, with the cold blue light of car headlights. And I saw him. Or it.

For, sensing the flare of light, it turned, and I saw it across the tops of the box-pews. A bald head, with blank black eyes that shone in the light. A broad chest, with what might have been a growth of black hair. And round the head and shoulders, not a ragged shirt, as Henry had said. But the green rags of a shroud . . .

Now there was a second police-car siren. Old Watkins must have had them homing in by radio from every point of the compass.

For a long moment the creature paused, like a badger brought to bay in its own wood. Then it seemed to sense that there would be no end to the lights and the noise, and the men with whom it had little quarrel. Men who could run it to earth and destroy and demolish and block it off for ever. Though the unreadable expression on the bald face never changed, I knew that it despaired.

The next second it was limping at great speed across the nave, towards the altar. I heard the grille to the vault clang, and it was gone.

Seconds later, a torch-beam cut across the nave from the porch. There was a fumbling, and all the lights went on; Sergeant Watkins must have known where the master-switch was. And then the place was full of flat caps and blue uniforms.

'Where?' asked Mike Watkins. I nodded towards the grille that led to the vault. He walked across, took something from his pocket and clicked it into place on the grille. He gave me a certain look, and I nodded. There are some things that are best not entered in policemen's notebooks, if only for the sake of Chief Constables and the judiciary.

'How did you get the lock?' I asked him.

'I confiscated it as material evidence,' he said ruefully. 'But it's better back where it is. I don't think we'll have any more bother, do you?'

I shook my head; but I rattled the old Georgian lock gently, just to make sure.

There was a gaggle of blue uniforms in the far corner, but it was parting; someone was being led out.

Dorinda was as white as a sheet, silent, eyes looking nowhere – all the signs of deep shock. But at least she was putting one foot in front of the other.

'I've radioed for an ambulance,' said Sergeant Watkins. The boys followed Dorinda out, with that same white, glazed look on their faces. Except Henry, who summoned up enough energy for a ghost of a grin and said, 'Cor, sir, you didn't 'arf fetch him one . . .'

I went to hospital with Dorinda in the ambulance; the boys went in the police-car. Halfway there, she opened her eyes and knew me.

'Geoff . . . thanks.'

But it wasn't the Dorinda Molyneaux I'd known. The unshakeable confidence had gone; the certainty that there was a practical answer for everything.

'I never realized . . .' She closed her eyes and was silent, then continued: 'I thought if you were decent . . . and kept the rules . . . God wouldn't let things like that . . . happen to you.'

I didn't ask what had happened to her. I just said, 'God lets road accidents happen to decent people every day. Why should that kind of thing be so different?'

'Yes,' she said, with the sadness you expect from an old, old woman.'Yes.' She reached out and grabbed my hand, and played with the knuckles. 'I like you – you're *warm*.' She went on holding my hand till we got to the hospital.

Mike Watkins joined me in the waiting-room; with his note-book.

'I suppose you're after the name and address of the accused,' I said, with a weak attempt at humour.

'Only for my own interest.'

'Must have been old Anstey, the Public Auditor. It was the Anstey vault.'

'Well, I'm not going down again to look – not for a superintendent's wages. But I don't reckon it was Anstey. Anstey's memorial was desecrated too. And I've seen a painting of him, in old age – a thin, elegant old gent, with lots of frizzy grey hair.'

'What I saw hadn't got grey hair.' I shuddered at the memory. 'Who d'you reckon it was, then?'

'The only memorial that wasn't desecrated was Thomas Dore's.'

'The honoured and paineful schoolemaster and benefactor of this parish . . .'

'Still publickly rebuking vice . . .'

'And discretely practising virtue . . . God, I feel sick. I'd like to blow the place to smithereens and him with it.'

'Nasty thing, repressed sex,' said Sergeant Watkins. 'We were shown a lot of that at Bramshill College. Prefer a pint of beer and a game of darts, meself. Don't fret, Geoff. He won't get loose again. I'll have a word with the vicar. He'll believe us . . . nobody else would.'

I took good care of Dorinda after that. Eventually, she got so she could walk into a church again; if I held her hand tight. She did that just before we got married. Which was the last day of Miss Dorinda Molyneaux.

# The Dumbledore

THE 1960s WERE a restless time for me. The trade went from bad to worse. The Americans, Dutch, Germans came in like locusts, buying up everything in sight. People like Clocky Watson threw it to them by the armful, the crateful, the container-load. Then when the cupboard became bare, people like Clocky invented helpful new categories: Victoriana; bric-à-brac. They even re-named 1920s tat 'art deco'.

In 1960, the poorest thing in my shop was a Regency wine-table, faded, but good value at ten pounds. In 1970, the worst thing was an Elvis Presley E P, in a greasy thumb-marked sleeve. That was ten pounds, too. If there are fools who'll pay . . .

My marriage changed, too. Dorinda inherited her father's estate, and we moved out to Barlborough. From being a nice relaxed rich girl, she was transformed overnight into a fully paid-up member of the landed gentry: took to wellies and quilted jackets, and talked endlessly about the cost-effectiveness of the home farm. Clocky Watson wasn't the only one who could've bought me up ten times over.

I worked like hell to make my way as a dealer. When we moved to Barlborough, I turned nearly every room in my old place over to antiques: good antiques. I could afford a full-time girl assistant. I was getting a name.

None of this impressed Dorinda. She allowed that I had business sense; she could use my help full-time with the estate. She wondered out loud at parties whether it was worthwhile my keeping on the shop. After all, we weren't pushed for pennies, and the shop kept me away from the children so much while they were growing up.

Once, at a party, I heard Lady Daresbury say, 'Dorinda's husband will get you a grandfather-clock. Such an *astute* little man, with a good eye.'

I struggled mightily to be more than Dorinda's husband. I did absurd things, like keeping one room at the shop furnished as a bedroom/office. Dorinda noticed, with a cocked eyebrow, but said nothing. She'd become very territorial herself; understood the need for territory in me. Twice, when we'd had really bad rows, I spent the night there.

But my main cure, in those restless years, when it all got too much, was to get into the Merc and drive into East Anglia. Looking for antiques, I said, and I always brought good stuff back. I had a lot of contacts there, and the farmers didn't know the value of what they had. You could get a Georgian dining-table and six chairs with carver for the price of the new vinyl three-piece the farmer's wife had her eye on in Downham Market.

But East Anglia meant more than that to me. I never took that turn beyond Melton Mowbray, into the Vale of Catmose, without my heart lifting. The sweeping fields of green corn and yellow mustard, lifting up into the sky, made me think irresistibly of flying. Then I'd pull off on to one of the disused airfields, and walk down the broad, cracked, weed-speckled runway, and feel free. The great spans of the hangars were still there then, though given over to storing grain. The control-towers still stood.

I only realized I'd been looking for East Cardingham when I got annoyed that I couldn't find it. It was always a joke in the old days; that it was easier to find East Cardingham from the air than the ground. Easier to get to it from Berlin than from Norwich. That every crossroads near East Cardingham had five roads leading into it and six leading out, none at right angles, let alone a signpost.

I got so mad in the end that I called at North Tewsham public library to check their Ordnance Survey maps. I was just getting stuck in with the grey-bunned, grey-stockinged chief librarian when a voice I knew said, 'Who wants East Cardingham?'

I spun round.

'Section-Officer Edmunds, I presume,' I said with great mock formality, to hide a rising excitement.

'Squadron-Leader Ashden, to the life. You've let your hair grow.'

She was not the same; sixteen years had seen to that. But I liked her better. The slimness of youth had given way to the slimness of discipline. The red hair that had emerged in a page-boy from under the WAAF cap was now swept up off her neck. She wore spectacles; but when she took them off, her eyes were just as big and beautiful as ever. We gave each other a chaste hug, cheek to cheek, under the eyes of her grey-haired superior. The boys in blue still had a memory of glamour in '61 – enough to stop her getting the sack on the spot.

I took her out that evening for the best dinner I could find, and heard her story. She'd married a travelling rep, and got rid of him for adultery. She'd kept the house, kept her figure and lost her way. She was very frank about it. When she asked me how I'd done, I shrugged her off with a detailed account of the antiques trade. I got on to old times pretty quickly, and got pretty tight. Afterwards, we sat on with brandies, till she arched her brows teasingly and said, 'D'you want to see East Cardingham, then?'

'You know the way?'

'I still drive out there sometimes. I think *I'd* better drive.'

She slid easily behind the Merc's steering-wheel. 'Nice crate . . .'

The entrance looked just the same in the headlights. In the dark you couldn't see that most of the glass had gone from the guardroom windows; that long dead grass grew against the guardroom door.

She drove round the perimeter track and parked on No. 1 runway, letting the headlights run out at full beam along the concrete, picking out the ruts and valleys with long shadows. I even glanced up at the sky nervously, expecting the first Lanc to get the green flare and come roaring and trundling in. Or a Jerry 88, on an intruder sweep.

She locked up the car for me, took an old RAF hooded torch

out of her handbag and led the way, letting the beam flicker here and there, like an usherette helping you find your seat in the cinema. I couldn't help wondering how many nights she'd come here. She led me straight to the old Mess. As I touched Chalky White's painting of Lancs taking off, over the ante-room fireplace, and the paint flaked off on my finger like powder, I grew in awe of her, as if she were a high-priestess of some old religion.

We even found the Adjutant's ashtray – an old aluminium thing, advertising Gold Flake. Somebody had put their cluddering great foot on it, but it was the Adge's ashtray all right. The one we'd stared at, while he tore us off a strip.

I was still clutching the ashtray like a sacred relic when she asked me in for a nightcap. I staggered across her doorstep, still babbling about the wonder of the bloody ashtray.

'Gin-hand-hit, Squadron-Leader Ashden?' She still had the cockney barman's accent to perfection. Had any time passed at all? When she brought the drinks, she'd let her hair down, and put an R A F officer's cap on top of it. Chalky White's second-best cap . . .

She'd always been Chalky's girl, till the night he got the chop over Darmstadt. She was Chalky's girl, but we'd all fancied her. We were still waiting for her to get over Chalky and pick somebody else when the War ended and we all went home.

So she'd never got over Chalky. Come back here when her marriage broke up, to be near him. I could see Chalky so clearly in my mind's eye. Always laughing; and twitching between the laughs.

Her blouse was starched and pale blue, like a WAAF officer's shirt; I hadn't noticed before.

I moved rather unsteadily towards her. 'D'you still miss him?' Her eyes were very close; she wasn't wearing her spectacles.

'Do you?' she asked.

'Yes,' I said, but I didn't. I hadn't thought of him for sixteen years.

There seemed nothing else possible to say. I put my hands on her slim shoulders . . .

After that, I always rang her, the night before I came over into

East Anglia. It couldn't have been much of an affaire, from her point of view.

But as she said, it was a lot better than drifting into middle-aged librarianship.

I don't know how long it might have lasted if I hadn't taken the short-cut that day, past Lower Wendlebury. I'd known Wendlebury nearly as well as East Cardingham, because I'd been liaison officer with the Yanks. My fighting war had been very short. Most of May, 1940. Flying Blenheim Mk IIs against the German breakthrough at Sedan. Going out in a flight of seven, including two new-boys, and coming back with four. That last time, I'd come back with one engine smoking glycol, a headless bomb-aimer at my feet, a wounded rear-gunner, and a very large piece of shrapnel in my leg. I don't remember much about it, except the wind blowing a gale through the shattered cockpit-cover, and my gunner shouting, 'Break right, for Christ's sake, he's coming again.' We got back at zero feet, and the crate fell apart around us as we landed, which saved the bother of scraping us out like sardines out of a tin.

Anyway, I'd saved the gunner, and when I got out of hospital they gave me a gong and posted me as liaison to East Cardingham. You can't fly a big bird with half your thigh-muscle gone.

Anyway, I was taking this short-cut past Wendlebury one rainy dusk in 1962, when I saw a series of mounds rearing up over the perimeter fence. Suddenly uneasy, I turned the Merc and drove in to investigate. God, it was awful. They'd been tearing up the runway with bloody great bulldozers. And that was some runway; the Yanks had laid concrete four feet deep to carry their big birds, their B-17s. Whoever had started demolishing it seemed to have bitten off more than they could chew, and abandoned the attempt half finished. The pieces of concrete rose up thirty feet high; indestructible, unless you were prepared to pay a million to have them chewed into manageable pieces. The Quonset-huts, the guardroom, the control-tower, hadn't proved so tough; they were gone, flattened.

Who could have done such a thing? I felt outraged, personally violated. I didn't mind the airfield being sown with wheat; or the Sunday driving lessons, given by nervous men to their nervous wives, where once we'd set off for the Happy Valley. I didn't mind the hangars being full of grain instead of bombs, or the courting couples having it away in the control-tower on wet and windy nights. That was a dignified decay . . . but this! I felt my way back to the past was being destroyed; as if my lungs were being torn out. I went on staring down that ravaged runway for a long time, thinking the blackest thoughts I had ever known. Remembering Major Stepanski and Captain Con O'Connell and Big Tex, and the way they died. *This* was their memorial, not that horror of white tombstones outside Cambridge. This was where their souls still came to fly . . .

I suppose that, being so upset, I didn't really think where I was going when I drove on. My mind must have picked up the old route in the dark; the route I'd so often travelled with them to whoop it up and forget, in the very limited fleshpots of Upper Wendlebury. There'd been a caff called the Dumbledore.

I drove up the main street for the first time in sixteen years. The street-lighting seemed the only thing that was different: low black-and-white thatched cottages, the same cat crossing the road in front of my wheels, in the same blasted place.

And then I gasped, and slammed on the brakes.

The Dumbledore was still there.

The same garish neon light the boys from the base had fixed up on V E night, saying 'The Dumbledore' in big Hollywood hand-writing. In the yard at the side were parked two Jeeps, with A E F white stars still visible on their bonnets. A big Buick command-car, and even a Dodge thirty-hundredweight pickup . . . And the juke-box was still playing . . . the sound of Glenn Miller's 'Ameri-can Patrol' came to my ears, right across the little windy square. The windows were lit up, but the place looked empty. I walked across, tried the door, then pressed my nose against the glass.

It hadn't changed. The tall bar-stools were still there, with their red leatherette tops; only the cross-bars, where people used to put their feet, were worn down into sickle shapes with time. There was the same old Coca-Cola advert, with the pigtailed girl playing the piano, and a nice young guy with short back and sides and a two-piece suit smiling down at her and turning her music. There was the three-bladed duralumin airscrew from a B-17, the Camels advert, the one for Lucky Strike. Same brown lino, worn in the same places, by the bar-counter . . . Not all the primitive neon lights, pinched from the maintenance hangars, were on. The place was full of shadows . . . there was Con O'Connell's chair with the Reb flag transfer on the back, and there was the corner where Tex used to sit on the floor, great legs bent up higher than his head. Tex and Little Charlene . . .

Then a door opened at the back. And she came through, silhouetted against the light. Hair back in a blonde pony-tail with a pink bow, seersucker dress, bobby-sox and white plimsolls. Little Charlene herself. Charlotte Hamlin really, but Tex always called her Charlene.

I tapped on the glass of the door to get her attention, but she passed, silent on plimsolled feet, circling the room, touching this and that; pausing at the part of the bar where Tex used to pick her up and set her down. Again I tapped, harder, hammered on the glass. She looked in my direction, but her eyes were blank; she looked straight through me. Then went on her way, touching things, like an automated doll in a glass cabinet. Finally, she went through the lighted door to the back; the door shut, leaving me with the shadows again. In the shadows, the record finished, the pickup arm swung over like a hand from a tomb, and the scratchy sound of 'Chattanooga Choo-Choo' filled the English night.

I felt I was going mad; had the sight of the airfield runway unhinged me? Was I seeing ghosts – the ghost of a café? I staggered to the side yard and sat in the driver's seat of one of the Jeeps – that was solid enough, not a ghost. Though the seat was soaking with rain, and the windscreen-wipers had rusted through, and the licence said 1945.

I don't blame myself for what followed. I had to find out what the hell was going on. So I went round the back, like we always did, for a Bourbon whiskey when the Dumbledore was closed by the old British licensing hours. I hammered on the back door; hammered and hammered. At last, it opened. Little Charlene stood there; it *was* Little Charlene. But closer, now, I could see she was no ghost. There were lines on her face; not many, but it made her thirty-four and not eighteen any more.

'It's Geoff,' I said gently, to her still, still face. 'Geoff Ashden – from East Cardingham.' Her expression didn't change; she didn't recognize me. 'I was a friend of Tex,' I said.

Then she raised her right hand.

It had a gun in it; a Colt .45 – Tex always carried a pair in cowboy holsters when he went over Germany. And that gun wasn't a ghost either; she had to use both trembling hands to lift it, and by the time it was pointing at my belly, I realized I'd better presume it was loaded . . .

I just made it behind the Dodge pickup before she fired. I heard the bullet whang off the Dodge's cylinder-block. She fired in my general direction five more times, till the gun was empty. I could hear the bullets cutting through the assembled vehicles with that peculiar noise a bullet makes piercing thin metal.

Then, her face still expressionless in the quiet lamplight, she closed the door and went back inside.

After five minutes, when I was sure she wasn't just reloading, I crawled out from under the Dodge, and dusted myself off.

I was in the middle of a small town, and she'd fired six shots, enough to wake the dead. And nobody had come. The lamplit streets were as empty and yellow as ever. There were lights on in all the house-windows (it wasn't more than seven in the evening) but nothing stirred. Silence. It was as if Wendlebury had turned its back on the Dumbledore; was pretending it didn't exist.

I decided I needed a stiff drink. There should be a pub called the Duke of Suffolk up West Street. I tried it, more in faith than hope.

But when I staggered through the door of the bar parlour, there was Tom Watkins behind the counter, polishing a glass and looking nearly as grey-haired and pot-bellied as his father had in 1943.

'Good evening, Squadron-Leader Ashden,' he said with a triumphant grin. 'The usual?'

'Make it a double,' I said. 'I've just been to the Dumbledore.'

He had been smiling; but now his face went curiously still.

'What the hell's going on up there?' I asked.

He looked round the bar, as if to make sure it was empty; then he gave me my drink, and took one himself, a lot bigger one than he used to, and said, 'It's a long story, Squadron-Leader.'

'You remember Tex?' he said. 'Big Tex?'

I nodded, took too big a swig of whisky, and nearly choked. He waited for me to wipe my eyes, then said, 'Remember the night we heard they got the chop?'

Should I ever forget it? The crew of the B-17 called 'Lizzie Borden'. The real-life Lizzie Borden had been an American axe-murderer in the 1920s. You may know the rhyme?

> Lizzie Borden took an axe, and gave her mother forty whacks
> And when she saw what she had done, she gave her father forty-one.

Well, the B-17 'Lizzie Borden' was one of the first gunships the US Eighth Airforce used. In their hardest time, the German fighters began flying straight at the front of their formations, head-on, to break them up before they could bomb. The answer was gunships, that would fly ahead of the American formations and draw the fire. They carried no bombs, but more guns and armour plate than a battle-ship. 'Lizzie Borden' went out *asking* for it. Stepanski had left her shiny metal finish, not the khaki-drab the rest were painted. She shone like the sun, like a mirror in the sky. And on her nose, this big impossibly busty near-naked blonde was painted, with long wild hair, busy putting an axe straight through Adolf's skull. Oh, yes, they went out look-ing for trouble, all right; and they found it. Which was funny, because they weren't really those sort of guys. Stepanski was old for a pilot, a quiet, thin schoolteacher from Chicago, with frizzy grey hair. But he was of Polish origin, and you remember how Poles felt about the Nazis . . .

And Con O'Connell's family were filthy rich. A little stocky dark guy, a medical-school graduate from Yale, who just couldn't wait for the War to finish so he could get back and find a cure for cancer.

And Tex was from Texas, and incredibly enough, he really had worked as a cowboy. He had a few fights about that, when the Yanks first came, because nobody would believe him . . . but he was usually a peaceful guy, on the ground.

Anyway, they asked for trouble, and they got it, and they coped with it, and came home. As time went by, the German fighters got to know them; they were mentioned four times on German propaganda broadcasts as having been shot down. They drew the enemy like wasps round a jam-pot, got shot full of holes, downed a lot of Huns. In the end, Stepanski had twenty swastikas painted on his nose, big, like he was a fighter plane. They came back on three engines, on two; once Stepanski landed, I swear, on little more than one. And 'Lizzie Borden' wasn't really one aircraft, but four; the first three were written off and towed to the knacker's yard. But not before the blonde with the axe had been painted on a brand new plane. They had a tracing of it ready; the sign-painters worked in the hangar all night. Next raid, 'Lizzie Borden' flew . . .

And in between, they made the Dumbledore their place, and Little Charlene their mascot. Especially Tex. She was so small, only a kid; and he was so big. He would swing her up on the counter, and sing her sad songs about Dixie and a yellow ribbon, and the siege of the Alamo. On big nights, at the base dance, he would walk round with her sitting on his shoulder. And before they went on a mission, the whole crew would kiss her for luck. Harmless fun, we thought, harmless . . .

Then came their last mission. Three more, and they'd have been going home. But it wasn't to be. They got hit on the big raid on the ball-bearing factory, hit bad, two engines out, and still over Germany. The group did their damnedest to cover them. Stepanski came down to zero feet to make it hard for the fighters, and three other un-hit Forts stayed with them, throttled right back. Even a group of Mustangs, fighters, got in on the act. But the Mustangs' fuel ran out over Belgium, and they had to come home. And two of the other Forts were hit and went down. And still, somehow, Stepanski kept 'Lizzie Borden' in the air. But the Germans . . . the Germans went mad. They had to down her, and to hell with the cost. One Me 109 actually tried to ram, but Tex picked him off the prop-blades and he blew up.

Lizzie crossed the Belgian coast, trailing a deadly mile-long plume of glycol. And still the Jerry fighters followed. She passed outside the range of the German coastal radar, and still they followed. They followed her to within sight of the Suffolk coast, where squadrons of Spits and Hurries were scrambling.

Too late. Within sight of home, they downed her. But still Lizzie's luck seemed to be holding; she pancaked neatly into a calm sea, and floated with her wings stuck to the waves, like a trapped moth. It must have been a crazy sight, with the other Fort still circling her at zero height, wanting to help, and screaming for reinforcements over her WT; the English home-defence squadrons starting to be visible dots in the sky, Stepanski and, they said, the whole crew except Tex standing on the wing, getting the dinghies inflated. That was the time for the happy ending . . .

But somehow Jerry must have known that while her crew lived, 'Lizzie Borden' would never die; they came in again, and machine-gunned the crew as they stood on the wings, as they struggled with the bullet-punctured dinghy in the water. They wiped out the lot; except Tex. He was still inside his dorsal turret, firing. Somehow, he must have known. He downed another Jerry, and he was still firing his guns as the water closed over his turret, the last thing to show.

The Jerries had left it too long, and they were close to the deck, sitting ducks. About four squadrons of Spits caught them, and not many Jerries saw Belgium again . . . when the air-sea rescue reached the scene – and they reached it quick – there wasn't a thing to be seen bar Major Stepanski's body, still floating in his Mae West.

'Yes,' I said. 'I remember the night they got the chop.'

'Another whisky, sir?' I nodded; he gave me another double.

'But do you remember a little feller called Jack Milton – little Jackie Milton?'

I didn't. 'Which mob was he with?'

'He wasn't with a mob, Squadron-Leader. He was a farmworker – directed to work on the land – a conchie – conscientious objector.'

'Oh, *him*,' I said. He wasn't a character I wanted to remember: a pacifist in the middle of a war; a man who chose to keep his lily-white soul clean, when hundreds were dying daily. He hadn't even had the decency to keep quiet about it: kept arguing with the Yanks that war was the greatest evil the human race was subject to. Clever, too, in a mulish way; argue the hind leg off a donkey. I wondered some of them didn't thump him, shut his mouth. And yet the Yanks, who were doing the real fighting and dying, were far more tolerant than I was. Part of it was that Tex tolerated him – more than that, made a pet of him. Bought him drinks in the Dumbledore, listened to his philosophical cant with a lazy smile on his face. Made him a pet, like he made Charlene into a pet. I could see Tex now, grinning, with Charlene on one side of him and Milton on the other. Little flaxen-haired Milton, with his khaki shorts and muscular hairy legs, and worn Harris-tweed sports-coat, open-necked shirt, gold-rimmed spectacles and old Scandinavian rucksack. The eternal college student.

'Yes,' I said, 'I remember Milton. Tex, Charlene and Milton, they always hung around together. We used to call them the Three Musketeers.'

'Well, Squadron-Leader Ashden, you left early that night, as I remember; had some work to do back at the base?'

I remembered. I hadn't really had any work, any more than usual. I just hadn't been able to stand the atmosphere, with crew after crew coming in, wanting to talk about Tex and the way he died. I'd run away, left them, and never gone back.

'Well, after you'd gone, Charlene was sitting in the corner, crying soft-like, and Jackie Milton was trying to cope with her, and everyone else was drinking and trying not to notice them. Only their whispering's getting more and more violent, and then suddenly Charlene stands up and throws off Milton's arm, and announces that she's pregnant.

'Well, her ma goes for her like an old she-cat – the aircrew have to hold her back, and she's still screeching at Charlene, wanting to know who the father is. And Charlene's just standing there, dry-eyed, and white as a sheet, saying not a word . . . and the aircrews are getting more and more uptight. Then Randy Leipzig . . . you remember Captain Leipzig, sir? . . . walks up to Charlene and asks her if the father was Tex?

'Charlene stands still an awful long time, with us all hanging on her every word so you could hear a pin drop, then she says, "Yes", and bursts into tears.

'And you know, when all the uproar's over, and we come to ourselves again, little Jackie Milton's nowhere to be seen, and he ups back to his lodgings and packs, and we never see him again in this village. But there's some as reckons that Tex being the father broke his heart, as he was sweet on Charlene himself.

'Anyway, a funny thing happened then. Charlene's ma keeps going on and on at her something horrible, about being a little whore and getting rid of the baby, and Charlene just going on crying, noisy. But the aircrews, they just keep staring at Charlene's mum, until the silence finally gets through to her and she turns on them and curses them for being oversexed and overpaid. Then Captain Leipzig . . . you remember what a gentle sort he was . . . but he wasn't that night. He walks over and takes hold of her mum's wrist in a grip that's liable to break it, until she finally shuts up as well.

'Then Captain Leipzig says, "Tex is dead, an' Tex died a hero, ma'am. An' this kid your daughter's carryin' is all we got left of Tex . . ." And Charlene's mum shuts up and never opens her mouth again. Then all the aircrews say goodnight to Charlene, real soft, and touch her hand like she's . . . if I was a Catholic, sir, I'd say like she was the Virgin Mary.'

Tom took a deep embarrassed swig of whisky, and wiped his mouth with the back of his hand. 'Well, the next day, the padre from the American base comes to the Dumbledore, and he doesn't go on like you'd expect from a sky-pilot. No, he says Charlene can have her baby in some big American military hospital when the time comes, and they'll drive her there in a big staff-car, and she's going to have a regular American allowance for the kid, of some sort, starting now. I think that had some part in shutting her ma up, if you ask me . . . Charlene thanks him, and goes on serving in the Dumbledore, all pale and strained, but kind of proud too, with her head up. And as far as the aircrews are concerned, she's St Joan and Calamity Jane rolled into one.

'Then she gets a letter from Tex's mum and dad in America. There's a lot of dollar bills tucked inside, and they say they'll get over to see their grandchild just as soon as the War's over, and to take care of herself . . . and it just goes on being like Christmas for Charlene and her old mum. I mean, her dad's dead, and they're pretty hard-up and just rent the caff. But after a bit, a deputation comes from the base, and all the aircrews have had a whip-round, and they've bought the Dumbledore for her, and the empty shop next door. And then the groundcrews chip in, even at the height of the attacks on Germany, and they strip out the two shops and rebuild them like new . . . and there's a juke-box, and the first neon strip-lighting I ever did see meself outside an American base. And when they announced that Tex had been given the Congressional Medal of Honour – that's their V C, as you know . . . well, there just ain't nothing any airman likes better than running down to the Dumbledore and seeing that Charlene's all right, for old Tex.

'Anyway, V E night comes . . . you'll remember V E night at the Dumbledore, sir . . . no . . . quite a night that was, sir, and little Charlene eight months gone and as big as a barrel, but still serving behind the counter to the end, like Tex at his guns. Then before V J night, the kid's been born, and the Yankee grandparents have come to see Little Tex. They wanted to take Charlene and the kid back with them, but she wouldn't leave her mum cos her mum wasn't well. When her mum finally died, they offered to give them a home again, and they could've afforded to, they were loaded . . . oil-wells, I think. But Charlene wouldn't. She said she'd stick to her guns, like Tex stuck to his. And when the base closed, after the War, they gave Charlene a lot of stuff, like the Fortress airscrew on the wall, and them Jeeps that stand outside. Useless stuff, of course – worn-out write-offs – but Charlene always liked anything American . . . said it made her feel at home.

'Well, a few years passed . . . quiet years round here. But Little Tex was a fine little lad, and helped his mum with the Dumbledore from the time he could walk. She never married – he was all she had. He wasn't big, which puzzled us a bit, 'cos Tex had been six foot two. And he had a mass of flaxen hair, whereas Tex had been almost bald at twenty-three. But we just reckoned he'd taken more after Charlene. Strong little bugger he was, though – you should've seen him lift down a full jar of sweets afore he was five.

'And then, of course, the Yanks started coming back, for holidays. Got themselves organized into their various squadron old-comrade associations, and came back by the bus-load every summer, with their wives and kids. We always felt a bit sorry for them, cos it seemed a miserable kind of holiday with nothing to see except that bloody great cemetery outside Cambridge, and the old airfields crumbling away, or lying under the corn. We used to lay on a slap-up tea for them in the village hall, and they'd keep asking, "Where's old so-and-so?" and more often every year we had to say "Dead" or "Re-married" or "Moved away".

'So you can imagine how the Dumbledore caught their fancy. It became a kind of shrine, like that Catholic place up Walsingham way, to Our Lady. They kept on bringing things – that bloody great press-photo of Tex in his flying gear – half covered the wall it did – did you see it? And what a fuss they made of Charlene. I reckon that's why she never married, 'cos she was still a good-looking girl, and she had plenty of offers. But they made an even greater fuss of Little Tex. It sort of . . . twisted him, as he grew up. He was the first kid round here to wear blue jeans. And every day a different tee-shirt: one day it was the Brooklyn Dodgers, and the next it was Notre Dame University. And when all the other lads had their Teddy-boy sideburns, young Tex still kept his hair in a crew-cut, just like the aircrew used to have. Made a lot of trouble for him at school with the other kids, and the teachers, especially when he insisted on speaking American all the time – he could speak every accent in the States by the time he was twelve. Used to have the Yanks in fits. And he chewed gum all the time, even if the Headmistress caned him for it. It only got worse when he got older – used to spend months in the States on holiday. Not just with the grandparents either, though they doted on him and were across here every year.

'It didn't help, either, how much Charlene prospered. She never said much about it – never bragged – but I reckon she had a tidy pile in the bank. Specially after she bought up the old Holmes house, and turned it into the Dumbledore Guest House, and charged the Yanks fancy prices to stay. Oh, she was into all kinds of things. Postcards – coloured postcards of the old caff – never missed a trick. Didn't make her very popular with the locals, but she didn't seem to care. She was all wrapped up in Little Tex.

'He was really bright – got to the grammar school in Norwich, and got a lot of O-levels, in spite of all the chewing-gum and canings. They say he could've gone to Cambridge, but he was all set up to go to the University of Texas, like his dad before him. Nothing English was much good to Little Tex.

'And so it might've gone on for ever . . . till one night I dropped in to have a word with Charlene – she pushed quite a lot of her overspill guests in my direction, and I was grateful.

'There was a car parked outside, and for once it wasn't a Chevrolet. It was an old Morris Minor. And inside the Dumbledore was a funny little guy – gold-rimmed spectacles, old hairy suit – Cambridge don written all over him. Stuck out like a sore thumb among the tourists. But he just asked for coffee politely, and then went and sat in a corner, and stared around like he was pussy-struck and couldn't believe it.

'Then Little Tex came in from school, and got behind the counter to help. I can remember him so clear, the blond crew-cut hair and the University of Texas sweat-shirt, and the little gold hairs glinting on his bare arm-muscles in the sun. And I noticed the little feller in the corner – he was just drinking his coffee when Little Tex came in, and he suddenly slurped it all over the Formica table-top, then started to wipe it up, all confused, with his handkerchief. Little Tex was over in a flash with a clean dishcloth – very fussy he always was, in the Dumbledore. And as Tex wiped the table, he looked down at the bloke, and the bloke looked up at him, and I could've *died*, Squadron-Leader . . .

'Their profiles were the spitting image of each other.

'The little feller went very pale; and Tex himself seemed a bit . . . baffled. I remember he shook his head, as if trying to shake some idea, some memory out of it, like it was a buzzing fly that was bothering him. Then Tex went back to the counter, and nobody else seemed to have noticed anything, but Tex was doing various Yank accents, to amuse the tourists.

'And then Charlene came in, her hands full of lists and things. And she looked up and noticed the little feller. She kept staring at him, and putting her hand to her throat, nervous-like, then looking away as if she was trying to ignore him. This went on quite a bit, and the atmosphere in the place getting worse and worse till even the tourists noticed, and drank up their coffee and left. That just left the three of them; and me.

'The little feller seemed to be trying to make up his mind about something. It took a long time. Then he got up, and shrugged to himself, like a man who's made up his mind, and went across to the counter. To Charlene.

'"Yes, sir?" she says, all bright and businesslike. But when she looks at him, her mouth seems to fall to pieces and she starts shaking all over, so she nearly dropped the plate she was holding.

'So the little feller says softly, "Don't you know me, Charlotte?"

'Her mouth falls open, and she does drop the plate. But she won't say anything.

'"It's Jackie," he says, "little Jackie Milton."

'"What do you want?" she asks, her face like death.

'"To see my son."

'Well, all hell breaks loose, Squadron-Leader. Charlene's screaming at him that he hasn't got a son, and to bugger off and leave her alone, and that he's ruined her whole life. Then she starts throwing things at him, plates and mugs and stuff. But he just stands there steady, looking at her, trying to fend off the things she's throwing with his hands, and tea and stuff sloshing all down him. Then Little Tex grabs her to stop her, and starts apologizing for her, because she seems to have gone bonkers.

'"He's *not* your father, he's not, he's not!" screams Charlene, over and over, and then runs out, still screaming.

'And the two blokes look at each other; young Tex is really baffled. And then Jackie Milton takes him gently by the arm, and turns him, so they're facing, side by side, the big mirror with Coke stickers all over it. And as I get up and look over their shoulders, I can see the two faces looking out at me, broad blond little faces, with beaky noses and big square jaws. There's no mistaking it; any court of law would believe it.

'And then Charlene comes raging back again, belting into Jackie Milton for all she's worth, and as I'm trying to get hold to calm her, I sense the kid slip out of the room.

'Then just as suddenly he's back, with his eyes forced as wide as saucers, and his face set white as marble, and I know he's gone clean out of his mind, and there's a big six-shooter, one of Tex's that some fool had given him, a-waving in his hand. And that shuts even Charlene up. It shuts us all up, 'cos we got a nasty feeling it's loaded and going to go off.

'"Give that here, son," I say, gently, "afore there's a nasty accident."

'"There's bin a nasty accident already, Tom," he says. "But it's not your fault. Stand back. I don't mean you no harm." And he points the gun at Jackie Milton.

'And I'll give it to Jackie, he has guts, for all he's a pacifist. If he'd tried to run or duck or grabbed for the gun, the kid'd have shot him. But he just says, gently, "If you shoot me, son, you'll shoot yourself just after." And again, he points at the mirror. And the kid turns and looks in the mirror, and starts to cry.

'"If you want," says Jackie, "I'll go away, and never bother you again – promise. But if you're going to shoot me, I think you ought to get to know me first." Ever so gentle and sad.

'And the kid turns to him and says, "Where've you been? Why'd you leave me?"

'"I didn't *know*," says Jackie. "I didn't know if you were mine or Tex's. How could I? Then? And who'd have believed me, anyway? Tex was a hero . . . and it was what your mum wanted."

'They both turned and looked at Charlene, then. And both their faces looked exactly alike; like the Day of Judgement. And Charlene ran out into the back again.

'"What shall I do?" asked the kid. And he put the gun quite natural on the counter, like it was a salt-cellar.

'"The car's outside," said Jackie Milton.

'The kid sort of moans, and starts taking off the University of Texas sweat-shirt. Then it tears, he takes it off so violent, like it was red-hot and burning him. And he goes on tearing it, till it's lying all over the floor in little shreds. Then he stares at his blue jeans, helpless, clutching at them with his fingers.

'"Everyone's wearing jeans," says Jackie softly. And he takes off the coat of his hairy suit, and drapes it round Little Tex's shoulders. "C'mon – we can buy what you need in Cambridge."

'And out they go, and we ain't seen hide nor hair of them since.

'And I went after them, but I took that blasted gun, and threw it in the dyke – good riddance to bad rubbish. Only . . . Tex always carried guns in pairs, and Charlene's still got the other one.'

It was late, and I was drunk, by the time I got to Section Officer Edmunds's house. She opened the door in a red-haired fury.

'Where the hell have you been?'

So I sat down in my usual chair in her lounge, and drank some more, and told her the lot. We sat till midnight; silent towards the end. Then she said, 'You want to come to bed?' But she knew that the answer would be no.

'I can't go on with it, Peggy,' I said. 'We've been on Cloud Nine, too. The War's over, Peggy. It's been over seventeen long years. Tex is dead, Chalky's dead. You're dead, I'm dead. I'm a dead middle-aged antique-dealer.'

'And I suppose I'm a middle-aged librarian?'

'No,' I said, 'not middle-aged. Not yet. You could start again . . .'

She shook her head at me, half sad, half comical, very thoughtful.

'I don't think I can come any more,' I blurted out.

She smiled faintly.

'What'll you do?' I was really sad for her, in a drunken sort of way.

She shrugged. 'I'll manage. Did you think you were the only one?'

'Only what?'

'The only lost RAF flyer, who couldn't find his way home to East Cardingham? My God, if you think I'm going to be lonely you're very much mistaken. I've got Tosher Norris, and Sid Stevens out of 'B' Flight; and Taffy Thomas, Chalky's old flight-engineer, is due to fly in tomorrow night. And Easby and Tullah, and Sproston and Gatesby and Micky Morris . . .'

'You're having me on . . .'

She pulled a desk-diary out of a drawer, with her old neat precision. I opened it. All the names were there; mine among them.

'You're not a woman; you're an old-comrades reunion.' I was too drunk to get up, thank God, but that didn't stop me being spiteful.

But she was beyond my spite. She smiled again, still half happy, half sad. 'Just call me the old home base. The flak wasn't all over Happy Valley. Some of them have never stopped fighting the war. Tosher Norris's wife walked out on him; Sid Stevens has got cancer.'

'And they all found the Adjutant's ashtray.' I was still bitter.

'It wasn't even the Adge's ashtray. I bought it in an antique-shop in Stalham. But it seems to make them happy, just the same.'

'Why?' I shouted. 'Why?'

'Chalky got the chop,' she said. 'It never mattered after Chalky got the chop. You remember . . . you were all waiting to see whose girl I would become, once I got over Chalky. Well, I never got over Chalky. So when they came flying back, all shot up with civvy flak, it seemed the least I could do.' She smiled a last time. 'You're tuckered up, Geoff – your eyebrow's twitching. Go to sleep.' With expert fingers, she loosened my tie and took my shoes off, and lifted my legs up on to the couch. Tossed a rug over me, gave me a beautiful salute in the doorway, and was gone into her bedroom, with the door locked, *snap!*

By the time I wakened in the morning, with one beauty of a hangover, she was gone. There was just a note saying:

*Please never come back.*

I never went back; but I still send her flowers for her birthday.

# The Woolworth Spectacles

BEFORE THE War, you could buy spectacles at Woolworth's. Dealers gathered in lost spectacles, uncollected spectacles, dead men's spectacles, and they appeared in a black, spidery jumble on Woolworth's counter. There were stranger ways of making a living in the Depression . . .

You merely walked up to the counter, tried them on pair by pair, and if a pair suited, you pulled out your sixpence.

Mostly, pensioners bought them, having more troubled eyesight and less money than anybody else. Certainly my cousin Maude Cleveland had no reason, one warm June afternoon in 1938, to be patronizing that counter. Her father, as the town's leading solicitor, would have disapproved tremendously. He would have sent her to the optician immediately. Perhaps that's why she was standing there fiddling, turning her large, blue, beautiful and myopic eyes to the door at intervals, in case anyone she knew came in and saw her.

She was only *slightly* short-sighted, but blurring small print, the need to hunch closer and closer, provoked her inordinately. Besides, if she went on squinting, it would make lines on her face in the end. She had been tremendously fit all her twenty-nine years; never been to the doctor since her mother died.

And once her father paid for spectacles, he would insist she wore them. All the time. In company. And men don't make passes at girls who wear glasses . . .

So she dabbled among the black, long-legged mass with her fine tapered fingers, holding her leather-bound New Testament in her left hand, open at the Book of Revelation, peering at it through each successive pair, in between peering at the door . . .

It was the feel of the strange spectacles that attracted her. The lively spring of metal, instead of the funereal smoothness of horn-rims. She disentangled them with difficulty: they seemed reluctant to come; then she realized they were on a chain, for hanging round the neck. This immediately disposed her in their favour. Lady Frome had such a pair, and fiddled and poked with them elegantly at meetings of the Parochial Church Council. And though Lady Frome was nearly fifty, her sprigged frocks and large hats were the quiet epitome of London elegance.

Maude examined the strange spectacles. Close to, her beautiful eyes had that near-microscopic accuracy that is the gift of short sight. The spectacles were very old-fashioned; half-moon lenses, with the palest green tint, and even a few tiny bubbles caught inside the glass. She could almost have sworn the frames were gold; and the chain, with its tiny links.

Her hand went to her purse swiftly. The shop could not know what it was selling . . . they were antiques . . . Mr Hazlitt who ran the little shop in Church Walk would be interested. She waved frantically for the assistant who was gossiping, arms akimbo, further down the counter.

'I'll take this pair!' She thrust the sixpence with force into the assistant's hand.

'Them's not ours, madam. We don't sell *that* sort.' The slow country voice quickened with contempt. 'Old-fashioned rubbish!'

'But they were here on the counter!'

'One of the old ladies must ha' left them, when she bought a new pair. Give 'em here, madam, an' I'll throw 'em in the bin.' The girl's plump hand rearranged the remaining spectacles protectively, as if they were sheep who'd had a wolf among them.

'But I *want* them!' Maude's voice rose to an indignant squeak.

'But they're not for sale, madam. Not ours. Lost property. I s'pose they should go along to the police-station, by rights.'

'Then I shall take them,' announced Maude triumphantly. 'After all, we don't want them ending up in the dustbin, do we?'

The girl hesitated, knowing she was lying. But Miss Cleveland was Miss Cleveland. And a complaint to the manager could cost her her job . . .

'Very well, madam. Shall I wrap them?'

'No thank you.' Maude clutched the spectacles even tighter, knowing she was being ridiculous. 'Are you sure I can't pay you? I wouldn't want you getting into trouble.'

'No, madam,' said the girl, tight-lipped with stubbornness.

Outside, Maude stood appalled. She had behaved in a most un-Christian manner. Lying, avarice, theft, uncharity to someone less well-off than herself. Sins that must go down in the back of her diary, towards her next confession at St Michael's. More sins in five minutes than she'd been guilty of in the last month . . . she felt almost shockingly excited about it. Was getting excited about sinning a sin in itself?

In the heat, the High Street seemed deserted. Maude felt a foolish urge to try the spectacles on. She moved well clear of Woolworth's doorway so that the assistant couldn't observe her, slipped the chain over her long smooth neck, felt her throat nervously and popped them on.

They were pince-nez; clamped surprisingly firmly on to the bridge of her elegant nose. Not painfully, like tweezers, but as if they knew where they belonged, and meant to stay.

What was more, they worked. Maude saw the world with a quite amazing clarity she'd forgotten existed. The black, half-shaven whiskers of that man coming towards her; the dirt-filled broken wrinkles descending cruelly from nose to mouth; the few greasy black strands fighting a losing battle across his balding pate. Worse, the way his beady black eyes roamed hungrily across her breasts and throat . . . It made her blush all over. Insufferable. She was a lady, but he was regarding her as if she was the lowest type of *woman*. A common working man . . . would she ever feel safe again?

She whipped the spectacles off, and relaxed back into her familiar peaceful blur. She was very good at reading that blur. That broad pink fuzz-patch approaching, accompanied by a smaller grey fuzz-patch, was undoubtedly what the county magazine referred to often as the genial Mrs Forbes-Formby and her charming daughter Patricia . . .

There was no time to remove the spectacles from round her neck; Mrs Forbes-Formby would certainly notice such a furtive gesture. Instead she tucked the spectacles down inside her discreet neckline. They lay flat, snugly, across the top of her breasts; a little chilly, but not unpleasant on such a hot day.

But some effect seemed to have lingered from wearing them. Certainly she had never seen Mrs Forbes-Formby so clearly in her life. How heavy she had grown in the haunch; how thick her ankles were, and how domineeringly she stood. Maude had always thought her a handsome woman, but now her nose, far from seeming noble, seemed merely too big and fleshy, and little beads of perspiration stood out unbecomingly all over it. The mouth, which had always seemed so decisive, drooped disagreeably.

Patricia looked worse; like a sweating sheep. Had her shoulders always drooped so much? Did she always keep her eyes down, so, when she was with her mother? She was two years younger than Maude, and she looked positively middle-aged. Gosh, thought Maude, you can't give up at *twenty-seven*! Do I look like that? She was seized with a sudden desire to peer into mirrors; to walk past reflecting shop-windows. The conversation did not prosper. Mrs Forbes-Formby looked positively affronted when Maude cut short her account of the cake-judging at the Melton W I gala . . .

Let her look affronted, thought Maude, passing her first shopfront. She treats her daughter like a child; and Patricia lets her.

Meanwhile, the shop-window showed her shoulders slightly rounded, thought not half as badly as Patricia's. She pulled them back, as she'd been taught at school.

It made her breasts stick out with disturbing prominence . . . another working-man passed and admired them.

It occurred to Maude that she had reached a crossroads in her life . . .

She went on, her shoulders well back.

The clarity of sight persisted. She noticed many things, few pleasant: broken upstairs windows above the shops' peeling paintwork, twitching faces. She had always thought Barlborough such a mellow town. There was a black-and-white cat sitting in the butcher's window, and several white cat-hairs on the meat. She went into Flatt's the greengrocer's. Mr Flatt gave her his usual genial greeting; she realized for the first time how shifty his eyes were . . . dipping down constantly to the apples he was weighing for her on his scales. It came to her quite suddenly that he was giving her short measure; something to do with resting his hand on the right side of the scales. She stared at the hand. His babbling increased; he broke out into a sweat and threw several more apples into the pan, bundled them all into a bag and couldn't get rid of her quick enough.

She had gained several apples, and lost a friend. The thought so disturbed her that she decided to go and see Mr Hazlitt. He always made her feel better, though he had to be used sparingly. For Mr Hazlitt was *persona non grata* at home, and it would not do for gossip to reach Father. Ever since the night he'd come to Barlborough Archaeological Society and disputed with Father a little too long over the dating of the Barlborough Crosses. On which subject Father was a lifelong expert . . .

She surveyed the front of Mr Hazlitt's shop with pleasure; the wall-clocks, the big brass Buddha she'd have loved to buy, the ginger cat . . . but the spectacles took over again, and showed her something less pleasant. The top corner of the shop-window showed damp; worse, green lichen was spreading everywhere. Worse still, the beam above was cracking into those little squares that could only mean dry-rot . . . and a widening crack meandered through the brickwork above, right down from the level of the guttering.

She knew with dreadful certainty. She rushed into the shop, breathless.

'You've got dry-rot. Your shop's going to fall down any minute . . .'

Mr Hazlitt looked up from his ancient book with a smile. He was intriguingly ageless. White hair above a young face, and very bright blue eyes. Tall and slim, like an undergraduate. His mouth intrigued her; cruel or kind? She could never decide.

But one thing the spectacles showed clearly; his smile was one he would give a precocious child. He didn't take her seriously, not for a minute. If only Mr Hazlitt would give her the kind of look those working-men . . . she brushed the thought aside, into the back of her diary.

'All right, Maude. Show me where you mean . . .' Amused, detached, kind, tolerant.

She showed him.

He suddenly ceased to be any of these things; he went berserk. He picked up the telephone directory and dropped it; trod on the cat; sent a hat-stand crashing to the floor; paced up and down like a caged tiger. She had never had anything like this effect on Mr Hazlitt before. It was she who finally got through to Theodore Brittan the builder, and calmly explained what was required.

By the time Theodore had come, and the window-beam was temporarily but safely shored up, Mr Hazlitt had flopped into his best Sheraton armchair, totally exhausted.

'I'll make you some tea,' said Maude, soothingly and greatly daring. As he did not reply, she went through the curtain into the back of the shop, where she'd never dared tread before. It was scrupulously neat and tidy, with a smell of clock oil, wood-shavings and tobacco smoke. Being so close to his life pleased her inordinately. She was satisfied he was what she would have called a proper man.

When she came out with the tray of tea (and some biscuits she'd found in a tin) he looked up at her in a new way.

'Maude, what would I have done without you?'

'Rung up Theodore Brittan yourself,' she said, with mock sharpness. But she blushed becomingly with pleasure, and thought she saw in his face not just a new respect, but the merest flicker, gone in a second, of the look that had been on the working-men's faces. Though much more refined, of course . . .

It was then that she noticed the time and remembered it was Wednesday. Wednesday was the day Father came home early; Wednesday was the day Mr and Mrs Dewhurst always came to tea. At four. And already it was half-past.

She hurried along, trying to work out why she was not reduced to a state of sheer terror. Not to be there to brew the tea and carry in the tray that cook had left ready . . . not to be there to pour, while Father and Mr Dewhurst delved deep into the business of the Archaeological Society, and Mrs Dewhurst stared carpingly round the room . . . it had never happened in all the years since her mother died. It was not to be thought of!

Father would be hungry, impatient, furious. Father would tell her off in front of everybody. Mrs Dewhurst would sniff disapprovingly; Mr Dewhurst would be sorry for her, in his slow, stately way . . .

It was all the spectacles' fault. She put her hand to her neck to take them off; then paused.

The spectacles had not let her down so far. Wearing the spectacles, she had put to flight Mrs Forbes-Formby, the greengrocer and Mr Hazlitt. Not a bad score . . .

She continued to wear them round her neck, under her frock, as she hurried up the drive, and saw Mr Dewhurst's grey car parked next to Father's black one.

Father reared up from the sofa as she entered; rather, in his black suit, with his drooping white moustache and bald head, like a bull-walrus defending his mating territory. She could not help smiling at the thought (quite unlike any thought she'd ever had before), saw he was disconcerted by the smile, and went directly into the attack.

'Haven't you started? You shouldn't have waited.' She glanced at Mrs Dewhurst, sitting like a full-bosomed judge about to pass the death-sentence . . . implying that Mrs Dewhurst could have poured boiling water into a pot, surely . . .

Her father opened his mouth three times to say something, then closed it again, and by that time she was past and into the kitchen, where she made firm, busy bangings with the kettle and taps.

Then she was back with the tray like a whirlwind, pouring cups of tea and passing round sandwiches with disconcerting vigour.

'Another cucumber sandwich, Mrs Dewhurst? Brown bread. Not at all *fattening*, I assure you.'

Then she sat back and watched them coolly, elegant fingers poised over her own sandwich. And the magic of the spectacles continued . . . She saw that her father was wearing a suit that had been made for a bigger man; the waistcoat sagged over his once-broad chest and belly, like the skin of a fruit past ripeness . . . his double chins, once full and pink, were pale and hung like empty flaps of skin. He had adopted, unnoticed, the habit of taking off his gold-rimmed spectacles and rubbing his eyes. He was well over sixty . . . growing old. Not much left of the frightening bear who had icily, legally, bullied Mother.

The righteous bulk of Mrs Dewhurst, as heavily corseletted as a knight in armour, appalled her. She could not be more than forty . . . what would she look like, undressed for bed, naked?

The thought shocked Maude. Another sin for the back of her diary? But Mr Dewhurst, about the same age as his wife, looked so much younger . . . Another bear of a man, but kinder than her father; red-haired, red-moustached, in his ginger tweed suit and big brogues. A ripe man, a man still full of juice, not dead, like the other two.

Her mind was running away with her. She'd never *had* such thoughts! The spectacles . . . but there was no chance to take them off here, as the other three munched steadily, holding out their cups for a refill as they discussed the inexhaustible topic of Hitler.

Except . . . Mr Dewhurst kept giving her more little glances than his requests for tea would seem to warrant. There was a look on Mr Dewhurst's face: tiny, timid, glancing. But that same hungry look again.

The utterly respectable churchwarden and local historian desired her, just like a common workman. It aroused a little devil in her. There were so many ways a woman could lead a man on . . . *ladylike* ways. The pensive turn of a head on a long neck; fingers stroking the soft down of her own cheek. Mr Dewhurst's glances grew bolder; till Mrs Dewhurst noticed.

'We must be off, Henry,' said Mrs Dewhurst, pulling on her gloves and inspecting her revolting green hat in the tall dark mirror of the sideboard.

'But we're discussing the arrangements for the outing to the fort . . .' Mr Dewhurst seemed disposed to argue; even Father looked affronted.

'Plenty of time for that later, Henry. Come, I must buy some Seville oranges for cook to make marmalade. Flatt may sell out.' She gave him a sharp look that got him on his feet, apologizing wretchedly to Father, looking a total, blushing, blundering fool. How could he stand her treating him like a lapdog in public? Then she remembered that his little book-shop hardly supported itself. He was no businessman; *she* had the money.

'I can't understand it,' bleated Father, when they'd gone. 'They never go this early. It's only five past five.'

'Obviously marmalade is more important than Roman forts,' said Maude.

'Woman's a fool . . .'

'Can *I* come to the fort? Mr Dewhurst's always so interesting.'

'I didn't known you were keen on the Romans.'

'Yes,' said Maude, 'Oh, *yes*.'

She lay in bed that night, thinking what she'd wear. The blue skirt was a little short. If she walked ahead of Mr Dewhurst, up the hill to the fort, looking back frequently over her shoulder to ask him questions, almost stumbling, so he would put out a hand to steady her . . . delicious!

Then she remembered she hadn't said her prayers. How had she forgotten to say her prayers? She never forgot to say her prayers. Father Whitstable . . .

At the thought of Father Whitstable, she realized the spectacles were still hanging round her neck, under her nightdress. How peculiar, that she hadn't taken them off! Except that they gave her a pleasant sensation as they slid around the valley between her breasts . . .

She shot upright. Maude Cleveland, you are a *sinful* woman! Get out of bed and say your prayers at once!

She still didn't want to. She wanted to go on lying in bed, thinking about the glint in Mr Dewhurst's eye . . . and other things. The feel of the rough texture of his jacket, the roughness of his hands, his faint tobacco smell.

She shot out of bed with a great effort of will, and knelt on the cold lino as a penance. But still she couldn't pray . . . not wearing those sinful, sliding spectacles . . .

She took them off with an even greater effort of will, and put them on her bedside cabinet.

Then she was able to pray. She was really very glad she'd taken the spectacles off.

She had never prayed so greyly, boredly, resentfully, in her life. The state of rebellion in her soul alarmed her. She would not wear those spectacles again.

She got back into bed and slept very badly, which was unusual for her. She dreamt about both Mr Hazlitt and Mr Dewhurst.

Next day, it rained. All day. The sky was the dull grey of a vicarage blanket. Maude attended weekday communion at St Michael's, but her heart did not lift. Father Whitstable preached badly, having a heavy cold. The sermon was all sniffs and handkerchief. He dropped his handkerchief three times and had to come down from the pulpit to search for it, and went on preaching as he searched . . . this did not do a great deal for the doctrine of the Transubstantiation, with reference to the Bishop of London's latest pseudo-scientific outburst. During the communion service, the knees of the woman in front creaked audibly; she was wearing a black hat with mauve flowers, that smelt strongly of mothballs.

Going round the shops afterwards, Maude could find nothing she wanted. She left her umbrella in Elliot's the stationer's during a brief break in the rain, and having to walk back for it, she got thoroughly soaked. As she took off her hat and coat in the hall, her face looked pale and pinched, and (as she said to herself) wrinkled like an old boot. Her hair drooped lankly; she looked as unlikely an object for lust, let alone love, as she'd ever seen, and as a result, she had words with cook.

As a further result, cook produced a truly punitive dinner; tinned oxtail soup, fat mutton chops, limp white boiled potatoes and watery green beans, followed by tinned peaches with over-solid rice pudding. And as an even further result of cook's vengeance, and the fact that she had eaten too much of that vengeance in a hopeless attempt to cheer herself up, Maude went to bed with indigestion, and woke with it in the middle of the night.

She lay and thought of life slipping like sand through her fingers. Next year she would reach thirty, the fatal watershed. One of her back teeth was loose, and wobbled more than usual; wobbled so violently that it threatened to come unstuck altogether . . .

More unhappy than she'd ever been, she reached in the dark towards the bedside table, for the glass of water and indigestion tablets.

Her hand touched the smooth glass of the spectacles. And she thought that if the rewards of virtue were so wretched, could the rewards of vice be any worse?

In that moment, she was a lost woman.

She slipped the spectacles round her neck.

The outing to the Roman fort was truly spiffing. The day dawned blue from horizon to horizon, so that Maude was able to wear her sleeveless blouse as well as the blue skirt that was a little too short. By the time the charabanc reached the foot of the suede-smooth green hill upon which the fort lay, it was really warm, which left Maude pleasantly and becomingly glowing, and Mrs Dewhurst sweating so badly that she got left behind over and over again as they climbed ramparts and descended counterscarps. Nobody was in the least interested in hauling Mrs Dewhurst up; she finally had to retire hurt back to the charabanc with a desperate migraine, and spend her time applying her own wet handkerchief to her brow, in between casting malevolent glances uphill to where Maude was having the time of her life.

Maude was, it must be added, the principal cause of that migraine. For her effect on Mr Dewhurst had been positively devastating. He seemed to have shed ten years as he made successful little jokes about vallum and fosse, and handed Maude up as athletically as a schoolboy. Nor was he the only one. Mr Hazlitt, similarly fascinated, was not to be outdone, either in handing-up or wit, and even Tony Smethurst, fresh down from Oxford and as boringly handsome as a Greek god, seemed to find Miss Cleveland irresistible, and was so bold to inquire what Miss Cleveland was wearing on that little gold chain around her neck? If it should be a locket, was there room for a lock of his own golden hair?

'Never you mind,' said Maude archly, 'you *naughty* boy!'

Which reference to his youthfulness he seemed to take more as a challenge than a discouragement, and grew bolder.

That was the moment Maude was to remember with pleasure for the rest of her days. The descending sun underlining every ridge and furrow of the earthworks, gilding even the individual stems of grass, and the wool of the few resident sheep. The warm early-evening breeze stroking the bare skin of her arms, and lifting her too-short skirt with gentle lasciviousness. Mr Dewhurst's face, looking so bronzed and alive; and Mr Hazlitt's and Tony Smethurst's, and those of the three humbler male hangers-on who stood slightly further off, hopefully, rather like the resident sheep. And the angry distant glare of Lydia Dewhurst . . .

She felt a queen, with her little group of courtiers. What fun, playing one off against the other, encouraging them to compete, excel, yet not letting any get so discouraged that they despairingly went away. There was a skill in it, a knack in it, she would never have dreamt for a moment she had. She looked up at the distant sea peeping through the gaps in the coastal Dorset hills, and thought, 'Can I do *anything*?'

Then innocent, harmless Tony Smethurst uttered the fatal words.

'Who's your partner in the mixed doubles this year, Maude?'

Now this was no trivial matter. Barlborough might have been despised as provincial in many things, but in tennis, never. The Tennis Club, even more than the Archaeological Society, was at the centre of Barlborough life. They had been county club champions the previous year; seven members had at one time played for the county and two actually at Wimbledon, one getting as far as the second round. Membership was by invitation, recommendation and reference. Once you were in, you were *in*; if you were out, you were nowhere. Maude, no mean player, had made a habit of losing gallantly in the quarter-finals of the ladies' singles.

Now they all looked at her, expectantly. In the past, she had partnered Jack Simcock; but Jack had moved to Brighton. Now she looked round them all, her lips slightly parted, aware of a particularly furious glare coming up from the charabanc. Greatly daring, she asked, 'Are you playing this year, Mr Dewhurst?'

'Good God,' said Mr Dewhurst. 'I'm thirty-eight, Maude. Nearly thirty-nine. I think I'll confine myself to umpiring again.'

But he'd been the one who'd played at Wimbledon; even after four years of umpiring, he was remembered. And suddenly, his face glowed with recalled youthful glory.

'Go on, Doug,' said Tony Smethurst. 'Show us there's life in the old dog yet.'

Mr Dewhurst put him in his place with a look. But it was a look containing as much pleasure as rebuke.

'All right,' he said, 'I shall show you, young Smethurst. If my first service goes in, God help you. But I'd better get some match practice.'

So, it was done.

Life had never been so full for Maude. Her father felt the draught at home. Dinner became a solitary meal for him; and once he found a newly-ironed shirt was missing two buttons. He spoke to Maude about it, but his icy diatribe had curiously little effect. She had this way of sitting back and looking at him these days, a little smile playing around her lips. His diatribe ran out of steam half-way, and he went back to his boring chop like a fugitive.

Maude *lived* at the Tennis Club, with its red gravel courts and low, pleasant green huts. Very often she practised with Mr Dewhurst. His first service terrified her deliciously, whether it whirled savagely up at her body, or whanged like the crack of doom into the net-cord. She liked to see him sweat, hear him grunt and groan, like a great red savage bear only separated from her by a three-foot barrier of netting. She saw and learnt his every mood and movement.

And there was the leaning close, discussing tactics. He gave off heat like a red furnace; she felt it on her bare arms. And sitting talking afterwards, as the shadows of the high wooden fencing that shut the world out crept across the court, and the swallows and swifts flew high and screaming in the dimming blue sky far above . . . there was no one left in the world but the two of them.

Of course, she never let him actually *touch* her. That was against the rules of the game . . . that would be playing into Lydia Dewhurst's hands.

She felt herself changing in many ways, as the gold spectacles bounced and joggled against the glowing pink skin of her breasts. Her own game, long based on good straight hitting, grew sneaky, in a way she would once have condemned. She tormented Mr Dewhurst with evil little drop-volleys; and her every stroke now carried a load of back-spin, top-spin or side-spin that could drift the ball back into the corner when everyone could have sworn it was going out. She admitted to herself that she was no longer a nice person to know. Sometimes she practised with Mr Dewhurst on Sunday mornings, instead of going to church. Her father grumbled that tennis was coming between her and her wits, and he would be glad when the tournament was over . . .

But she didn't neglect Mr Hazlitt. Especially when she discovered, on his single shelf of antiquarian books, a couple of medieval herbals. The one by Gerard she liked so much that she drew out every penny she had in the bank to buy it. Mr Hazlitt gave her a good discount, and they discussed the book frequently. When Maude read it at home, it seemed so often to fall open at certain pages.

'Fox-glove, called by the ancients *digitalis*. A little taken strengthens the heart, but over-much killeth.'

Mr Hazlitt was struck by her discrimination and eagerness to learn about antiques. He explained to her the significance of an object being parcel-gilt; how to tell a Sheraton commode from a design by Hepplewhite. She respected Mr Hazlitt. His mind was good. She sensed that his thoughts were gathering towards a proposal; but she held him back gently. Certainly, not yet . . . Mr and Mrs Dewhurst were *much* more fun. For she found Lydia Dewhurst's seething, leaden hatred – totally denied expression even when she and her father went round to tea in the Dewhursts' great rambling house, full of strange uncouth African objects collected by Mrs Dewhurst's missionary father – even more exciting than Mr Dewhurst's great dammed-up bear-like passion.

But sometimes she mentioned the herbal to Mr Dewhurst. What secrets were locked up in an innocent English hedgerow! How easy it would be to poison, without arousing suspicion! When, greatly daring, she gathered foxgloves to decorate the lounge, and when they were past their best, did not throw them in the bin but boiled certain portions down, she showed the little bottle to Mr Dewhurst . . .

His finger lingered on it, till she snatched it away; and a look lingered on his face that was not lust, but something curiously, blackly like it. As before, she knew his moods. He was happy with her, bitterly unhappy at home. He often arrived for practice white and shaking; and when the time came to part, a look of sombreness would creep across his face.

On the night before the tournament, they had booked a final practice, late. The sun had dropped from the sky before she arrived on her bicycle, and the last members, snugly tired, with towels tucked round their necks, were getting into their cars and waving goodbye. She sat on the old wooden bench alone; she had time to think for the first time in weeks.

Something surfaced in her mind, something of what she might have called the old Maude; the Maude she had been before she first put on the spectacles . . . Recently, that little, weak, buried Maude had only approached her in dreams, leaving her to wake in the mornings with a feeling that something indefinable was terribly, terribly wrong. That she was running down a hill – keeping her feet, just, but having to run faster and faster, so that she couldn't stop now if she wanted to. Then, as she got dressed, the little fearful Maude would fade out of sight, banished by the busy excitements of the day, the spite, the scheming, the power. Am I breaking into two, she wondered? She shivered, as if someone had walked across her grave . . .

Shadows were gathering; it was late; he had not come.

Something was terribly, terribly wrong. He had never been late before, usually ridiculously early. The longer she sat, the more frantic she got. In the end she got back on her bicycle, shoving her tennis-racket into the large basket on the handlebars, and cycled to his house. If she just cycled past, saw the lights on, she would be reassured.

She passed the gate; his car was in the drive; the house was in darkness. She turned the bike, and cycled back. She was so worried now that she would even brave the cold, leaden dragon's wrath . . . all these weeks, little lost Maude had wanted her to feel sorry for the dragon, to understand. Little Maude had said that even the dragon had once been a baby . . .

But it had been no good; the dragon had never been a baby; had never been kind, or friendly, or even happy. She was a total blot on the light; the world would be better off without her . . . what use was she, for all her money – fat, ugly thing?

She cycled up the drive, rather wobbly, and rang the bell.

No answer.

But he never went anywhere except in his car! Had he had a heart attack? He was big; not young; he'd been pushing himself very hard . . .

She crept round the side of the house, holding her breath, peering through the windows at the darkness inside, shading the glass with her hand.

But when she reached the conservatory, he was plainly visible, among his beloved potted palms. Ready, wearing his tennis-whites, but leaning forward in one of the cast-iron chairs, his head in his hands.

Was he ill? She tapped gently. He gave a start and reared upright, as if in terror of her. And his pale, staring-eyed face was spotted . . . all over, with dark brown. And so was the front of his tennis-whites. The dragon had thrown gravy all over him, ruining his clothes. That's why he hadn't come. But he might have let her know.

She tapped again, more insistently. Slowly, like an old man, he rose, came across, and fiddled with the catch on the French windows.

What was the matter with him? A bit of gravy . . .

It wasn't gravy; it was red. It was blood. His tongue, like a little child's, came out and licked exploringly at a splash on his face.

'What? Where?'

He nodded limply, in the direction of the hall and staircase. She walked through.

He'd done it all right. The vast bulk of the dragon, in a vile purple afternoon-frock, was sprawled at the foot of the staircase. Her skirt had ridden up, revealing pillar-like legs that had always been hideous and were more hideous now. The top of her head was crushed in like an egg, and an African knobkerry, pulled from the wall, lay beside her, thick with matted blood and hair.

In that moment, she should have screamed. But, the spectacles cool and reassuring against her chest, she did not scream. Instead, her eyes noticed very clearly that the knob on top of the staircase newel-post was nearly the same diameter as the knobkerry he had used . . .

She felt *what* for him? No longer lust, certainly. Rage, at his unplanned spontaneous clumsiness, that had ruined everything. Disgust at his pathetic total collapse. A certain pity . . . and a rush of realization that if he came to trial, the cause of the quarrel between him and the dragon would certainly come out in court. Her whole future would be ruined. The papers . . . she would be painted a scarlet woman . . .

She walked slowly up the stairs, her eyes scheming, clear, conniving . . . She took hold of the landing banister-rail directly above the knob on the newel-post, and began to pull at it. It was not very securely fastened to the wall. It began to sway from side to side, under her urgent hands . . .

'Yes, that will do for now, I think, madam.' Inspector Groves, her father's friend and a keen member of the Archaeological Society, closed his official notebook with a snap. 'Thank you for all you've done. A sad accident to a well-liked lady.'

He led her out into the hall. The body of the dragon had been removed; and the matted hair and blood that Maude had so carefully removed from the knobkerry and transferred to the knob of the newel-post. And the broken banister, that had lain

so convincingly under the dragon by the time the police arrived.
'That handrail was always loose,' said Maude. 'I must have
warned her about it a dozen times.'

'And she was a big woman,' said Inspector Groves, 'a heavy
woman. It's a sad blow for him. I thought he took it very hard.
I've seldom seen a man collapse like that . . . though it's a shock-
ing accident, of course. Think he'll be all right? I was all for
sending him to hospital . . .'

'Daddy'll have him at our house by this time. And that doctor
gave him some pretty heavy sedation. He'll sleep the clock round.
We'll look after him, Inspector, don't worry.'

I shall, too, she thought. What a mess of a man! Clinging to
her, crying like a baby, while she commanded his brute strength
to do what was required. All men were weak, weak. But the worst
was past. The fatal evidence was dispersing.

'Can I give you a lift, madam?'

'No – I've got my bicycle. If my light works.'

'What's that you've got in your bike-basket – oh, spare tennis
things!'

'We were going to play. That's why I called.'

'A rare shock for you, her falling like that, and you in the very
next room . . .'

'We were just talking . . . I heard her call out as she fell.'

Just at that moment, a dog came trotting along the pavement,
out of the gloom, in the busy way dogs do. By the bicycle it
stopped, sniffed eagerly upwards at the basket.

Maude stood frozen as the Inspector moved forward. But he
only kicked mildly at the dog. 'Gerraway, you brute.'

'It's the smell of . . . sweat he's after, I suppose,' said Maude,
delicately.

The dog howled in pain and departed. The Inspector drove off
past her with a wave, and Maude cycled home, only a little
fatigued.

It was autumn. The wind had plastered wet yellow leaves along
the bottom of Mr Hazlitt's repaired window. Mr Hazlitt and
Maude were sitting drinking tea, as dusk fell. They were very

close now; Mr Hazlitt was a proper man. He would do as a husband.

'Any news of poor old Dewhurst?' asked Mr Hazlitt.

'Had a card two days ago. He's landed in New Zealand. Went as soon as he got probate. Sold up the lot.'

'Don't blame him,' said Mr Hazlitt. 'Think I'd do the same. This town would always be full of memories – he would expect to see her on every corner. Lucky they had no children.'

'Yes,' said Maude.

Mr Hazlitt switched on the shop-light, and it winked on the gold chain round her neck that held the spectacles. 'What *is* that thing you wear round your neck?' He reached across with the privilege of a fiancé and pulled up the spectacles . . . removed them.

And immediately went frantic, more frantic than he had been about his window.

'Why, Maude, where did you get these? They're old . . . really old . . . hand-made . . . hand-ground lenses. Why, these are the kind of spectacles they wore in Hans Holbein's time . . . if they're genuine . . . fifteenth, early sixteenth century . . .' He pulled out a little round black jeweller's lens and screwed it in his eye. 'There's a goldsmith's mark . . . and a little salamander . . . a salamander stamped into the gold.'

'Oh!' said Maude weakly. The removal of the spectacles from round her neck was having a very strange effect on her. Suddenly she was her old self again; shy, diffident, half blind, helpless, terrified at the memory of the things she had done.

'A *salamander*, Maude. Symbol of the old royal family of France . . . why, Maude, Catherine de Medici could have worn these spectacles.'

'Who's she?' Maude managed to ask tentatively.

'*Who's she*? Only the Queen of France. The poisoner, you remember. Formidable woman. When I went to Blois, five years ago, they showed us the hidden wall-cabinet where she kept her poisons. What tales these spectacles might tell! I must send them to the Science Museum . . . they'll know. You don't mind, do you? I expect they'll pay you a great deal of money for them. Where on earth did you get them? Family heirloom or something?'

'I bought them at Woolworth's,' said Maude, and broke into frantic weeping at all she had done.

'There, there,' said Mr Hazlitt, hugging her as any good fiancé should. 'You're a funny one – you're not the same woman two minutes running. I shall have to get used to coping. How many women *are* there inside you, Maude?'

Maude continued weeping.

How was she going to put all this to Father Whitstable?

# Portland Bill

I N T H E April of 1964, my wife and I took a few days off. I grow restless in the spring; every year the first wind-torn daffodils seem to promise something I will never find. My wife knows me in this mood, wise woman, and comes along as well. We share a snug world of fleeting sunshine, resting on the back of winter; of half-timbered cottages and a roaring fire after a massive meal; and, often, of breaking the ice on the pitcher-and-ewer set on our dressing-table. Having the money to live in style, we enjoy being poor for a few days. A hard-up courting couple on a guilty week-end. Dorinda even has a brass wedding-ring she wears for the occasion, to tantalize the nosier landladies. Even our Mercedes doesn't totally spoil the illusion . . . and we return half quieted, half satisfied.

But other things beside the Mercedes can spoil the illusion. We were driving west from Wareham, Dorset, when my wife suddenly smacked her palm to her forehead and gave that muted female shriek that is a mixture of discovery, exasperation and new en-deavour.

Had I not remembered, she asked, that Claire Farnaby had settled somewhere near Wareham after her marriage? Since I knew my wife had been at Roedean with Claire, I made muted impossibility-noises: about the time, the weather, and our need to reach our destination before midnight. I might as well have saved my breath to cool my porridge. Claire, I was informed, would be *heartbroken* if she ever found out we'd been her way and not looked her up.

I pointed out that discretion on my wife's part would ensure Claire's eternal safety from grief . . . but my wife said '*Stop!*' in a voice that brooked no argument, and was out of the car, across the road and into a red telephone-box almost before the Merc had pulled to a standstill. I watched her dial a number, thumb in directory. Saw her speak, wait, and then a grin of manic glee crossed her face that banished all hope. Within ten minutes of the phone call, we were sitting down over pre-lunch drinks in a very presentable Stuart manor house.

Had I been left alone with Claire Farnaby, I would doubtless have spent a most enjoyable time. She had elegant legs, what we used to call a pert nose, and large brown eyes of real warmth. Undoubtedly a very cultured and intelligent young woman; as was Dorinda, my wife. But they had been at Roedean together, and that was enough to banish all sense. We ate to the sound of belly-laughs and feverish inquiries as to what Fluffy Rossiter thought she was up to, writing for the *Telegraph*. Worse, as time passed a sort of mutual shorthand revived between them, so that a line of dialogue as short as 'You remember the time she fed Tiddum's cat . . .?' could send them into gusts of laughter for several minutes. Their cheeks became more and more flushed; their legs were flung out in a manner more suited to shin-pads than mini-skirts. Given the economy of such dialogue, there was no reason why the session shouldn't drag on for several weeks. In the end I began to prowl the long dining-room, losing myself in the set of twelve Chippendale chairs, the Regency sideboard with its brass rail and urns intact, the little oil by Cuyp, the fine circular array of naval cutlasses over the high fireplace . . .

'Oh, God,' said Dorinda, when she finally noticed what I was doing. 'We'd better let him off the leash, Claire, or he'll be making you an offer for something.'

'He can make me an offer any time,' said Claire, with an undertone indicating that she, at least, was tiring of lacrosse-sticks, starting to see a wider world beyond the dorms of Roedean.

'Why don't you go for a drive, darling?' said Dorinda. 'Work off your lunch. Chat up some of your little competitors and find a bargain? You'll only get the hump if you stay here with us. Come and pick me up about four? That's all right, isn't it?' The last remark was addressed to Claire.

'Yes . . . yes,' said Claire, half closing her eyes momentarily at the prospect of another two hours of '*Esprit de corps*, Number Four'.

An enormous cold rage seized me. Oh, the waste of good things! The waste of a whole day of our holiday; of the chance to enjoy Claire Farnaby's mind, Claire Farnaby's furniture, Claire Farnaby's elegant legs. And being grandly dismissed as if I were the boot-boy. Oh, the bloodiness of marriage, of being tied to somebody else's insane and piffling desires.

'I'll go and take a look at Portland Bill,' I said bleakly, as I let Claire help me on with my coat.

I only knew Portland Bill from the weather forecasts, but Portland Island could not have suited my bleak mood better. A ghostly place, built entirely from the stone it stands on. And that stone, unlike the warm, golden Ham stone of Claire's manor, is pale grey, nearly white. Grey walls, grey slate roofs, grey roads. Mostly, for some reason, the doors and windows are painted white. It looks bleached, like a black-and-white telly once you've got used to colour. And the grey roads are ground by the traffic into a fine, grey, powdery dust that blights the very green of the thin, starving grass to greyness.

And since the island contains the austerities of a naval barracks, a prison and a Borstal, and much of the rest is working quarries, still chewing inexorably away at the ground they stand on, it is as bleak to the spirit as to the eyes.

Portland Bill, on the southern tip, is bleakest of all. A bare rock plateau on which nothing blooms but crisp-bags and fleeing, ragged, wind-blown polythene, wire fences and parked cars. Seaward hung a grey mist that the eternal wind breached from time to time, letting in a cold white sun. And standing tall, striped red and white like a frozen jester, like a great phallic barber's-pole, was the lighthouse.

It bellowed at the hovering fog like a nervous bully; and the echo, bouncing back off the fog, seemed to shout faintly back. That shouting voice destroyed conversation, thought, on the whole cliff-top. One was either shuddering at the body-breaking impact of it, or waiting cowering in the intervals of silence for the next blow.

Perverse, I walked around the shaped tower to where the mouth of the foghorn pointed, to where it would do its worst; and waited.

The shock of sound was unbelievable; it made the bones vibrate within my flesh. Yet I walked on, endeavouring to withstand it.

The ground-rock wasn't clean, like that of a Hebridean island. It had been nibbled at by many feet, as mice nibble at cheese, leaving a trail of grey crumbs to be ground into mere grey dust. A huge jagged boulder, twice human height, was lying on the flatness at the tip of the cliff, carrying a rusting iron plaque dedicating the place to Thomas Hardy. Hardy lay right in the teeth of the foghorn's blast. But his shade was not there; how he would have hated it.

Yet it was the place for a shade . . .

Reaching the cliff-edge, I gasped. In every crevice offering shelter from the wind, on every rock-platform descending to the stony sea, sat holidaymakers in deck-chairs, beach-bags and thermos-flasks beside them, as if they sat on a warm golden beach. And there was no sand at all . . .

Mainly, they were brown, hard-wrinkled pensioners who had come by ancient, highly polished cars, bringing their own deck-chairs to save money. They were wrapped up in overcoats, tucked deep into tartan rugs, determined to enjoy Easter Sunday as was their right. Ardent worshippers of a sun that came and went like a ghost.

The cross-Channel ferry was emerging from the harbour, her siren shouting back at the lighthouse like another bully, blustery in red funnel and black hull and bold white lettering on her side. Then, slowly, the encroaching mist stole the life and substance from her; she faded, faded and died, becoming another ghost.

I liked it all better and better; it's a rare luxury in this life when the outside world so perfectly echoes your inner mood.

I drifted on to the wooden café, perched like an empty matchbox on a stony table. It lived by keeping up the spirits, and the illusions, of the pensioners – with tea and coffee at sixpence a cup, and hot

Oxo, and celluloid windmills chattering themselves to pieces in the never-ending wind. Everything for the beach was available – buckets and spades, where there was no sand; plastic beachballs, where there was no place to play football without the hungry wind snatching them and whirling them out to sea, to float and roll across the waves and be swallowed by the greyness that had swallowed the ferry. I laughed at the pointless madness of it all.

And then I saw the woman watching me.

She was tall and thin, in trousers and a well-cut tweed coat, holding the collar up with one hand to keep the cold from her throat. Her long, straight, honey-coloured hair flapped round her face like a flag in the wind. I noticed she wore cherry-coloured brogues on her feet – once as polished as conkers, but now scuffed and scarred white from climbing on the rocks.

There was a song I'd always liked, from the musical 'South Pacific':

> Some enchanted evening, you may see a stranger,
> You may see a stranger, across a crowded room . . .

I saw my enchanted stranger through a vista of tough old pensioners, busy spinning out their cups of tea, checking their change, and turning up their collars against the wind. She hovered on the fringe, with them, but not of them. A million pounds away from them; she would not count pounds as they counted pennies . . .

It was extraordinary, the way her bright blue eyes, watching me, seemed to annihilate the twenty yards between us. With that kind of invitation, who could have resisted walking over?

As I squeezed between the last pairs of pensioners, she turned on her heel and began to stroll away in front of me. I loved the arrogance of that; her certainty that I would follow. It went with the quality of her tweed coat, the narrow elegance of her hips and bottom beneath it, that had never heard of starch and stodge, the long lithe legs that had plenty of leisure to swim and play tennis at the club . . . You don't survive as a dealer long without getting an eye for class, in a chair, a racehorse or a woman.

We walked, still one behind the other, as far as a little huddle of fishing gear in the lee of a corrugated-iron shed. She perched her elegant bottom on the gunwhale of a tarred and broken boat. I sat down two yards away; a respectful distance. My weight made the boat rock alarmingly, made me feel a clumsy oaf.

She turned her face to me. Never tell me that the daughters of the gentry have faces like horses; their ancestors have married too many famous beauties. If there are girls with faces like horses in your county magazine, they are the daughters of successful suburban dentists.

She was too thin; but not in a way that did any harm. I was lost in wonder at the finely chiselled lips and curve of the nostril; Grinling Gibbons could not have done better. But certainly she was not happy. This was a lady in trouble. Is it my fault if beautiful ladies in trouble bring out my lust?

'Can I help you?'

'Have you seen a little boy?' she said. 'A little boy about seven, with red hair and a blue anorak? He's missing.'

'Your son?'

She nodded, biting her lip and looking down, as if to hide tears.

'How long missing?'

'Two hours he's been gone. I've looked *everywhere*. He's not anywhere. He's carrying a teddy-bear called Brutus . . .'

I looked around the desolate stone plateau. Nothing in sight but pensioners, and gulls foraging for the pensioners' crumbs.

'Haven't you rung the police?'

'Yes. They won't do anything. They don't seem to believe me. They won't come.'

'We'll soon see about that,' I said. 'C'mon. I'm a magistrate back home. I'll move them.'

'You're wasting your time,' she said hopelessly. But I got off the boat, which rocked alarmingly again, and strode off towards the solitary red telephone-box that stood perched on the stone, looking as out-of-place as everything else.

When I looked back, I saw she was following listlessly, at a distance.

I had a hell of a battle getting through to the police; the phone-book had half its sheets ripped away, and several of the panes of glass in the box had been vandalized, and the wind whistled past their jagged edges like a dozen harpies. When I finally got through to directory inquiries, I had nothing to write down the number with.

But I got through eventually.

'Police; Portland.'

I put on my best Establishment voice; my retired colonel, chairman-of-the-Bench voice. It was not easy to sound convincing, the way that wind was whistling.

'I want to report a small boy missing. Age seven. Red hair – blue anorak.'

'What's the boy's name, sir?'

That took me aback. 'I'm afraid I don't know.' I felt such a fool. Looked out of the window for the mother. She was still coming; still a long way off. 'I can find out in a moment. Any-way, the main thing is, he's *missing*.' I was off balance, at a dis-advantage; starting to disbelieve in myself and bluster. Never a good thing to do with the police.

'You'll be at Portland Bill, sir?'

'How the hell did you know that?' I thought the sound of laughter came down the line, from other policemen in the police-station. I thought I heard one of them, not the one I was talking to, say, 'Oh, God, not that *again*.' But it might have been the wind. It was so hard to hear anything.

'What is your name and address, sir?' There was something odd, almost mocking, about the policeman's voice now. It made me start to get really angry.

'What the hell's that got to do with it?'

'Just routine, sir. We must follow the routine.'

Striving for patience, I gave my name and address. The sound of Barlborough Hall shook him a bit. I followed up my advantage. 'Well, how soon can I expect someone, sergeant? The lad's been missing two hours already; the mother's frantic!'

'Can I have the lad's name, sir?'

The woman was standing outside the box now, staring in at me

through a broken pane. I opened the door and shouted, 'What's
his name?'

'Ronny Smythson,' she said, mouthing it exaggeratedly so I
could make it out over the wind.

'Ronny Smythson,' I told the police. 'With a "y", that'll be,' I
added, striving for authority.

'Ronny Smythson, with a "y", sir,' said the sergeant doggedly.
I could almost see him licking the end of his pencil between every
word. And again came that hint of derision from the voices of
policemen in the background. I thought I heard somebody shout,
'That's the one!'

'And the lad's address, sir?'

'For God's sake!' I shouted. 'Does it matter? The kid could be
lying injured . . . dead . . . drowned.'

'Please allow me to know best, sir.' That had been a stupid
thing; to shout at him. He was going mulish on me. The background yattering in the police-station grew more derisive, I
thought. Or it might have been the wind and my imagination.

I got the address and gave it to him; the phone began its
warning pips, and I had to scrabble in my pockets for more
money. I hadn't liked to use 999 . . .

'Well, you're coming up then, sergeant? The mother really is
frantic . . .'

A background voice in the police-station said, 'What do we *do*
with these jokers?'

'You are coming, sergeant?' The wind was driving me nuts. I
heard that squeaky noise down the phone, which meant the sergeant had put his hand over the mouthpiece at the far end; probably to quell the revellers with a sharp word. They sounded drunk
down there. Then he came back on the line.

'I'm sorry, sir. We haven't got anyone to spare. There's been a
spot of bother at the Borstal.'

'What sort of bother?'

'I'm not in a position to say, sir.' He'd gone mulish on me again.

'But for God's sake, a kid could be drowning!'

'You get a lot of lost kids this time of year, sir. They usually
turn up.' His voice sounded final; he was going to hang up on me.

'*Look*! I'm a magistrate at home and . . .'
Too late. He had hung up.

I came out of the telephone-box.
'I told you so,' she said. Her eyes were pools of sadness; old, weary sadness. 'They wouldn't listen to me, either.'
'But they'll bloody well listen to me. I'm going down there.'
'Don't . . .'
'Try and stop me! Show me the way!' I grabbed for her hand, half in rage and half from a desire to know how it would feel. Slim, cool, a little bony, exciting . . .
She gave a small movement of ladylike rejection, and avoided my grasp. Putting me in my place as a lout; but ever so gently.
'My car's over here.' I led her across to the Merc, held the passenger-door open for her. She got in gracefully, if reluctantly. As if she were used to having car-doors opened for her.
The noise of the wind stopped; the Merc has good sound-insulation. The smell of her came from where she sat close; but no closer than the space demanded. She leaned wearily against the door on her side, head down on her hand. The perfume of her came across; I sniffed at it, surreptitiously, trying to place it. Nothing like Dorinda's Chanel No. 5, or Claire's Dior . . . More a sea-like smell, evasive, like mist, salt, seaweed. Must be a new and *very* expensive one; mixing with the mob I did, I thought I knew them all . . .
I turned on the ignition. 'Which way?' I drove showing all my fury, but it didn't seem to scare her. She just said listlessly 'Left . . . right here.' She obviously knew the way.
The police-station was small; right on the road. I braked, pulled up with a screech.
'I won't come in,' she said in a low voice. You could tell she was exhausted, beaten. I didn't bully her. I went in alone.
'Yessir?' said the desk-sergeant. Pretty pushy and off-putting. Trying to put you in the dock.
'I've come about that child who's missing . . .' That caused a stir among the two or three young coppers lounging in the back room behind the desk. I was at least glad to know that they

existed; were not an effect of the wind. The sergeant got up, said, 'Shut up, you lot,' and closed the door on them.

'Yessir?'

'Before we discuss this matter further, sergeant,' I started, 'and as I was just about to say when you hung up on me, I happen to be a magistrate back in Cheshire. Perhaps you would care to look at these and satisfy yourself that I am what I say I am.' I passed him several items that proved I was a J P.

He inspected them very thoroughly; but they wiped that look off his face. The one person a copper is always respectful to is a magistrate; magistrates talk to other magistrates.

'I'm sorry I hung up on you, sir. My apologies. It just so happens that we've had a lot of hoax calls from the Bill, all about children going missing; been a right plague of them this year. And the child always seems to have red hair. And it's not kids mucking about, either. Most of the hoax calls are from grown men. But there's never anybody waiting by the box when we get there. So you can see, we get a bit fed up . . .'

'Well, I can assure you I'm no hoaxer, sergeant. I've got the lady in question waiting outside in my car.'

He got up, raised the flap of his counter, and walked across to the window. I walked with him. We stared out. She was still sitting in the passenger-seat, slumped on her hand as I had left her.

'She's pretty shattered,' I said. 'But who wouldn't be? I asked her to come in, but she won't. She said you wouldn't listen to her the first time.'

The sergeant did not reply. I looked at him, crossly. There was a totally unreadable look on his face. As I watched, little beads of sweat grew visibly on his upper lip. He was without doubt a very shaken man. Well, he'd bloody asked for that . . . the English police may have slipped a bit, but they haven't got round to ignoring mothers in distress with impunity yet.

'Well?' I said.

'You're on holiday, sir?' he asked cagily. 'Alone?'

'With my wife.'

'But she's not with you today?'

'She's spending the afternoon with a friend of hers. Mrs Farnaby. At Cootisham Court. What the hell has that got to do with it?'

'Er . . . nothing, sir.' But for some reason he sounded relieved. 'Well, I'm sorry, sir, but we can't do anything about this business, I'm afraid. It's not as if it was a crime. We're rushed off our feet at the moment . . .'

'Trouble at the Borstal?' I said sarcastically. 'I suppose these three idle young constables in your back room are up to their eyes investigating the trouble at the Borstal?'

'No, sir . . .'

I'm afraid I lost my temper then. And said a lot of things about falling standards and police callousness, and contacting Chief Constables with complaints and bringing it before the Dorset police committee. All of which left him unmoved; though the sweat was by now freely trickling down his face, and it was not a hot day. I mean I was blasting away, and not anywhere near sweating. In the end I stamped out, breathing fire and thunder.

I looked back through the glass swing-doors. He had dived for the phone the moment my back was turned.

Or maybe the phone had just rung; maybe I was getting paranoid in my old age.

She looked up as I got into the car.

'I told you . . .'

'It's incomprehensible. The world seems to have gone mad. Somebody's going to pay for this . . . I'm driving into Weymouth . . .'

'But what about Ronny?' she asked. Her eyes were desperate. 'It'll be getting dark soon . . . he'll be so *frightened*.'

'God, I'm sorry . . .' I said, reaching for her hand to comfort her.

Again, she moved back, avoiding me, keeping me at the proper distance. We drove back to the Bill in silence. She stayed sitting, until I walked round and opened the door for her. Then she said simply, 'Please help me look. There are places I haven't looked yet. I got so discouraged on my own.'

'All right,' I said. 'We'll ask at the café.'

The open-air part of the café was emptier than before. What warmth there had been was gone from the day, and we'd met a succession of ancient Morris Minors full of wrinkled faces, homeward bound. But we went from table to table.

'Excuse me,' I said, each time. 'You haven't seen a little boy anywhere today – a little boy with red hair and a blue anorak? He's this lady's son. He's lost. He was carrying a teddy-bear. He's called Ronny . . .'

The old people looked at me, at first with astonishment, and then, affronted, they said gruffly, 'No we haven't seen anybody, have we, Emma? Nobody at all.' Or, 'We've just come . . .' Then, abruptly, they turned their backs on us, pulled up their coat collars, and went back deliberately to finishing their tea or counting their change. Except when we were well clear of them; then they would turn and stare at us, rudely, and whisper among themselves. Then they would get up hurriedly, gather their bags and baskets, and hurry away.

Before I could ask at every table, the whole area was empty.

It hurt. I can tell you that it hurt. It hurt me as an Englishman. Were these the people that had helped each other so much in the Blitz?

'I suppose,' I said bitterly to Mrs Smythson, 'they think that the old have enough troubles of their own, without adding other people's. I never knew the old were so *selfish*.'

'You're wasting your time asking people,' she said. 'People don't care any more. I've learnt that this morning. Oh, yes, I've learnt that. I didn't realize it, all my life, until this morning. When real trouble comes, everybody walks away. Nobody wants to know.' I have never in all my days heard anyone so bitter.

'You've got me,' I said. 'I won't walk away.'

She smiled; a tiny, weary smile, dragged from the depths. She was beautiful; my bowels moved with lust for her. But I only said, 'D'you want a cup of tea? You look so cold.'

'I just want to find Ronny, before it's dark.'

So we went.

God, was there every so dreary a place as the cliff-top of Portland Bill? We kept dipping into little hollows, without a visible sign of humanity. Except for the never-ending crisp-bags and crushed Coke-cans, lying embedded in the grey ooze of mud that lay in every gully of the cliffs. And the sea, coming out of the mist and breaking at the foot of the cliffs, and the endless shouting of the bullying lighthouse. At every rise I hoped to see a little shape, running towards us, tear-stained, daring to cry now his mother had come and it was all right . . .

Nothing. Except the body of a dead gull, decomposing back to brown string and bone and soaked pinion-feathers, washing about with a dreadful semblance of vitality in a circular eddy at the foot of one cliff.

Dreadful. And yet I didn't *want* to find him, in one way. Because then she would be full of effusive thanks; then only concerned about the boy, chiding him, scolding him, hurrying him back to her car and driving off with a grateful wave, and I'd never see her again. Every time I caught her sad, shy eye, I lusted after her lithe slender body more. Lie down with me here, and I will give you another child, a child who will never get lost, whom I will never allow to get lost because he will be made of you and me . . . I felt mad urges to throw her down on the thin grey turf and take her, unconsenting; mad urges to grasp her in my arms and throw both of us down into the sea to drown with him. What an ending!

Because more and more, as the mist closed in and the light began to fade, I was convinced that we would not find him. He was gone. If we saw a little figure now, running towards us, carrying a teddy-bear and waving, he would be a little pathetic ghost . . .

But still she kept on and on, her hope getting more desperate as her strength ebbed.

And then, we heard a cry. As we ascended a slope of the cliff-top.

'It's *him*!' Her eyes looked at me, huge and flaring with gladness. 'This was always our favourite place. He must have come here, knowing I'd come here to look for him.'

'It sounded like a gull to me,' I said doubtfully.

'No, *listen*!'

The cry came again. Was it a gull? Or a child crying, 'Here!'

Against the sea, and the foghorn's distant bellow, it was hard to tell.

Then the cry came a third time. It *was* a child's voice. Mrs Smythson's voice echoed down the high cliff, loud in reply.

'Darling! Ronny! Hold on, we're coming! Oh, thank God, thank God! He's down there, on the little beach. And he's still got Brutus.'

I peered down, and could see nothing but the strands of mist drifting up the cliff, and through them, vaguely, losing and finding, a narrow nail-paring of bouldery beach, and the froth of breaking waves, endlessly swirling.

'Hang on,' I shouted to her. 'Let's think. Let's get organized.'

But she was already lowering herself over the cliff-edge. I tried to grab her back, but she was below my reach. She stared up at me, her face scarcely human with the strain of urgency.

'Come *on*. *Help* me!'

'Let's go and get help! Ropes. Let's get organized.'

She went on climbing down.

'This is dangerous,' I shouted. 'We need help.'

'Haven't you got any guts at all?' She was ten feet below, now, clinging on for dear life to what looked like two blades of grey grass and a knob of rock no bigger than a tea-cup. 'Call yourself a *man*?' Then she turned her head from me, and went on descending into the mist.

'We need help!'

'No time – the tide's coming in. He'll drown. I know the way down – we always come this way – it's much safer than it looks.'

And still I hovered. And still the child seemed to call. And the tide *was* coming in . . .

You will think me a pretty poor sort of coward. But it wasn't that. I'd done my share of rock-climbing, in the Cuillins on Skye, before the War, when I was a young man. I had a mountaineer's eye for rock. But sea-cliffs are always murder, and this was worse than most. The strata of the rock was fractured; what looked like good footholds were cracked, starting to come away from the main cliff. And even what wasn't cracked was sloping gently seaward, and carrying that little slick of grey mud born of dust and sea-mist. The place was a death-trap.

She crawled out of sight beneath an overhang, but I could still hear her shouting to the child.

'Hang on, Ronny! Mummy's coming . . . it's all right, darling.'

With a groan, against all sense, I swung myself over the edge after her.

Within six feet, my foot slipped and I nearly fell. Every trick I knew, I used. I found a bit of a chimney, and went down it, with my back braced against one side, and my feet braced out against the other. It worked, just, till I got to that overhang, and there I could see no way over at all. I heard her call, desperately.

'Hurry, hurry, help me! I'm *stuck*.'

But there comes a moment when you face stark reality. When all hope and faith and courage run away like sand through your fingers, in the face of the inevitable rock. I knew that I was trapped: a step forward was a step into nothingness; a step into death. In spite of her cries, I had to go back up. Somehow I'd missed the way she'd taken. Well, if I got back up, I could try again. I'd be no good to her as a broken heap of blood and bone at the foot of the cliff . . .

A lot easier said than done. I had already come a long way on footholds no mountaineer in his senses would have used. For a long time, I could not move up at all. And then I got out my handkerchief and wiped the slick of mud carefully off what looked like the least crazy of the footholds. Then I wrapped the hanky round my fingers to give them extra dry-traction and heaved up with all my strength.

My foot slipped; then, on the very edge, held. I felt muscles crack, felt my lungs suck breath like a dying man, felt the pain grow in my shoulder-blade like seeping acid.

And I was there; I'd gained two feet in height and I was exhausted, trembling in every limb. I breathed deep to quieten my middle-aged heart, and started wiping the next handhold with my handkerchief, looking with hate at the Coke-can and crisp-bags wedged safe, indestructible, within a foot of my nose. They served only to remind me that I was a middle-aged bag of heavy flesh and frail bone . . . Steady, old lad!

And that was how it went on. Twice I despaired; twice I prayed to a God I hadn't prayed to since I left school. He must have heard me. Because somehow I was lying on the sodden grass of the cliff-top, waiting for a heart to quieten that I thought would never quieten again. Listening, listening for her, and only hearing the endless shouting of the lighthouse.

In the end, I got to my feet; my hip-bones ached, my knees shook, my ankles turned under me. In the dusk, the lighthouse had begun to flash. The fog was thicker, turning the light into a faint, fuzzy aureole which I thankfully made for, staying well clear of the cliff-edge. She must be dead . . . perhaps the police would listen to me now. I felt a dreadful sense of guilt at being still alive, and yet overwhelmingly thankful it wasn't me who'd died.

There was a tall figure, standing on the next rise of the cliff-top. I shouted . . .

She turned. Pale blur of face, and blowing hair.

'Are you all right?' she called.

'Are you?' I said, staggering up to her, full of thankfulness.

'Yes. It's quite easy if you know the way.'

'Where's . . . the boy?'

'He wasn't there. You were right. It must have been a gull. Did you get lost? What can we do now?'

'I can't go . . . much further . . . I'm knackered. Let's have something to drink . . . if that café's still open. We can . . . sit and think.'

She walked alongside, silent, obedient. But I could feel her pain, her terror, mounting again, coming to me through her silence.

The café was open, thank God; though the owner had taken in his balls and buckets and whirling windmills, and seemed reluctant to serve me, glancing at his watch.

'Two teas, please!'

He gave me a curious glance, then poured out two teas from a well-stewed pot, adding fresh hot water and punishing the soggy tea-leaves with a spoon. I turned to her, called out over my shoulder, 'Do you take sugar?'

'Half a spoonful,' she said, low and weary. I spooned in half for her, and three spoonfuls for me. Then I looked up and caught the proprietor watching me, like I was some kind of nut-case. In fact he stared at me so strangely that I looked down at myself, to see what he was staring at.

My trench-coat gave the answer. One of the lapels was torn, and the whole thing was plastered with drying and cracking grey slime. I must have looked like a tramp. I paid him hurriedly in case he thought I couldn't afford to pay at all, and carried the teas to the table, where the mist was starting to lay a dew on the bare pine boards.

'Look at the state I got myself into,' I said. 'You haven't got a spot of it on you . . .'

'I knew the way,' she said, with a weary, twisted half-smile that made my heart turn over, knackered though I was.

I drank my tea; at least it was hot and sweet, and my mouth was like a desert. I drank it so enthusiastically that it ran scalding down my chin. She didn't touch hers; just sat staring at it.

'Don't you want it?' I asked. 'Can I get you something else?'

She shook her head, her face hidden by her hair. 'I can't touch a thing. I'm too worried about Ronny. Would you like my cup as well?'

'Not sweet enough for me. I'll get myself another.'

The proprietor was staring at me more fixedly than ever; probably wondering what a tramp like me was doing talking to someone as beautiful as she was, at this time of night. I carried my cup back; I'd bought her some chocolate, which I laid beside her cup. 'You must eat,' I said gently. 'You must keep your strength up.'

But she just shrugged. I said, 'Look, we can't stay here all night. We can't search in the dark. These cliffs will be a death-trap now. Are you staying at an hotel? Shall I take you back there? We could ring your husband . . .'

She looked at me very straight, very close. She leaned nearer to me, across the table, than she ever had before. 'I have no husband,' she said. Her words had a kind of faint promise in them; her scent, that sea-like scent, came to me on the wind. 'I have no hotel, either. You'll have to find me one.'

I had a vision: of finding her an hotel; of helping her up the stairs of some near-empty place, her leaning against me with help-less weariness. Of taking her in my arms, in some bare, cheerless bedroom . . . I looked up. She knew. She didn't seem to mind. Then she leaned further towards me . . . reached out a hand and nearly put it on my wrist.

'Look – there's one more place I think he might be. Can we just look there? After that, I'll know it's hopeless for tonight. You're right: these cliffs are a death-trap in the dark. If he's not there, I'll come with you . . . we can do it your way. I'm past caring what I do . . . you can do what you like . . . only come with me to this one place, first . . .'

The proprietor came out and began putting up the shutters of the café, blotting out, one by one, the bands of lamplight that fell across the empty table and us. My loins tingled with a cold, crazy excitement.

'OK,' I said. 'Let's go. Where is this place?'

'We'll have to be careful,' she said. 'It's very steep and very dark.'

As I was about to rise, there was the distant sound of a car coming very fast down the Bill towards us.

'Hey,' I said, settling back on the hard, damp wooden chair. 'That looks like somebody in a hurry. Help at last?'

The car headlights swung across her. But there was no trace of fresh hope in her face; only a deepening sense of loneliness.

The car drove to the car park, and stopped, cut its lights. I wondered whether it could be the police; it was a big car, a Zephyr, the kind the police sometimes use. Two people got out; one each side, the way the police do. But it was too dark to tell if they were police or not. Their footsteps on the rock came towards us, drawn by the last lights of the café. Then I heard their voices: women's voices, rather urgent, calling to each other. They switched on torches, to help them across the uneven ground.

Policewomen? I didn't think they let policewomen drive the big cars.

She rose and said, 'It's not help; let's go.' Rather urgently.

'Sit down. This won't take a minute; they might be willing to help. They've got torches.' Reluctantly, she sat down again.

The women came up to us; sat down at the table on either side of us. One biggish woman; one tall, but slender. I looked at the big one's face, a request on my lips.

'What the hell have you been up to?' said Dorinda. 'Just look at the state of you.' She reached across a proprietorial hand, and began to wipe my lapel with her loose glove. The touch of her hand was heavy with . . . anger?

I frowned. She looked different . . . very solid, somehow. The full curve of her cheekbone; the bright red of her lipstick; the yellow fat glint of her big gold ear-ring. She seemed somehow . . . more solid than solid, more real than real.

I looked the other way . . . Claire, Claire with her big brown lovely eyes full of worry for me. I remember thinking the guy who'd married beautiful Claire must be a lucky man. She too seemed different; more solid than solid, more real than real. And in the cold night, a breath of real warmth came off her.

Why did they feel more warm and solid . . . than Mrs Smythson? Just the warmth of the car, while we'd been wandering around in the cold?

I looked at Mrs Smythson, starting introductions.

'Dorinda . . . I'd like you to meet . . .' I stopped.

Mrs Smythson wasn't there. Only an empty gap on to the night. She didn't get up, or walk away . . . but she wasn't there any more, and the night-wind blew through the gap where she'd been, across her cold un-drunk cup of tea, and the red wrapper of the uneaten chocolate.

'Where are you?' I said, stupidly.

Dorinda grabbed me by the hand. 'Geoff, Geoff, pull yourself together. Who the hell are you supposed to be talking to?' I looked from one to the other. Dorinda looked outraged; Claire looked very, very worried for me.

'You're not going to believe this,' I said, 'but I think I've spent the last three hours with a ghost.'

Because it all came back to me in a flash. The way she'd got me to open the car-door for her. The way she'd never touched me. The way she hadn't drunk her tea. The way the policeman had looked out of the police-station window . . . he must have heard me babbling about what seemed to him a totally empty car. And the way she'd climbed down a cliff where there were no footholds . . . a cliff that was death to descend . . . she had been luring me to my death and she'd damned near done it. If I hadn't been a wily old mountaineer, I'd be a pile of human rubbish washing at the cliff-foot.

And *then* the hair stood up all over my head.

'You can come out now, sergeant,' called Dorinda, arrogantly, commandingly. I heard the Zephyr's door open and shut again; the heavy beat of a constabulary tread. 'He's stopped being potty, I think – for the moment,' she added reassuringly.

'I'm not sure potty's the word, madam.' It was my old enemy from the police-station.

'Sergeant Yarwood rang us about you – he was worried. So we came as fast as we could. Good job he did,' Dorinda added, 'with you sitting alone at a table with two cups of tea, babbling to your-self.'

'There's a bit more to it than that,' said the sergeant, taking the empty chair and blocking out the night, comfortably. 'You see, there *was* a Mrs Smythson. She used to come here for her holidays, most years. And she did have a son called Ronny – a little lad with red hair. They were a regular sight round here – they loved it, for some reason best known to themselves. The husband was never with them, though – too busy he always was, to come on holi-day.'

'And the child drowned . . .' said Claire sadly.

'No, madam – as far as I know, the lad's as right as you or me, only living in California – he'll be ten by now.'

'But . . .' said Dorinda.

'But the husband and wife . . . the husband had a lot of fancy women – a company director, I think – you know the sort. And he'd send his wife and kid down here for a holiday, and then he'd make hay while the sun shone, back in London. Well, a lady got her hooks into him and it seems she was too good a chance to turn

down. An American woman – daughter of one of those big financial empires. She came to him with a lot in her hand. But seemingly
she couldn't have children herself – she wanted the boy as well –
Ronny. And one morning they came and took the kid from his
bed early, while the wife was walking on the Bill here. When she
got back, the kid was gone, with them. On his way to America
and never coming back.'

'There are courts for that kind of thing,' said Dorinda indignantly.

'I believe money talks in the American courts, madam. Anyway,
she wasn't that sort of lady – not a fighter. She . . . went out of her
mind, madam. Thought the kid was lost on Portland Bill, where
they'd been happy. She must have come to us a dozen times. We
took her seriously at first; then we made inquiries, and it all came
out. But she wouldn't believe it – kept on coming to us, asking us
to help her search.'

'She should have been put in hospital,' said Dorinda.

'That's not for the police to say, madam. We're not in the habit
of putting people in hospital. And the social services couldn't do
anything either . . . she wasn't a danger to anybody else, and they
couldn't prove she was a danger to herself – till she'd done it.'

'Done what?' asked Claire in a low voice; though we all knew
the answer.

'Drowned herself from this very place, three years ago. Her
body was washed up in a little cove that way . . .' He jerked his
head towards the direction I'd come from.

I remembered the faint scent of her perfume . . . fog and salt
and seaweed.

'We've had a lot of hoax calls since then, madam, about the
little boy with red hair and a blue anorak. Always from men . . .
some young . . . some quite middle-aged.' He looked at me.

'She must be *very* lonely,' said Claire.

'Aye, madam. Though I don't know why she should be.'

'What *do* you mean?' said Dorinda.

The sergeant leaned a little closer. 'This is off the record,
madam. Between you and me. It wouldn't do to have it appearing
on any police report . . . more than me job's worth. But I have a

sort of responsibility for the Bill, madam, when I'm on duty. Not official – but I was born here, and I've known every nook and cranny since I was a lad. So when there's trouble up here, they tend to send for me.'

'And?' said Dorinda, impatiently.

'And . . .' said the sergeant, 'there's always been accidents on the Bill – it's a dicey place even in daylight in summer . . . people fall, people get drowned, once in a while. But there's been a lot more fallen and been drowned these last three years. And nearly all men, barring one little girl, and that was a true accident, for her mother was with her. And very much the same kind of men, madam . . . decent fellers who've lost their way a bit, and come to stare out to sea. Going bankrupt . . . broken marriages . . . fellers on their own. Is your business all right, sir?'

'My business is flourishing,' I said, shortly.

The sergeant cast an eye at Dorinda, and Dorinda had the grace to flinch.

'We'll, you've got him back safe and sound this time, madam. And he's as sane as you or me, I do assure you. You'd just best look after him, that's all.'

And for once, Dorinda had nothing to say.

# The Ugly House

*I* suppose I am growing old. All my restlessness seems to have
gone, and I miss it. I still watch the girls go by, but I stay to finish
my beer now. I suppose I am happy with Dorinda. My kids are
growing up, and I think of their problems instead of my own.

The separate shop in town is gone, sold at a good profit. But I
still sell antiques at Barlborough Hall; the servants' hall is my
patch now, and Dorinda respects it. With our weekend conferences
and dinners for rich Americans, we prosper and are busy.

Until the Rotary lunch last week, I thought the ghosts were
gone, too. (Rotary is the one thing I still bother to keep up in
town.) And there I met a little balding chap from the Council
called Dave Dobson, ordinary as pie, you would have thought.
But odd things still happen to people, even though they no longer
seem to happen to Geoff Ashden.

This was the story he told me in his own words.

———

'It's incredible,' I said. 'I don't know what you people have
been *doing*.'

'There's been problems,' said Tetley.

I glared at him; Tetley had problems all right. A thinning-hair
problem that wouldn't be solved by combing a few greasy strands
over a lard-white pate. A weight problem that creased his suit-
jacket dramatically, now he had it buttoned against a biting Essex
wind. An eating-lunch-at-his-desk problem; egg on his green zip-
pered cardigan. God, don't let me stay in local government as
long as Tetley . . .

But, to the problem in hand. The unfinished approach-road.

To the hypermarket that was due to open in two months' time. Already the hypermarket's red-brick, blank-eyed bulk dwarfed the thatched roofs of Besingfield. If it opened without a completed approach-road, it'd choke the High Street with cars. And choke the Council with complaints. All of which would land on my desk.

'There's your problem,' said Tetley. 'The Ugly House.' My eye followed the smooth sweep of the approach-road through the rubble and grass of neat bites of demolition. To where it stopped in the middle of nowhere, at a pair of closed gates with glassless iron lamps on each gatepost. Behind, the Ugly House had a kind of cramped solitariness, like the last stump in a toothless mouth. Stone, so blackened you couldn't tell what kind of stone. But each carefully masoned block was huge. There was a crumbling, illegible date above the front door. The three-storey house leaning dramatically leftwards, on baulks of timber like crutches. It had a miserable sooty grandeur, like the lodge of an ancient hospital or Victorian mortuary.

'It's a Grade Two protected building,' said Tetley. 'The lower walls are sixteenth-century – or earlier.'

'*That* won't save it.'

'Don't worry. Nevinson had it downgraded, first thing he did.'

'Nevinson.' I disliked having Nevinson mentioned. Nevinson had wrapped his Jaguar round a flyover on the M1, and I got his job. Dead man's shoes. Which is why I was Chief Technical Officer to Besingfield District Council, the youngest CTO in Essex.

'I'll be going then,' said Tetley abruptly. I stared at him in disbelief. He was supposed to be showing me round the district.

'Got a lot to do, back at the office. I'll have the report on your desk by four o'clock.'

I shouted, more to hold him than anything else, 'How soon can the contractors finish the approach-road, once the house is demolished?'

'Three weeks, Harrison says. They're slack at the moment. If we don't move by Monday, he'll have to start laying men off.'

He said, 'By Monday,' without hope, as if he was talking about winning a million on the pools. And went on backing away towards his car like a fat, conciliatory crab. And drove off with a spurt of gravel. Inevitably, his car was a P-registration maroon Viva.

I was left standing alone by my Volvo, facing the Ugly House. No sign of life, except for a flutter of pigeons' wings in the back garden. No smoke from the tall hexagonal chimneys. Yet I had a feeling of being observed. And a much worse feeling that if I just got into my car and drove away, it would be the beginning of defeat.

As Nevinson had been defeated.

I told myself not to be stupid. I hadn't had time to read the file on the Ugly House. Didn't know what Nevinson had done. Didn't even know the owner's name ... Tetley had no right to drive away and leave me like that.

I started walking up the access-road; meaning only to *look* at the house.

The front door was oak, silvery with the grey sheen of centuries. Studded with hand-made iron bolts. The knocker was a diabolical head, a bit like the one at Durham Cathedral, holding a ring in its slightly rusty teeth. As I reached up to knock, my fingers looked very pale and soft against that iron mouth.

The door opened immediately, making me step back.

'Come in, Mr Dobson!' The man smiled, showing gold among his teeth. How the hell did he know my name?

He led me through a narrow, dark-panelled hall that leaned and twisted dustily to the left. There was a little cramped fireplace, a rusty grate spilling cold ash on to the black-and-white tiles. Who has a fire in the hall these days?

I followed his upright back, elderly but solid. His dark-blue jersey failed to do anything for his brown trousers and carpet-slippers. Grey hair, short-back-and-sides, combed greasily but neatly on top. A retired fisherman?

He took me into a dark room with very small windows; he didn't put the light on. Something caught my sleeve, creaked, wobbled and began to fall. I grabbed to save it, then had to bite my lip to stop myself screaming. Since childhood I've had a phobic horror of fur and feathers, and what I was holding was a large stuffed white owl, with only one eye and a dangle of thread where the other should have been. I desperately struggled to put it back on the shelf, but somehow it wouldn't balance. I had to go on grabbing it, twisting it desperately to make it stay so that I could get my hands off it.

He took it from me gently. 'Hard to come by, these. Not many made any more. Not fashionable. I've been a lifetime collecting.'

I stared round, wildly. The dark room was full of shapes, writhing in stillness. A fox glowed red glass eyes at me, a dead rabbit drooping from its mouth. On the mantelpiece, a giant misshapen eagle with a sagging broken wing perpetually prepared to launch itself at my face. They weren't even in glass cases; the dust of dead fur and feathers tickled my nostrils.

'Admiring my bittern, Mr Dobson? Haven't seen one round here for a few years. They're extinct now, in Essex.' His East Anglian accent was heavy and ignorant, the voice rising at the end of every sentence. The accent of charladies, shouting 'Goodnight' after Bingo. Yet he didn't look an ignorant man, as he settled himself in a chair by the window, his back to the light, his face hidden in shadow, his hands folded in his lap. He reminded me of a doctor in his consulting-room; or my grandfather, who was a Methodist preacher. The same uncomfortable certainty of a cold faith.

'Sit down, Mr Dobson. You'll have come to inquire after the lovely pen you lost?'

'Pen?' I asked stupidly.

'Your gold pen, Mr Dobson. The one that tells the time as well. The one you lost, first day you were in Besingfield.'

'How the hell did you know?' Amazement made me rude. He lifted one hand gently, the way a headmaster quietens an overnoisy schoolboy.

'You do set great store by that pen, Mr Dobson!'

That shook me even more. That pen was the latest thing; with a built-in digital watch. Linda had bought it for me, to celebrate getting the CTO's job. A good-luck talisman, and I'd lost it my first morning . . .

'But how did you know?'

Again he raised the soothing hand, and did not answer my

question. 'I'll tell you where it do be, Mr Dobson. You remember, that first morning, you went up inspecting the gravel-pit? And it came on to rain, and Mr Tetley fetched you his old donkey-jacket? Your pen be still in the pocket o' that, a-hanging in your staff cloakroom. You won't leave it there no longer though, will you, Mr Dobson? Mrs Charles, who cleans that cloakroom, has had it out and looked at it three times already. We wouldn't want her *tempted*, would we?'

'Oh no,' I said. 'No, of course not.' And stared at him.

He paused, putting a big-knuckled hand to his bony forehead. 'Now, there's something else you need . . . oh, yes, that cottage you've a-bought. Limetree Cottage, Manningtree, they calls it now. Have you found the well in the back garden yet? No? Well, it's there if you look. In the corner of the orchard, by the back hedge. They'll have filled it up wi' rubbish, the last people . . . the water do be fine for plants, but don't let your Linda go drinkin' it – not if you do want to have childer.'

'Have *what*?'

'Childer, Mr Dobson. Little babbies – boys an' girls. You'll have a boy first, then a girl. If you don't let your Linda go drinkin' from that well.'

I stared at him again, incredulous. He stared back . . . professionally. Like a vicar, or a doctor. Someone who didn't expect to be argued with.

I was so angry, all I could do was get to my feet.

'You off, Mr Dobson? Never stop to draw breath, you young folk, these days. Well now, that'll be five pounds, Mr Dobson . . .'

'Five pounds? For what?'

'For finding your pen, Mr Dobson. And the well.' He paused at his front door. 'You don't have to pay me; till you find them.' He was quite certain I'd find them. Somehow, so was I. I took out my wallet and gave him five pounds. He drew out a battered black notebook held together with an elastic band, and put the note inside, snapping it shut.

I'd walked back to the Volvo before I realized I'd never mentioned the demolition. But I would have seemed very foolish, walking back to the house again.

I drove straight back to the office. The pen was where he said. Mrs Charles, the cleaner, gave me a funny look as I passed her. I drove home at three in the afternoon, a thing I'd never done in my life, and went straight down the garden without letting Linda know I was home.

The well was there, too, exactly where he'd said. A low rim of masonry, overgrown with couch-grass and full of broken brick. I could have lived there for ten years and never have found it. As I was coming back to the house, my hands all grass and earth stains, I met Linda and Tigger coming to meet me. Tigger sat down short of me, and started washing his whiskers with a thoughtful paw; cats don't like coming too close when you're upset. Linda said, 'Darling, what's the matter? You look like you've seen a ghost!' She tried to give me a kiss, then felt the stiffness of rage and shock in my shoulders.

'C'mon, tell me about it. Over a whisky.'

'No!' I couldn't bear to tell her that vile old man had been discussing her body.

'You know you'll have to tell me in the end. You always do!'

It was a relief. Especially when she laughed.

'Oh, Dave. You are a cuckoo! Really, getting in such a sweat. You know what country people are. Of course they're discussing every move you make. You're the biggest thing that's happened for months in this one-horse town. They notice your gold pen that can tell the time . . . and of course they know where you're living . . .'

'How did he know it was in Tetley's coat?'

'Because Tetley told him, stupid. I'll bet he's thick-in with Tetley . . . maybe that's why his house hasn't been pulled down, yet?'

'You mean, they suckered me? All a put-up job?'

She shrugged. 'Why not?'

'And I fell for it,' I said, bitterly.

'My God, Dave, you are hard to please. Would you rather believe in witchcraft, or that people make suckers of other people?'

'I'll show them who's a sucker!'

'*That's* my boy! Now drink your whisky and let's go upstairs. Why waste a free afternoon?'

I read the file on the Ugly House first thing next morning. Then sent for Tetley. He was supposed to be my assistant; had been Nevinson's.

'Why didn't Nevinson make a compulsory-purchase order?'

'He tried. D'you mind if I sit down?' He settled himself comfortably, pudgy hand compulsively checking the row of pens and pencils that made his breast-pocket bulge. Half of them didn't even work. He kept those for lending to other people . . .

'Well?'

'We couldn't trace the owners.'

'Surely he's the owner?'

'He's not. Only the tenant. Says his grandfather paid rent to a Mrs Yoxford, who died in 1910. She left it all to a nephew, who vanished.'

'Have you been through the records *thoroughly*?'

'Not just here. County records . . . Public Records Office . . . last wills and testaments. You name it, we looked. No owners, so no compulsory purchase.'

'Except by Act of Parliament!'

'For one little piddling access-road? Besides, there's not time – we have to open in two months.'

'We'll have to get him with a Notice of Time and Place.'

'Nevinson tried all that.'

'Well, we'll just have to try it again, won't we? Shouldn't be too hard. House is leaning like a drunken sailor.'

Tetley put his head on one side. 'Why don't you leave poor old Burridge alone? He's not doing you any harm. He just wants to go on living in the house he's always lived in. Like you and me.'

'He's defying the law.'

'He was defying Nevinson . . . there's another way the access-road could go. Up through Rufus's Yard. Old Rufus would sell for a song – wants to go and live with his daughter in Clacton. It's a bit swampy, but nothing twenty tons of chippings wouldn't cure.' He pulled a crumpled site-map out of his pocket.

'But we'd lose fifty yards of made-up road . . . ten thousand quid.'

'Burridge is willing to buy that bit off us. Made a very decent offer.'

'*Has* he? Who's he made the offer to?'

Tetley had the grace to lower his eyes. 'Me. After Nevinson . . . copped it. Before you came.'

'You mean – nothing on paper?'

'No. But he's willing.'

'Does he think he runs the town? Who does he think he is?'

Tetley shrugged. 'He's retired. But he's not pushed for a penny.'

'You seem to know an awful lot about him!' I took out my gold pen.

He didn't flinch. 'Everybody in Besingfield knows old Burridge.'

'Oh? What's he famous for?'

'Oh, he makes up herbal remedies . . . herbal smoking-mixtures. Now he's retired.'

'Retired fisherman?' I asked sarcastically.

'In a way,' said Tetley. 'You could call him a fisher of men . . .'

I gave him a sharp look, but his face had returned to blandness. Might as well try to read small-print through a pound of lard.

By a Notice of Time and Place, you summon someone before the Housing Committee; either to tell him to get his premises repaired pronto, or to tell him you're going to demolish them because they're past repair. You do a very thorough survey of the premises beforehand, I can tell you. But in my case, I could see another problem coming up. Some councillor might start shouting that I was victimizing Burridge, carrying on an old vendetta. So I needed a complaint about the Ugly House from a member of the public.

It should have been easy. I was making friends among my fellow-workers, as well as enemies. Someone should have known of someone willing to make a complaint against Burridge. For the price of a drink; as a favour to be remembered; or as an act of spite.

Nobody would. Not for ten quid, not twenty, nor even fifty, which I offered on the QT and nothing in writing.

'Burridge would get to know who did it,' said Mike Hargreaves, the Chief Planning Officer.

'So?'

'Burridge has lived a long time in this town; he knows everybody; he bears *grudges*.'

'So?'

He shrugged, grinned shamefacedly and shrugged again. 'People are frightened of him. He'll know you're doing this, you know . . .'

'Bollocks!'

'O K. Go ahead and find somebody. Bet you a quid you can't.'

'Done.' And it did cost him a quid. I got a mate of mine over from the Architects Department at Ipswich. I invited Gordon down after work one night, and Linda gave him one of her best American dinners. I got him mellow with a couple of bottles of Chablis, and drove him down to the Ugly House. We parked about fifty yards away; quite close enough to see how much it was leaning. But Gordon was out of the car in a flash, walking right up to the Ugly House, which wasn't in my plan at all.

'Fascinating,' said Gordon, peering over Burridge's withered hedge. 'Practically a history of English architecture in its own right. Gorgeous.'

'This,' I hissed, 'is the place I want demolished.'

'You're joking,' bawled Gordon. 'You don't want to demolish a place like this. I wish I had something half as good on my patch.'

I began to realize I had overdone the Chablis. Burridge must be hearing every word. He'd be in need of a deaf-aid if he wasn't.

'Look at the way it's leaning,' I hissed.

'Leaning doesn't mean dangerous. You wouldn't want to demolish the Leaning Tower of Pisa?' He pushed open Burridge's gate and began pinching away at the door-moulding like it was

Sophia Loren's thigh. At that point I left him to it. When he came back to the car, he seemed more sober.

'Is there no way you can save it?'

'No – the hypermarket access goes straight through it.'

He gave me a sad look. 'I don't understand you, Dave. But I've eaten your dinner, so I'll write your complaint. Give me your pen.' He wrote it with set lips and gave it to me. As he did, I felt a wetness on the sleeve of his jacket. 'What's that patch of damp?'

He looked at it, baffled. 'Something must have dripped on it, from the house. Leaky downspout, maybe.'

'That's a start,' I said grimly.

When we got back to my place, he got his coat, said goodbye to Linda, and drove straight home.

At least, we thought he'd driven straight home. Till we got a call from the Manningtree police.

Gordon had swerved his car off a perfectly clear road at seventy. The police said from the skid-marks, it almost looked as if he'd swerved to avoid something that was no longer there. He was in intensive care. They'd found our instructions for getting to our house in his pocket.

It sounds silly, but I blamed Burridge. When I'd finished with Burridge's house, he wouldn't know what had hit him. I summoned all my forces for the attack. I'm a qualified building-inspector – most CTOs are. So was Tetley. Besides that, I had an old inspector called Reg Totton within months of retiring, and a young trainee called Martin Francis.

When I had them all into my office to brief them, the night before, Reg and Martin looked at each other.

'We did that place last March. With Nevinson. The report's on file – sound as a bell.'

'There's no report here,' I said.

'Item number seven, in the file,' said Reg.

I looked. There were some yellowed sheets of paper, looking far older than the rest. And faint brown traces, where typescript had been. But only the figure '7' remained, hacked in savagely with Biro.

There was a long, haunted silence, then Tetley said, not looking at anybody, 'That bloody photocopier is always going on the blink.'

'Am I to assume,' I said icily, 'that all the copies of this report will be in the same condition?' They made half-hearted phone calls, to the Planning Department, the Secretaries Department. From the indignant squeaks that came back down the phone, all the copies were. We trooped down to the photocopying-room to dig the original typescript out of their files.

It was nowhere to be found.

'Well,' I said, 'we'll have to start all over again, shan't we?'

'Bloody photocopier,' said Tetley, with purely ritual annoyance.

Reg and Martin said nothing at all.

I drove in next morning through an Essex landscape draped in mist. Line after line of trees swam up at me, and departed behind. I felt so unreal I could hardly bring myself to believe the road-signs, and I got lost twice. The unreal feeling had started the previous night, as I briefed them. I had this ghastly feeling that what I was saying was not entering their minds. They were sluggish, miles away. When I asked them a question, they started and bumbled like men wakened from sleep. I had the growing conviction that my carefully worked-out instructions were meaningless gibberish; a growing conviction I was discussing an event that was never going to happen. It had given me the most restless night I had ever spent in my life.

I went into my office and saw to my post. Totton's wife rang in. Reg had developed one of his migraines – the three-day sort.

'He should be retired by this time,' she said accusingly. 'He should've retired years ago, only they couldn't do without him.'

'Give him my best wishes,' I said, with false bonhomie. Even the best doctor in the world can't tell whether you've really got a migraine. Migraine, like backache, is invisible.

Then young Martin rang in. From Cromer in Norfolk, of all places. He'd driven up to see a girlfriend overnight, and now his car wouldn't start. Also, a dense sea-fog was covering most of Norfolk and Suffolk.

'Get in as soon as you can,' I said, with a grate in my voice. In that sea-fog, Martin's car must be as invisible as Reg's migraine.

'Sorry,' he said, sounding as real as a three-pound note.

'*You* feel all right?' I asked my one remaining henchman. 'No backache, fallen arches, ingrowing toenails?'

'Don't know what you mean.' Tetley was never a witty man.

Burridge checked through our documents thoroughly.

'Your friend's improving,' he said. 'In the hospital.' He didn't sound glad or amazed. He might have been talking about a paper-clip.

'How do you know?' I asked rudely.

He ignored me. 'Well, I'll leave you gentlemen to it. We've got shopping to do, haven't we, Legion?' He addressed his remarks to a black labrador that lay at his slippered feet and stared at nothing. It was oddly like Burridge; old, with a greying muzzle, but durable. Solid, without being fat. Its coat was curiously dusty and lacking in gloss, and its skin lay in wrinkled folds round its neck, exposing grey skin through the black hair at the top of each fold.

Burridge turned to me. 'I expect you'll find all you need.' He wasn't hostile, or even interested. He was bored; bored like the dog; bored like old Reg and Martin had been last night. He picked up a curious mixture of shopping-bags that lay in a chair; old brown or black leatherette, most of them, but there was a straw fish-bag among them, that clinked with bottles. We listened to the front door close behind them.

'I'll check the outbuildings and the yard,' said Tetley.

'Sure you still feel OK?' I asked sarcastically. He went out the back door without bothering to answer, and I was left alone with the house.

I went straight for the thing I was most afraid of; the room full of stuffed birds. Get the worst over first . . .

There wasn't a single stuffed bird to be seen. Bare as a prison-cell. I whipped from room to room, thinking I'd got the wrong one. Nothing to be seen on the ground floor, nothing on the first floor. I was just going up to the top floor when I caught myself. I was acting like a child. I was meant to be looking for dangerous structure, not stuffed birds . . . but at least now I knew that Burridge had been playing a game to frighten me, bloody charlatan.

Except how did he know I was afraid of feathers? I was still wondering as I went down to Burridge's stone-flagged kitchen at the back.

Hundreds of dull black eyes watched me from the table-top. A mass of little white animals? I couldn't see properly; couldn't make out what they were at all, in the gloom . . . I wanted, like a child, to run away. But I made myself go over . . . touched one . . . pulled my hand back sharply as it touched the dreaded feel of feathers.

Chicken heads. Dead chicken heads, severed at the neck. Still staring at me with a ghost of life. Each with a different expression. Some fear; some alertness; some anger. All dead, that had been alive. So many done to death; envying my life . . . What ghastly thing had Burridge done? Spent the night murdering every chicken in the neighbourhood? Was every hen-cree in the district full of headless corpses? The police . . .

Then I laughed harshly. There was a massive broiler-farm down the road towards the coast. It gave us health problems. Especially the mountains of chicken heads that built up outside, bringing the threat of rats. Anybody could have a hundred chicken heads for the asking.

To frighten the new CTO with? I couldn't see they could have any other purpose. I'll get you for that, Burridge, you bastard. And there's only one way to get you. My skill as a building-inspector. My skill against yours, whatever that is.

I examined the kitchen thoroughly, tapping for detached plaster, sniffing for the smell of dry-rot, insidious as evil. Poking for structural cracks or the small holes of woodworm, or the larger holes of death-watch beetle.

Nothing. Sound as a bell, as old Reg Totton had said. Had old Reg really got a migraine? Was Martin really stuck at Cromer? Or were they frightened of Burridge? I glanced out of the smeared kitchen-window, to make sure Tetley was still with me. He had dragged a crate of bottles out of a hole in the wall, and was kicking it with idle spite. I tapped on the window, making him jump, then he vigorously attacked a window-frame with the spike of his army knife.

Was Tetley afraid to come indoors? His cowardice made me feel braver. I pressed on. It was a funny house. A big house if you judged it by the number of rooms; a veritable nest of rooms, stairs and twisting corridors. But small in total volume. As if a lot of very small people had lived there, closely packed together, long ago. What they'd have considered grand, in the sixteenth century. Most of the rooms, Burridge had no use for. Pointless. Take this one. An old table; two wooden chairs standing on the table. An old tin bath, half-full of some rusty liquid. And a picture on the wall. That might be a laugh. I could do with a laugh, just at present. I brushed the coating of fluff off the photograph with my sleeve.

Little boys in the photograph; little footballers with adenoids and cropped hair, sticking-out ears and long, long shorts. Arms folded across their hooped jerseys, they stared alertly, fearfully, angrily, at the camera. Somehow their bright button-eyes reminded me of the chicken heads. Because they'd be dead too, most of them. Inscribed on the football held by the one in the middle was 'Champions 1911–12'.

Was one of them the infant Burridge? Could he be *that* old? I ran my eye along the faces, looking for the beginnings of that long skull, long nose, long jaw. The eyes would give him away, small, close together. None of the little long-gone footballers looked like they could possibly have turned into Burridge. Another pointless exercise. Why couldn't I keep my mind on the job in hand? Then I looked at the men behind the boys, moustached, bowler-hatted, self-important.

The un-moustached one at the end was Burridge.

And he was already a middle-aged man. Not much different from how he looked now. A middle-aged man in 1912 . . .

Oh, give over. Burridge's father . . . or grandfather. Long noses must run in that family. I hung it back on the rusty nail.

Then went back and had another look. Could anyone, even Burridge's father, replicate so closely that cold, watchful, *weary* look?

For God's sake, I told myself, you've come here to survey a house.

I did my work thoroughly, sniffing, tapping, stamping on floor-boards, as I worked my way upstairs. I could find nothing wrong, and I was really concentrating. But the place was in fair nick. Gloomy and cold, but not damp. Dry as dust. Paintwork peeling, but sound wood beneath. With my completion of the ground floor, half my hopes were gone. Any surveyor will tell you, you find trouble at the bottom of a house, and at the top. Never in the middle.

Suddenly there was shouting from outside. Tetley wildly ges-ticulating. I had a terrible struggle to get a small rusty window open. Why didn't he come up, if he wanted to tell me something?

He was shouting about a forgotten meeting with the Chairman of the Amenities and Recreation Committee. On site, at eleven. And as he said, jabbing at his Mickey-Mouse watch, it was already eleven-twenty.

I let him go. I hadn't much option. He was into his maroon Viva before he'd finished shouting, and away like the clappers.

I felt pretty lonely, even with the Volvo parked outside. And there was still half the house left to do, including the attics and the soot-laden roof-spaces. And it was *cold*; a grey shadowy cold that ate into your bones and killed hope. The very thought of central heating or double-glazing seemed ridiculous. Might as well put roof-insulation into Castle Dracula . . .

Mind you, Burridge was no Dracula. You get a feel of people, doing their houses, as refuse-collectors get one through their dust-bins. You ought to hear Ron, our refuse foreman. Give him a dustbin, and he starts prophesying: 'Three cats, one dog, two young kids. Vegetarians, but the wife's a bit of an alcoholic. Go to the Costa Brava; she dyes her hair, he plays billiards . . .' Brilliant.

Well, I can do the same with a house. This was the house of an old man, a bored man, a stoical and enduring man. Not a stick of creature comfort. No pathetic touches, like mementoes. You couldn't even feel sorry for the man.

I was doing his bedroom (faded striped pyjamas, grey socks laid on the window-sill to dry) when I heard the sound of paws in the corridor outside. Dog's paws, with little blunt claws that tapped like tiny hammers on the bare boards.

It surprised me. I thought he'd taken the dog shopping with him. Then I thought, he's left that bloody black thing to keep an eye on me. I'll try and chum up with it; anything for company in this bloody hole.

I'm usually good with dogs. So I poked my head round the door.

No dog, though there were a couple of half-open doors he could've nipped through. I called out.

'All right. Play hard to get. I'm not chasing you.' And went back to work. The bedroom seemed darker than it had been; the corridor must be brighter . . .

Again, tin-tack paws on the floorboards just outside the half-open door. Again, I shoved my head out.

Nothing there.

The next time, as I crouched to check a skirting-board, I heard the paws come through the door, and into the bedroom. I whirled.

Nothing there. I went cold all over. I knew it wasn't a trick of the wind; I've surveyed too many empty houses. I know the sounds wind makes.

One of your tricks, Burridge? Like the chicken heads? I'm not easy to fool twice. So I went on working. I'm not scared of dogs, ghostly or otherwise. So I went on working, crouching, tapping the length of skirting, hoping for dry-rot.

There was the sound of sniffing behind me.

I went on working.

A little cold breath in my ear. Cold breath from a cold nose. Dog's breath isn't warm like humans. There was the strong smell of an old dog; the big black presence of black dustiness pressed against my back . . .

I whirled, nearly fell, staggered to my feet. There was nothing there. Yet the sound of the paws continued, round and round the room. I could follow it with my ears. And the dirty smell of dog, and the sniffing.

The room got a lot colder – or maybe it was just me. Cold

creeps up on you slowly when you're doing an unheated building. Then I went goose pimples all over. They crept up my spine, into my scalp. I reached upwards with amazement, and found my hair was standing on end, like a frightened cat's. And that really managed to scare me.

I grabbed wildly for my clipboard. I was on the point of running out of that house. Nothing would have stopped me, and I'd never have gone back.

Except that I began to feel anger. The anger oozed into me, strong and red and bright, like the first whisky after a cold day's work. The funny thing was, I thought then that it wasn't *my* anger – it was directed against the thing that was padding round the room. It got stronger and stronger, and it held me upright. I had never felt that angry in my life. I'm normally a fairly placid sort of bloke, or so Linda tells me. But this anger was like a dam bursting.

And then, suddenly, the sound of paws and the sniffing and the smell of dog were gone. The house was truly empty. I looked through the window and saw old Burridge just coming in through the gate, his shopping-bags full. He was holding open the gate for the obese, waddling dog.

I went to the head of the stairs, still full of the red anger, as he opened the front door with his key.

'Hello, Mr Burridge,' I said. My voice came out high and harsh, so I wouldn't have recognized it. It must have been the anger I was feeling.

He looked up, and I thought his face looked terrified.

'I'm still here,' I said.

He raised a hand to his face. Maybe it was to protect his face, or maybe just to shield his eyes against the light. There was a staircase-window on the landing behind me, putting my figure in silhouette.

'You don't get rid of me that easy,' I said. These strange phrases just kept coming into my head, so I said them, in that funny high voice. I began to walk downstairs towards him.

He gave a whimper, and half fell into the corner by the grandfather-clock. He nearly knocked it over; its metal innards jangled together. He continued to watch me, hunched in his corner, eyes like saucers, showing the whites all round. I thought that was how a man might look who sees his death coming towards him.

Then he said, 'Who *are* you?' And then, 'But you haven't got red hair.' And a great sigh exploded out of him, and his fear-face fell apart, and began to put itself together to look normal. In a moment there was the normal, immovable Burridge, except that he was very pale, and there was a sheen of sweat all over his face that shone in the dim light of the hall.

'Of course I haven't got red hair,' I said. 'What d'you mean, I haven't got red hair?' The anger had left me; my voice was back to normal. To tell you the truth, I was feeling nearly as rocky as Burridge.

'Nothing, Mr Dobson,' he said. 'I was just wool-gathering. When you get to my age . . .'

'How old are you?' I asked, suddenly remembering the football photograph.

He ignored my question, as usual, with that wave of the hand. Pretended to be solicitous. 'You'll be cold, Mr Dobson. Could you do with a cup of tea? With something in it?'

'Like what? Some of your famous herbal mixture?'

He pursed his lips, as if noting a point. 'No, Mr Dobson. I thought, a spot of whisky . . .'

'No thanks. Can I use your phone? If you've *got* a phone?'

'Oh, I have a phone. One of the things this modern world sells its soul for . . .' He sounded bitter.

He had a phone; an old black thing, pre-war. He'd have got a few pounds for it, in a flea-market. I noted the strange old number; Besingfield 342. Then I rang to inquire after Tetley and his on-site meeting. Tetley came to the phone himself; just got back, he said. I reminded him he had a job of work to do. With me, here. He sounded funny, disorganized. As if he hadn't expected me to ring . . . Then he said he had to go, he was going out to lunch.

I snarled that if he was going out to lunch, he might just call at Burridge's on the way. He might consider buying me a lunch, considering I'd been doing his damned work for him all morning.

To my surprise, he gave in meekly. I reckoned he must be suffering from shock. Mind you, he took me to a vile snack-bar where I sipped a poisonous cup of coffee, and cut a coldly soggy pork pie into cubes and played chess with them while I watched him demolish two Cornish pasties, mushy peas and chips. He must be a wow at our annual office dinner. I let him get thoroughly stuck into a large mock-cream éclair before I jumped him.

'If I hadn't rung, Tetley, how long would you have left me?'

He bit off half the éclair at a gulp, which gave him nearly three minutes' chewing-time to work out how to reply.

'That site-meeting with Amenities was *real*. Look in the diary, if you don't believe me. Ask the Chairman.'

'And suppose I ask him who fixed it up – you or him? And before or after I fixed the inspection of Burridge's place?'

He solved his problem this time by choking. Did it rather well. Turned slightly blue; sprayed crumbs and spit all down his floral tie. But he didn't have to tell me the answer. I knew.

'That site-meeting was about as real as Totton's migraine or Martin's car breaking down, wasn't it? Are you a mate of Burridge, Tetley?'

'Burridge doesn't have mates,' he said, sullenly.

An inspiration struck me. 'You must be a mate of Burridge, Tetley. You were seen going into his house one night last week.'

This time, he blushed.

'Tell me about it, Tetley. How much did he slip you, to bugger up this morning?'

'He didn't slip me anything. I went for something different.'

'Like what? I'd hate to have to report you for corrupt practices involving Council legislation . . .' He blanched; he had an unfortunate wife and three unfortunate kids to keep.

'Baldness,' he said, into the crumbled and forgotten remains of his éclair.

'What?'

'He's curing me of baldness. He gives me ointment to rub on.' I leaned over and smelled his head. The stink, close to, was horrific.

'What in God's name *is* it, Tetley?'

'Rat grease.'

'*What?*'

'R A T G R E A S E.' The woman behind the counter actually came out of her glaze of boredom.

'Smells like rat shit.'

'Aye, some of that as well. But it's working. I've got little bristles all over me scalp.'

'They're not bristles, mate. That's a fungus that only grows on rat shit.' The woman behind the counter was laughing so hard that she gave her bosom a painful burn on the tea-urn. I got Tetley away, before she reduced herself to a stretcher-case. I slapped him on the shoulder.

'Tetley, old mate, for rat shit I can forgive you anything. Let's get back to that survey.'

I drove home late, in a pretty vile temper. Tetley and I had put in five more hours, and found absolutely nothing wrong with the Ugly House. It leaned, but the leaning was centuries old; even perhaps a mistake by the original builders. No cracks or movement. It would lean no further, for the foundations were on rock. Burridge hadn't wasted any money on paint, but it was watertight. The slates were fastened on with best copper nails into oak purlins so hard they bent your finger-nail. Nothing, except for a cellar-door Burridge refused to open. And since, as Tetley pointed out, it was tunnelled into solid rock, there couldn't be anything wrong there anyway.

Tetley summed it up. 'Not a fault. We might as well have been looking for Besingfield Castle.' That was a famous local saying. Besingfield had had a castle once, but it had totally vanished. Even the site wasn't known. It must have been one of those timber motte-and-bailey structures that just rotted away.

The only compensation was that Burridge hadn't gloated. He'd let us out looking very subdued. With anyone else, I'd have said frightened. He gave me a long, lingering look as he closed his grey front door. But whatever I was going to get him on, it wasn't going to be a Notice of Time and Place.

Ah well, another day, another dollar, as Linda would say. As an American girl, she'd been taught how a husband should be welcomed home, if you want to keep him. Dry Martinis, newly-iced; an Ella Fitzgerald on the stereo. It was getting dark early; heavy grey clouds, feeling like thunder. Maybe she'd have the candles lit on the dinner-table. I could do with forgetting work.

I put the car in the garage, round the back, and walked up through the unkempt orchard, whistling feebly. I hadn't got round to the orchard yet; the old crab-apple trees had grown together, blocking out the dull sky. The grass was waist-high. Last year's leaves, and the leaves from the year before that, crunched drily underfoot. It was very dark under the trees. But I could see the windows of my house; every one was lit, upstairs and down. I wondered why . . .

Till I heard the other footsteps behind; following me. I pulled up, thinking they were an echo of my own, expecting them to stop. They didn't. They went on, pattering around me in a semi-circle to the right, in the shadows among the long grass. Getting between me and home. Two sets of small footsteps . . .

Like a big heavy dog might make.

They came nearer, circling.

I ran at them, wildly.

Nothing there.

But the footsteps began again, behind me. Again I ran at them; doubled back suddenly, wildly circling every tree and clump of grass.

Nothing. Except that I could hear the sniffing now. The same sniffing, the same smell, that I'd had at Burridge's house. I was just going to make a panicky run for the house when that strange anger that I'd felt before came to my rescue again. This time I welcomed it, felt it surge through me and, at the same time, heard the footsteps begin to retreat. Through a growing red mist of rage, I followed them, to the edge of the ploughed field that stood next to our house.

The footsteps left the orchard; the sniffing ceased. But nothing showed across the darkening field.

When the strange anger began to fade, I knew that the thing, whatever it was, had gone. I felt light, carefree. Whatever it was, I had the better of it. I was whistling again as I opened my front door.

Linda didn't run to meet me. She came slowly, like an old woman.

'Linda, what's the matter? Are you ill? Have you called the doctor? Sit down, I'll make you a cup of tea.'

To all of which she said nothing. Just came and sat down. I put an arm round her, and she leaned against me, limp, like a lost child.

'What's the matter?'

'Oh, it's nothing. It's silly . . .'

'*What's* silly?'

'Oh, take no notice of me, Dave.'

'I will take bloody notice. What's the matter?'

'Oh,' she pushed back a strand of hair wearily, 'I keep imagining things – it's so silly. But when you're alone all day . . .'

'What things?'

'Dog's feet, padding. First outside the house . . . then inside. And a smell . . .'

She wouldn't let me send for the police. What could we have told them?

'There must be somebody we can talk to.'

She looked up with half her old smile. It had cheered her up that I'd been hearing the same things; she'd been wondering if she was going round the bend. 'If Burridge is doing this – and I still can't believe it – we need to talk to somebody who's lived here all their lives. Newcomers like us, they'd just laugh.'

I thought, and said, 'Reg Totton – he owes me one for today.'

'Ring him up!'

'No – let's just go,' I said, with half a grim smile.

Reg opened the door himself, a bottle of Sainsbury's red plonk in one hand, and a corkscrew in the other. He was wearing an open-necked check shirt and an open navy cardigan, and looked not at all like a man getting over a migraine. The worst thing you can do with a migraine is drink.

'Evening, Reg!'

'The wine's for the wife,' he said, clutching it defensively.

'Come off it, Reg. It's a fair cop!'

He grinned engagingly, showing his missing teeth. All the rest are his own, as he'll tell you ten times a day, if you let him.

When his wife grasped that I wasn't going to sack Reg on the spot, and deprive him of his pension, she grew amiable enough to ask us to stay to dinner. It shows how the Tottons spoiled themselves that none of us went in the least hungry. I eyed Reg's comfortable paunch, and decided there was such a thing as growing old gracefully.

But she tensed right up again when I mentioned Burridge. 'Reg is not going back to that house. The last time he went, wi' Nevinson, we had bad luck for months. We're only just clear of it now. He's *not* going back.'

'What kind of bad luck?'

Reg moved uneasily in his chair, but he couldn't stop her.

'All sorts o' bad luck. Every year Reg takes a prize for his tomatoes at Besingfield Show. As long as we've been married. Barring one or two Highly Commendeds. Well, this year, the day after he went down Burridge's, all the plants died overnight. Fine an' healthy in the evening – a mass of grey mould by the morning. Couldn't save a single bit o' fruit, even for bottling.'

'C'mon, Greta – maybe I over-watered them.'

'After forty years? Maybe you were over-watering the cats as well – three dead within the week. And we nearly lost our first grandson wi' a miscarriage – it was touch an' go for four days. It doesn't pay to cross Burridge.'

I watched Reg. He was wriggling with embarrassment, but he wasn't denying any of it. He was pulling at his lip.

So I said quietly, 'What gives, Reg?' He gave me a shrewd look.

'You had trouble, Mr Dobson?'

I told them.

'That settles it,' said Greta. 'Go on, Reg, they're entitled to know.'

'Well,' said Reg 'I want to be fair. I'd lived fifty-odd years alongside Cunning Burridge, and he never did me no harm. Did me a bit of good, once. Me mam took me to him for warts. All over me face, I had 'em, and the other kids called me "Pig". I was bloody paralysed, going into that house, I can tell you. But he just told me to be brave, cut a potato in half, and rubbed it all over me face. Then he wrapped it up in newspaper, and told us to throw it into the first field we passed where there were pigs. When the pigs nosed open the packet an' ate the potato, me warts would go. And they did, like magic. Cost me mam five shillings.'

'That's witchcraft,' said Linda.

Both the Tottons stared into their fire uncomfortably. Finally Reg said, 'Well, there's witchcraft an' witchcraft. Burridge is all right, if you don't cross him. He's done a lot of good in his time and no harm. Till Nevinson got across him.'

'How was that?'

'Nevinson got across everybody. A right bastard to work for. Not like you, Mr Dobson. There was only one slacker when Nevinson was CTO – Nevinson. Off for long lunch-hours, drinking wi' his contractor mates. Shifty, too. You'd think he'd gone off for the whole afternoon, then he'd come back at five to five, and bawl you out for having a game o' shove-ha'penny.'

'There was more to it than that, Reg,' said Greta, viciously poking the fire, her mouth set like a rat-trap. 'There was sending workmen off into the back of beyond, then calling on their wives . . .'

'Aye, he was a wicked womanizer. An' he didn't stop at a slice o' the cut cake. He was after the unmarried ones as well. And at the Council, bloody fool. They reckon he scored with every typist in Secretaries . . .'

'Till he come to Susan Myerscough,' said Greta, with another vicious poke. 'Susan fixed him, wi' his tom-cat ways.'

'How?'

'She went to old Burridge about him. It weren't fair, Nevinson should've left Susan alone. She weren't fair game. Susan's the marrying sort, unlike some. He got her pregnant, an' he wouldn't marry her, so she went to Burridge.'

'What happened?'

'That's not for us to say. You go an' ask Susan if you're that interested. Susan Nevinson, as she is now, and I never saw a merrier widow. Fine little boy he left her with, I'll say that for him. And a fine whack o' life insurance. Now not another word, Reg!'

Reg looked at me, shrugged helplessly. I hope there never comes a time when Linda does that to me.

After a silence, Linda said, 'What do we do, now?' I knew that even there, in the solid, chintzy warmth of Reg's sitting-room, with the Dralon curtains drawn against the night, she was still listening for those paws, that sniffing. And tomorrow morning was only ten hours away, when I'd have to leave her alone again.

'Aye,' said Reg, after a long pause. 'Burridge has got a hold on both of you. Did you leave anything at his house, Mr Dobson? Belonging to you or Mrs Dobson? Something small, like – a used handkerchief, or a stub of pencil? Hair and nail-parings is best, of course, but cloth or a pencil would do it.'

I thought carefully. Made a mental check of all my gear. I'm the careful sort. 'Nothing.'

'You sure? A pencil you've sucked, or a stamp you've licked?'

'Nothing, I tell you.'

'He couldn't have stolen fluff out of your coat pocket, when you hung it up?'

'I kept my coat on!' He was starting to get on my nerves.

'Get on wi' it, Reg,' said Mrs Totton, nearly as tense as I was.

'Well, did *he* give *you* anything?'

'No . . . yes. He was carrying a mug of tea, the first day I called; he stumbled and spilled some on my arm. How does that bring in Linda? Is tea enough?'

'Tea drunk, no – goes straight through you. But tea spilt on your arm . . . leaving a stain on your coat, your shirt. Where's that coat now?'

I glanced at my donkey-jacket. 'I'm still wearing it.'

'And where's the shirt?'

'In the laundry-basket at home.'

'So he can reach you, and he can reach Linda . . .' He made a great play of tamping down his pipe and lighting it. I looked at Mrs Totton. She nodded, grimly.

'That's ridiculous,' said Linda. 'That's *medieval*.'

'So's Burridge.'

'What is he – some kind of *witch*?' Her New England accent was very strong.

'He's a cunning-man, Mrs Dobson. The old 'uns still call him Cunning Burridge. There's still a few cunning-men, plying their trade in Essex. In me grandfather's time – afore the National Health Service – there were three or four in every town. People would come from miles away, like to doctors. And I'm not sure they didn't do us more good than doctors.'

'Lay off, Reg, this is the twentieth century!'

'In London maybe, Mr Dobson. Not in Essex.'

'So,' said Linda, in a flat, beaten voice, 'suppose you're right; what do we do next?'

'Well, you can do one of two things. Either go and ask him to take the witching off you voluntarily . . . but he'll want something in return . . .'

'Like not demolishing his house?' I said. 'What's the other alternative, Reg?'

'Well, if the cunning-man has used something to put a witching on you, they do say that if you cut that thing up and burn it piece by piece on your fire, the witch will be driven to your door afire wi' fever . . . in a muck sweat. And he'll go on burning till he's taken the curse off you, see? You've got him, see? An' if he won't take the curse off, an' you burn the last piece, the witch dies . . .'

We all stared at each other, aghast.

'We'd better be going,' I said. 'Thanks for the meal, Reg. Smashing cooking, Mrs Totton.'

'Tek care, lad,' said Reg.

I put away the car, and followed Linda up to the house. She had all the lights on again, and she was standing holding open the front door, with the light streaming down the path.

'I heard it,' she said. 'I heard it as soon as I unlocked the door. It's inside the house.'

'That's *it*,' I said. I went to the dirty-laundry basket, and grabbed the shirt I'd worn to Burridge's. It was one of my favourites – green with a white stripe and white collar. 'Where do we burn it?'

'But it's nearly new . . . suppose nothing happens?'

'If we burn it and nothing happens, we've got one less thing to worry about.'

'Oh, God, I'm so *cold*, Dave. Let's sit by the Aga. Want a whisky?'

'A bloody big one.'

It was snug by the Aga. We sat in our old wooden rockers, Linda cutting the shirt into half-inch strips, and me lifting the Aga lid and popping them down one by one.

'It's gone,' said Linda, after a bit. 'The sniffing thing . . . I just suddenly feel, know, it's gone.'

'Yes,' I said, 'but it could come back. Let's go on. It's too late to save the shirt.'

She held it up with a giggle. The tail was gone; and most of the front. 'Shall we try a bit of the tea-stain itself?'

'Why not?' But some streak of caution made me add, 'Only a bit.'

'There,' she said. 'Snip.' A tiny piece of tea-stain fell on the floor, and I picked it up and put it in the Aga.

After another half-hour, Linda said, 'I feel silly. He's not coming, is he? It's not going to work. Let's go to bed – I'm whacked.'

I looked at my watch; gone midnight. I felt whacked too. But something hard and fierce was growing in me, like a backbone I never knew I had, that made me say, 'Give it another half-hour. We're six miles from where Burridge lives. And he's an old man. And I don't think he's got a car.'

Snip, snip, snip. I recharged our whisky-glasses. A cruel hunter's excitement began to grow in me, a sadistic joy I'd never known.

'I think it's working. I *feel* he's coming.'

But the hammering on our front door still shook me rigid. One minute we were snug and giggling, and the next we were terrified. The knocking was so wild, so endless. I've only heard that kind of knocking once before, and then it was a car crash. Linda stood and stared at me, white, open-mouthed.

'Get on the phone to the police,' I said. 'Dial 999, and keep the fuzz talking. Pretend we've lost Tigger or something. While I answer the door.'

I picked up the remains of my shirt and the scissors, and shoved them into the pocket of the duffle-coat I was still wearing. I passed Linda as the police answered, and opened the front door.

Burridge fell through, on to the doormat on his hands and knees. Sucking in great gouts of breath, his back heaving, the back of his neck a colour that is dangerous in an elderly man. He made no attempt to speak, just knelt there, fighting for breath. On and on. I was terrified, not of him, but that he might die on my doormat; at the same time I had never felt colder towards any human being in my life.

I signalled the horrified Linda to get off the phone, before Burridge's stertorous breathing brought the whole Essex Constabulary thundering down on us. I felt I could cope with Burridge now. Linda made some quavering response about pussy just walking through the door (I ask you, at twenty past one in the morning!) and hung up.

Together, we got Burridge into a kitchen rocker. Hard going. He was a heavy man, and slippery with perspiration. He stank of sweat; his overcoat was soaked, though it was a dry night.

I loosened his collar and tie, and played the hypocrite in a heartless way that shocked me.

'Hello, it's Mr Burridge! Are you ill, Mr Burridge? Shall I call an ambulance? Linda, ring for an ambulance!'

With that gesture of his hand, Burridge cancelled the order. But it was a frantic version of that gesture. He kept throwing himself about in the rocker; nearly rocked it clear across the room. His eyes were trapped and desperate; he rolled his head from side to side; there was dried scrum round his lips. Though he wasn't dying, yet.

'The shirt. Give me the shirt!'

I took it out of my pocket and looked at it mockingly. 'I'm afraid there's not much of it left, Mr Burridge. Best throw it on the fire, eh?'

I lifted the Aga lid. He screamed, as I have never heard a man scream.

'Give . . . me . . . that . . . shirt.'

'Why? So you can use it to work other spells on us? So you can send your sniffing-thing bothering my wife again?'

In spite of his sufferings, his eyes were contemptuous.

'If . . . I . . . take . . . back . . . the shirt . . . it's all over.'

Linda moved across, snatched the remnant from my hand, and gave it to him. He snatched it as a refugee might snatch a crust, and immediately became still. His head drooped, his eyes closed. I might have thought him dead, but his breathing was steadying, and the puce colour was seeping out of his face. I noticed the state his clothes were in – boots scuffed, trousers torn, overcoat smeared with yellow mud. He looked, with his grey hair in tats all over the place, like an old tramp.

I poured him a small whisky and gained his attention by tapping its wet rim against his hand. He sipped it slowly, head still down. He wasn't sweating any more, but his soaked clothes steamed from the heat of the Aga and the stink was horrific.

But when he finally looked up, he was his old calm, sure self again.

'Who told you?' he asked, as if he had a right to know. 'Who told you what I'd done to you? And how to cure it?'

Suddenly, I was terrified for Reg and Greta. And not just for their tomato-plants, either. I didn't know what to say, while his eyes bored into me.

And then that strange blessed anger came to my rescue again. And I said words I didn't understand myself. In a voice I didn't recognize as my own.

'You're up against two of us now, Burridge. You won't fool me again.'

His eyes dropped. He said one word I couldn't make out, heaved himself out of the chair, and stalked out of the house, leaving the rocker swinging. We stood silent, till we heard the front door slam.

'Good riddance to bad rubbish,' I said, with an attempt at a laugh.

'You were *horrible* to him.'

'He wasn't exactly nice to us.'

'But you weren't . . . *you*.' Her face twisted up in bafflement.

'Oh, I have hidden depths,' I said, still trying to make a joke of it.

'Have you?' she said. 'Is that why he called you Nevinson?'

It was after that that I stopped worrying about Burridge, and started worrying about Nevinson. Or rather, some funny changes in my own behaviour.

For myself, I'd have been content to let Burridge stew. He'd tried to do us an evil turn, but he'd paid in full. I had the impression we'd very nearly killed him. And I'm not one to bear a grudge; I was too happy with Linda and Tigger.

But I found myself reading the local paper, with an eye cocked for Burridge's doings. And every afternoon, about three, I'd get this urge to drive up and stare at the Ugly House, for no particular purpose. It was as insidious as the sight of a Mars bar to a slimmer, or a whisky to somebody on the wagon. Mostly, I fought the urge off; but once or twice it got too strong, and I'd make excuses to my staff. Once, the urge came on so strongly during an afternoon meeting of the Highways Committee that I broke into a cold sweat resisting it. Every night I had to pass the turn for the Ugly House on my way home, and unless I was concentrating very hard I took that turn without thinking, and was sitting in my car staring at the house before I realized. Not looking at the house as I normally would, looking for loose slates or leaking downspouts, but staring with a kind of blank avidness, like a cat at a mousehole, for any sign of Burridge. I said to Linda it was as if some other person was using my eyes as a television camera. I'd sit there, my body complaining it was hot, or hungry, or tired, but my eyes, with a life of their own, would go on searching for Burridge.

This feeling I began to think of as 'Nevinson'. That, and the terrible rages. I wondered, half idly, half terrified, whether I was going potty. I contemplated going to the doctor. But word gets round in a small town, and who wants a potty CTO? Linda let me talk it out of my system. She was a great support. It was she who suggested we look up Nevinson's death in old copies of the local paper.

He had died on the M1, a hundred miles from Besingfield,

driving towards London. The evidence was scanty; it was after midnight and raining heavily, with little traffic. He had overtaken, in the fast lane, a car that had admitted to doing eighty. 'Well over a ton,' the other driver had said, 'like all the devils in hell were after him. I saw him coming up behind and got out of the way quick. He was slewing all over the road, like there were two drunks inside, fighting for control of the wheel. Then he went straight into the bridge-support, straight as an arrow. Didn't even brake – never saw his brake-lights go on.'

The speedo had stuck at 129 m.p.h., when they prised it out of the wreckage.

His wife did not know where he was going. She did not know where he had been all evening. He had left home as usual that morning, never rung her. She hadn't worried unduly, or rung the police. Nevinson was often not home for dinner; out till all hours. His habits were erratic.

He had no luggage; not even an overcoat. No London hotel had booked him in; no friend had been expecting him, though an appeal was made for people to come forward. But his suit, what was left of it, had been damp when they got him from the wreckage, as if he had been out in the rain, and his shoes were caked in yellow clay, as if he had been walking across some construction site. The clay was similar to that on several sites in the Besingfield district.

There had been a tea-stain on his sleeve.

Nevinson had never been known to drink tea.

I looked up Mrs Nevinson in the phone-book. She was still living in the big house Nevinson had bought cheap from a contact in the construction industry. I rang her. She didn't seem unduly surprised; but she'd rather we came round the following evening.

We found her in the garden, busy with gloves and secateurs and a gardening trug. The setting sun was gilding everything; the garden seemed abnormally full of bees, until you saw the quality of the flowers. I have never seen a garden full of such huge blooms; hardly a patch of bare earth to be seen. If anything, they were over-lush, almost cocky in their splendour, a little wild-growing and overwhelming, as if we humans were only there on sufferance.

Mrs Nevinson did not look like a four-month widow; she looked the picture of contentment, kneeling, secateurs poised, listening to the distant note of a bird, with her head cocked. Then she got up and took her gardening gloves off to greet us.

My God, she was a beauty. Five foot ten, maybe taller. Slightly plump, in a way that made Linda in her jeans look boyish and inadequate. What my father would have called appreciatively 'a big woman'. Ash-blonde hair, plaited up over her head. Rounded brow, upturned nose, gently rosy cheeks. Disappointingly, her blue eyes when she turned them on me were rather small.

Still, she shook hands graciously enough, and took us to see her vegetable-garden. Again, I've never seen such vegetables. The bursting roundness of cabbage, turnip, marrow and tomato were disturbing, almost sexual. I suppose that should have warned me . . .

She took us inside, offered us sherry or Martini. She did it gracefully, but as if she found them unreal toys. I felt she would have been more at home offering us parsnip wine, or last year's elderberry. It was hard not to giggle. I kept on looking at her lushness, then taking quick, shamefaced glances back at Linda, who seemed to be becoming more disappointingly boyish all the time.

Linda missed nothing: when she'd had enough of it, she said sharply, 'Did it ever occur to you, Mrs Nevinson, that someone might have wished your husband harm?'

'Harm?' Mrs Nevinson drew out the syllable very long and Essex. 'Now whatever did put that in your head?'

She had all the surface airs of a lady, but underneath, the peasant showed.

'That he might have been trying to get away from somebody when he crashed?'

Her white forehead wrinkled. She couldn't be more than twenty-six, yet she sat like a matron.

'But there weren't no one near him, 'cept the poor man that found him.' She sounded a good deal more sorry for the poor man than for her dead husband.

'There was a tea-stain on his sleeve when he crashed. Any idea how he got it?'

Her small eyes flickered. Linda had hit the mark. Then she said, 'No – he were more of a coffee-drinker really. Or gin. And whisky.' It came out spitefully.

'But he hadn't been . . . drinking . . . when he crashed?'

'No. He were stone-cold sober – for once.'

'You don't sound too fond of him,' I said.

'I weren't.' The accent was stronger now. 'He got me pregnant, see? Then he wouldn't marry me. Laughed at my dad, when my dad went to see him.'

'So you went to Cunning Burridge about him?'

'Oh, don't look so shocked. Yes. What's the point of trying to hide it? Half the town'll have told you I went to Cunning Burridge.'

'What did *he* do?' asked Linda. Now she had genuine feminine curiosity in her voice, and Mrs Nevinson spoke entirely to her.

'He give me a love-potion, didn't he.'

'A love-potion?' Linda's laugh was only half incredulous.

'Yes, he did give me a love-potion for him, an' I slipped it in his coffee at work, an' he never noticed. An' the same the next day and the next. Then he was mad for me, but I wouldn't have him again, till we were wed. He was just usin' me for his fun. It was time he paid.'

'And then?'

'After a bit I left off the potion . . . he was wearin' me out, day an' night. I watched him come back to his senses. He used to wonder out loud why he done it. In front of me. He wasn't the marryin' sort, Nevinson. But we made him pay for his fun.' She looked around her beautiful house, with a slow, serene smile. 'Well insured, he was. I saw to that, afore I left off the potion. He cut up for a nice pile, when he went. He didn't love me no more, by then. But he hadn't bothered to make a will, so I got the lot. He was going to divorce me.'

'Why . . . was he going to divorce you?'

Mrs Nevinson smiled, as she might have smiled at the question of a five-year-old. 'Some kind friend told him what I'd a-done with Burridge. He went mad. Then he started gunnin' for Burridge. That's when he thought up the access-road to the hypermarket. He tricked the Council, see. The plan o' the access-road he showed 'em didn't show them the road goin' right through Cunning's house. None of 'em could read a map anyway. But they'd-a never voted for knockin' down Cunning's home if they'd known. But once they'd voted, they couldn't un-vote it, see? It was just pure spite, Mr Dobson. That road could just as easy have gone through Rufus's yard. Can't you see to it? Won't do you no harm to have Cunning Burridge grateful. He do be a reasonable man, if he's not provoked. Nevinson provoked him.'

'So Nevinson died, with a tea-stain on his sleeve,' I said.

Again those small eyes flickered, but did not drop.

'Drunken pig . . . fit for neither man nor beast.'

'So you went to see Burridge about him again.'

'No need.' She smiled. 'He'd provoked Cunning enough already.' It wasn't a nice smile.

'How do you know so much?'

'I do be a friend of Cunning's. The whole town do know anyway.' But there was a smugness in her smile . . . the fruitfulness of the whole garden.

'You're . . . his mistress,' said Linda, her voice bleak with disgust. 'That old man . . .'

'Don't you speak of that old man!' Suddenly Mrs Nevinson's face was equally bleak. 'I been a-walkin' in the country wi' that *old* man. When he walks in the fields, the hares come and eat from his hand. Burridge knows, and he knows what women like, too. And I'm not the only one . . .'

She sat back, smug, fulfilled, beautiful in her assurance.

'Do you know what you've just said?' I asked, coldly.

She looked back equally coldly. 'Sayin's one thing; provin's something else. Try going to the police, Mr Dobson. Probably lock you up in the loony-bin. There's a lot round here has reason to be grateful to Cunning. And one or two policemen among them . . . There's more of us than there is of you, Mr Dobson. You'd do well to remember that.' She cocked her head. 'There's young Nevinson, a-cryin' for a feed.' She stirred her large, shapely breasts, in a way that said quite clearly that she was feeding him herself. 'Impatient, the Nevinsons are!'

'This . . . is one Nevinson you approve of?' There was as much anxiety as sarcasm in my voice.

'Some days I do, and some I don't,' she said, stretching lazily. 'Some days he reminds me of our family . . . and some days he reminds me of Nevinson. There's plenty of time to make my mind up . . . accidents can happen. You have to be careful, don't you, Mrs Dobson?'

'We have no children,' said Linda, shortly. But, like me, she took it as a threat.

After that we had no desire to linger, even though she asked us to stay and have something to eat. Especially after she'd asked us to have something to eat.

I saw nothing of Burridge; but the pressure he was putting on was everywhere. Councillors came to see me in my office when I was alone. Some were smooth about it; some ended up pretty nasty. But Labour, Tory or Independent, they said the same thing. Forget Burridge's house, or your days in Besingfield are numbered.

Then the Chief Executive had me in his office to meet the representative of the hypermarket company, who was worried that the access-road might not be finished in time. After the hypermarket man had gone, the Chief Executive was pretty blunt too. Go through Rufus's yard, or get out. The pressure built up like a thunderstorm. And strangely enough, the worst of it was Tetley's bald head.

Where he'd rubbed the rat grease on, a blue-black shadow was growing across it. When I went over, pretending to ask him something, I saw it was bristles of hair.

'Go on,' said Tetley. 'Feel it if you like. I'm going to have a better head of hair than you. What did you think Burridge was? A party conjuror doing a few tricks for the kids at Christmas?'

Reg Totton urged me to give up on the Ugly House for my own sake; he was the only one concerned for *me*. When I said the law must take its course, he told me to be careful what I ate.

I asked him what the hell he meant. He just stared out of the window and said nothing.

My application to join Besingfield Rotary Club was turned down, though the Chief Executive had said it would be a doddle. And it turned out that the local golf club had no vacancies after all . . .

Soon, it wasn't just Burridge who was crossing the street to avoid speaking to me. I got pretty lonely.

But I still had Linda and Tigger.

I remember I got home late that night. Ken Wright's secretary had rung up from British Waterways. One of the drain bridges was badly cracked; its footings had given way. Could I meet him there urgently? I drove down to the canal at Earisbury; but Earisbury is a warren of minor roads, and there are about ten canal bridges, and they're supposed to have number-plates on them, but most have fallen off over the years. Suffice it to say that I spent three frustrating hours, and never a sign of a cracked bridge or Ken Wright. I didn't bother to go back to the office but drove straight home, hot and tired. It was getting on for dusk, and I saw the house-lights shining down through the orchard.

Tigger met me in the garden, told me all his day's news, then ran ahead, patting at the front door with his paw.

I let him in; all the lights were on (Linda has a transatlantic disrespect for electricity bills). There was a record running on the record-player – my favourite LP of John Williams. And the most fantastic smell coming from the kitchen.

'Linda?' I went through to the lounge. 'Linda?' I called upstairs.

There was the sound of someone splashing in the bathroom, and her usual kind of humming. I nearly went upstairs to say hello, but the smell from the kitchen was too intriguing.

A small army of Cornish pasties lay cooling on a wire tray on the broad window-sill next to the stove. It wasn't something she'd ever tried before, but she was still enjoying coming to terms with English cooking. And the nice thing about Linda was that she didn't mind me helping myself. I mean, she counted them afterwards in a mocking way, but she loved me doing it really.

I'd just picked one up, and put the end of it in my mouth, when the phone rang. Cursing, I put it down on the kitchen table, went out into the hall and picked up the phone.

'Hi!' It was Linda. Her voice sounded crackly and far away.

'Where *are* you?' I shouted, completely baffled.

'London. At Aunt Lou's. They telegrammed me she was ill. I rang you at the office, but they couldn't reach you.'

'How is the old darling?'

'That's the baffling thing, Dave. Her flat's locked up; they say she's gone to Venice for a fortnight. I remember now she wrote and told me she was going.'

'But . . . but . . . you're in the bath . . . upstairs.'

'Dave, are you crazy or something?'

'Hold on'. I dropped the phone and ran upstairs. The house was full of her presence, her perfume. If she was in London, who had put the LP on, who had baked the pasties, still warm from the oven? Who was in the bathroom? Still splashing and humming, in that inimitable way?

The door was locked; I smashed it down.

The bath was dry and empty. A small red tape-recorder lay on the green plastic seat of the bathroom stool, the spools turning. It was Linda's voice all right . . . I banged it off and ran back downstairs. What the hell was going on? If she was in London, who'd baked the pasties?

Then I remembered Reg Totton telling me to be careful what I ate.

I ran to the kitchen. All the pasties were gone; only the smell lingered. I stared transfixed at my own reflection in the kitchen window, against the darkening night outside, wondering if I was going mad.

Then I pushed at the closed window. It opened at the touch of my finger; the catch wasn't fastened. Open the window, take away the pasties . . .

Even the one I'd left on the table? Gone too; but not so completely. Only as far as the floor. Half of it still lay there, in the midst of a scatter of broken pieces and crumbs.

Tigger, hungry, had struck again.

'Tigger, Tigger!' Suddenly I was terrified. I ran from room to room, calling. I couldn't see him anywhere, till I heard a faint mew.

He was huddled up in the dark space under the kitchen cupboard. I dragged him out and he fought me, and desperately crawled back again into the dark. The second time, his struggles were weaker, and I was able to hold on to him. He kept on shaking his old head, as if there was something he couldn't quite believe. His mouth was a little open, and his protruding tongue wasn't its usual healthy colour. His eyes were wide, the pupils unusually large. And they had a dull film over them.

I somehow knew he was dying. I ran for the phone again, to ring the vet. But as I ran, he died, wetting himself in a great scalding stream down the front of my shirt. I laid him gently on the table. He was already gone, just a bundle of fur, ruffled in a way he would never have allowed in life.

When I finally reached the phone again and saw it was already off the hook, I realized I still had Linda on the other end. She was amused and slightly baffled.

'They've poisoned Tigger,' I shouted. 'They tried to poison me, but they've poisoned Tigger. He's dead.'

'Oh my God,' said Linda. Then, sharp as lightning, 'Get a grip on yourself, Dave. Get a grip. Phone the police! Are you alone? Lock the doors. I'll be home as fast as that car will carry me.'

A chill hand clutched my heart. Another car driven fast, late at night . . . Nevinson . . . Gordon. 'Don't drive yourself,' I shouted. 'Come by train. Get a taxi from the station . . .'

'But Dave . . . the expense . . .'

'Damn the expense.'

When I put the phone down, I was calm again. Became the technician. It hurt less that way. I had evidence against them, Burridge and Mrs Nevinson. A dead cat and a half-eaten pasty. Even though they'd removed the rest of the pasties, as if they'd never existed. My God, suppose they'd stolen Tigger's body? I ran back, frantic again. But he was still where I'd laid him. I tried the kitchen window, found I'd fastened the catch without thinking, and thanked God. The crumbled pasty still lay on the floor. I went round and checked and secured every door and window. Then I started to ring the police.

Which police? Not Besingfield police. Maybe the Inspector at Besingfield had had *his* warts removed by Cunning Burridge as a boy. Or was having his baldness cured.

I rang Manningtree police. We're just on the border of the two sub-divisions. The phone played me up something cruel. I couldn't hear the 999 operator for the buzzings and clickings, and she certainly couldn't hear me. I tried over and over again. At one point I could have sworn I heard Burridge's voice say, 'It's no good, Mr Dobson.' But I couldn't vouch for my state of mind by then. Then I tried a dash for my car, but that wouldn't start either. I ran back into the house, terrified they had removed the evidence in my absence; but double-glazing is pretty stubborn stuff to break through.

I realized that Burridge was putting the hex on everything I was doing.

I should have to be very, very primitive.

I had a new garden shed, a few yards from the kitchen-door. In it is a spare gallon can of petrol. I soaked the shed in petrol and set alight to it by throwing in a burning ball of paper. I didn't want a nasty accident that would leave me a mass of flames.

The shed burnt nicely; my neighbours, bless them, came running, and phoned Manningtree police from their own houses. I suppose there were so many trying to phone in the end that Burridge couldn't hex them all.

I must hand it to the Manningtree police: they were pretty sharp. They had a lot of trouble getting to me. Cars inexplicably broke down; radios suffered from a lot of static. But they got to me in the end and listened to my story. (Thank God I managed to keep my voice cool.) When I mentioned Burridge, they ran the corpse and the pasty straight into the path. labs in London. They had no more trouble, once they crossed the Deben. Cunning-men, apparently, can't use their powers across large stretches of running water . . . or so the Inspector told me. He also told me they had their own cunning-man in Manningtree, who sounded rather nicer than Burridge. Not that they were against cunning-men, but attempted murder was attempted murder . . .

They told me later that the London forensic boys had a lot of trouble tracing the poison. The stuff inside poor Tigger had metabolized, and was no longer traceable. But they got a trace in the pasty, after a rare struggle. Something to do with toadstools . . .

'If we hadn't found that, sir, we'd have thought the cat had died of heart failure.'

'Or me?'

'Yes, sir. Point taken.'

They caught Burridge and Mrs Nevinson at York, heading north on an overnight coach. Burridge had nothing to say. But Mrs Nevinson turned Queen's evidence and sang like a canary. About Nevinson as well. It promised to be the kind of trial that would double the circulation of the *News of the World* overnight.

Once they were lodged in Colchester Gaol, a flatness came down. We buried Tigger – what was left of him – under his favourite tree in the orchard. The marks of his claws were still clear on the bark. Then there was nothing left to do but wait.

Except that my old restlessness to see the Ugly House persisted. In the evenings now, though. I'd hold out, sometimes till near midnight. Eating apples and biscuits obsessively, playing records, watching telly. Anything to jam the tug of the Ugly House. But by midnight I'd be in the car and driving. Then I'd sit for hours, staring at its dark, empty windows. Almost as if I was waiting for it to fall down. Always feeling that strange, patient, waiting hate, like a cat at a mousehole. Linda would always come with me and sit silently. Only once she gave way and burst out, 'What does Nevinson want? What does he *want?*'

Then, one night, Reg Totton called, before I could get really restless; he stood in my hall, cap in hand.

'He's dead!'

I didn't need to ask who.

'Heart attack?'

Reg shrugged; told me what he knew.

Burridge had been put in a cell in Colchester Gaol with two

other men. Hard nuts, associates up on a robbery-with-violence charge. He had protested; explained his need to be on his own. The Governor had refused his request.

Next morning, both the hard nuts had requested interviews with the Governor; asked to be moved. Request refused. That evening, there was a terrible fight in the cell. The pair of them half killed each other and had to be hospitalized. Two more men were moved in with Burridge.

The same thing happened again; only that time, when they were moved out to the prison hospital they were not replaced.

Next morning, the men in the cells on either side had asked for transfers, and been refused. All five of them. By nightfall, one had fallen down a spiral staircase and broken his leg. Two more were in hospital, doubled-up with stomach cramps. Another, left alone, tried to hang himself.

They checked the last man; he held his wrists behind him, but they saw the blood trickling down the whitewashed wall.

That little cell-block was now empty, except for Burridge. Wardens grew reluctant to go down it, to check on him. It was strangely cold, they said; far colder than outside. And it was damp, increasingly damp. Flagstones glistened that had always been dry. And the smell. Prisons are pretty smelly places, but . . . One warder had called it a *hating* smell, not a human smell at all.

And Burridge just *sat*. Whenever they looked in, he was always sitting in the same place. Not eating, not drinking. Not looking up when he was spoken to.

That night the warders on duty failed to check Burridge out. They didn't say anything to each other, but they both knew they'd lost their nerve. They could no more walk down that short whitewashed side-corridor than fly in the air. By the time the morning shift came on, the smell, the cold, the wetness could no longer be ignored.

They went along and found Burridge still sitting there. Dead. Rigor mortis had set in; they couldn't get him into his coffin till the next day. They said he looked about two hundred years old, but that grim little smile was still on his face.

All I said was, 'Thanks for letting me know, Reg. Now we can get on with the access-road.'

Reg looked at me like I was mad. 'You maybe had a chance when he was alive, Mr Dobson. He might've changed his mind. But now . . .'

'Have a drink, Reg. You're upset!'

'You wait and see,' he said, turning to go.

Burridge had no relatives. But he had a lawyer. I got a court order to remove his belongings. The lawyer shrugged.

'Nobody will move them. Only a cunning-man would move another cunning's belongings.'

And nobody would, not for twice the asking price. I went as far as Norwich and Ipswich.

'All right,' I said, 'we'll bulldoze the lot.'

'You won't,' said the lawyer. 'You won't find anyone to do it.'

I found them. An Irish demolition firm in Grantham. Fervent Catholics to a man, and fearing neither man nor beast, drunk or sober.

'We'd demolish the gates o' hell themselves, if the price was right, yer rivirince.'

They arrived next evening, with their big jib and swinging iron ball. Only ten hours late.

They'd had no trouble till they crossed the Deben.

There was a big crowd next morning, way back down the access-road, stationed in the little shortened street-ends the demolition had left. Not coming too near, but you could see them bunching, peering between the houses.

Nearer, but still not very near, every senior Council official who could wangle his way out of the office on any excuse whatever: the Chief Executive and his deputy, the Treasurer, the Chief Planner, the Chief Architect. I could tell from their muttering that they were making bets; the Treasurer was making the book, and I gathered the odds were against me doing it.

The jib-and-ball had been parked in position overnight. Now it refused to start. The Irishmen fiddled with it, removed various bits of the engine and blew through them and put them back again. But still nothing happened.

I heard laughter behind me; and that set off the last burst I ever felt of that terrible rage I had come to know as Nevinson. I pushed through them, jammed the bits back on the engine any old how, got into the cab and pressed the starter like a man possessed.

She fired first time.

I've never used a jib-and-ball; but I've watched one being used often enough to get the hang of it. Anyway, I was so seized with this rage that I was beyond caring. I shoved the thing into first, and manoeuvred for my first swing, just above the front door. I heard warning shouts, but I ignored them.

And then the jib, the ball, the whole machine on its caterpillar tracks began to tilt. Slowly, slowly, like a great ship slowly sinking, we heeled over until it, and I, were lying on our sides, the engine roaring irrelevantly.

I believed in witchcraft at last.

Only it wasn't.

The Chief Architect was dragging me out of the cab. The Chief Architect was pointing. Beyond the jib, where the earth had fallen in, was the broken end of a tunnel into darkness. An arch, and a pointed arch at that. The Chief Architect was babbling about Early English groin-vaulting, and crypts, and priceless finds, and finally his sincere conviction that the broken arch, and the base of the Ugly House itself, were part of the long-lost Besingfield Castle . . . a priceless find, a new jewel of heritage for the nation, please contact the National Trust . . .

You've won, Burridge, you bastard. We'll never be able to pull it down now . . . I looked up at the windows of the Ugly House . . .

And I saw him looking down at me. Maybe other people would say it was just a collection of ragged lace curtain and shadow playing hell with my guilty conscience. But I knew it was Burridge looking down at me, clear as day.

I looked round, quite calmly, to see if anyone else had noticed. Oh, yes. Tetley was standing three yards away, staring up at the same windows, so close that I could hear the panting of his breath, and see the paleness of his face, and the dew of sweat that broke out all over it. So I knew I wasn't mad.

It made me feel quite kindly towards Tetley. So when I had calmed the demolition foreman down and reassured him he wouldn't be the loser financially, I took old Tetley out for a stiff whisky. I looked across at him fondly. His whole bald head was covered with half-inch bristles of new hair. But whereas his previous remnants were blond, the new hair was dark . . .

'You saw him,' I said.

'Yes, I saw him,' he said, taking a deep gulp of whisky.

'So he won – he's got his rotten house for ever now.'

'Who?' he said.

'Burridge,' I said. 'You saw him. You came out all in a sweat.'

'I saw him. But I didn't come out in a sweat for *Burridge*. I knew he'd be there.'

Suddenly, it was as though somebody had walked over my grave.

'Who, then?'

'Didn't you see him, in the window next to Burridge?'

'*Who*, for God's sake?' I was yelling now. Heads were turning all over the pub.

'Nevinson,' he said, and drained his glass. 'Nevinson was in the next window. They've got each other for ever now. In that house.'

'How do you know it was Nevinson?'

'Nevinson had red hair.'


The Ugly House still stands. The National Trust received it gratefully, and there was talk of opening it on Sundays, but nothing came of it. It stands heavily locked and empty to this day, and people prefer not to walk past it at night.

I moved away from Besingfield, and lived with Linda happily ever after. We had, as Cunning Burridge forecast, first a boy and then a girl. They gave Tetley my old job. I met him at a conference of CTOs last month. He had enough hair for all the Beatles put together, but it's still dark in the middle and blond round the edges. People think he has it dyed . . .